Aisling and Oth...

PETER TREMAYNE

AISLING

and other Irish Tales of Terror

BRANDON

A Brandon Paperback

First published in 1992 by
Brandon Book Publishers Ltd

This edition published 1998
by Brandon
an imprint of Mount Eagle Publications
Dingle, Co. Kerry, Ireland

© Peter Tremayne 1992

The author has asserted his moral rights

ISBN 0 86322 247 1

This book is published with the assistance of
the Arts Council/An Chomhairle Ealaíon, Ireland

Cover design by the Public Communications Centre Ltd, Dublin
Typeset by Koinonia, Bury
Printed by The Guernsey Press, Channel Islands

CONTENTS

CONTENTS

I

Aisling

To my brother in Christ, Brother Antonio Urbino, *Ordinis Sancti Benedicti*, at the Pontifical Irish College, Rome; from his friend Father Máirtín Ó Meadhra, *Ordinis Praedicatorium*, priest at Inis Deisceart, in the county of Kerry, Ireland. 11 September 1852.

I have commenced writing this epistle to you today although I know not when I shall end it for the boats to this isolated, windswept rock of an island are so few and infrequent that it may be months before I can despatch it. I shall therefore content myself to begin my letter, to pick up my pen as and when I feel able, in order to tell you of the most extraordinary events that have occurred since I left the seminary at Rome and came hither as a priest to a handful of heathen.

I delight in writing to you in English, our common tongue, for I need practise in the language, there being no one in these parts who speaks or understands it in any degree. I find myself forgetting it from want of use which is troublesome for I have resolved, God willing, not to remain a rural priest all my life. English is a necessity if I am to remove in the better parts of the country among the people of education and quality. For while our Irish tongue is spoken by many, it is now in a decline from which I doubt to see it recover. Two million of our population have been lost in recent years due to the most unprecedented famine; one million by death from starvation and attendant disease and one million by migration to the Americas. Most of those people were Irish-speaking and therefore their destruction and going has dealt a blow to the language from which only a miracle will allow recovery.

The cities of Ireland, in this particular, are English in manner and speech and the remaining rural population will eventually follow their example. Dublin, our chief city, is representative, for only 3,426 souls are to be found there who speak the tongue, of whom just 27 are in total ignorance of English. Therefore, the only way to move in society is through the English tongue. Yet in the remote area in which I reside, ignorance is no handicap for here the old tongue is strong and virile still.

But, my dear brother in Christ, I will come to particulars.

You will recall how we celebrated my ordination to the Order of Preachers that last day which I spent in the Eternal City? How I yearn for the hot Italian sunshine and the cool white wine of the country. After I had bade farewell to you and my tutors, I set out on the long journey to my native land. It seems like a lifetime ago and yet it was only in the spring of this year. I reported myself to His Grace, the Archbishop of Armagh, who is the apostolic delegate in this country, for I had been given letters to bring him from Rome among which was a warm letter of introduction and recommendation which the Father Prior of the Irish College had written. I found His Grace most singularly occupied for the Archbishop of Dublin had died but recently and His Grace was to give up his See of Armagh for that of Dublin. I had hoped, on the recommendation I brought with me, that His Grace would take me to his new office and employ me as some under-secretary in Dublin. God's will be done.

His Grace instructed me to repair to a tiny island off the west coast of the county of Kerry to administer to the needs of a small flock there. Having been born and raised in the hills of Idagh, in the county of Kilkenny, I was informed that my fluency in Irish was needed among a people who spoke no other tongue. Being educated in the language, I protested that the Irish of my native province of Leinster would differ from the dialect that was spoken in the western islands. The Archbishop rejected my protest and lectured me on the need to acquire the humility to accept God's purpose.

So it was that in the March of this year I came to this island.

If I had known then what I know now I would have prayed that a great wave had dashed the boat which brought me against the rocks and sent me to a watery death. God between me and all evil!

The island is called Inis Deisceart which means "southern island" for it lies to the south of a group called Na Blascaodaí, or, as some pronounce it in English, The Blaskets. They lie in a group off the coast of the Dingle Peninsula and are, indeed, the most westerly group of islands off the Irish coast. They are strange lumps of land, like the peaks of hills cut off from the mainland and surrounded by restless, brooding Atlantic waves. Islets surrounded by jagged granite rocks leaning seaward in a perpetual defence against the furious onslaught of the ocean.

Inis Deisceart, seen against the setting sun, is a curious serrated crag of an island, rising nearly six hundred feet above sea level at its highest point, shaped like the comb of a fighting cock.

It was late afternoon when I arrived, heralded by the haunted cry of the gulls and other soaring sea birds, curlews and plovers which flocked above the little craft which brought me from Dún Chaoin, a small village, isolated and lonely, yet the nearest point of civilisation on the mainland. I had been three days at the village before a boat from the island had landed there. Three sun-bronzed and burly islandmen awaited me at the single quay of Dún Chaoin with their frail looking curragh or, as the natives call them, a *naomhóg,* which literally means a small boat. They are of light wooden lath framework, over which taut canvas is stretched and coated with tar. They are high bowed and ride lightly in the water so that they tend to skim the waves rather than slice through them.

"God and Mary to you, Father," cried one raw-boned man, greeting me in Irish. I replied courteously and asked if they had word of my coming and if they were waiting to take me to the island. A spokesman replied that they had not heard of me but nevertheless would transport me to the island if I so wished it. I confess, in spite of my disappointment at not getting a stipend in a more salubrious parish, I was eager to see what, after all, was to be my first living. So I placed my bags within the boat and climbed into the stern. The six short and almost bladeless oars caused a ripple in the water and the *naomhóg* worked its way out of the harbour, along the shoreline under the cliffs and then turned due west, running towards the dark silhouette of the island. It ran rapidly over the waves answering the faintest suggestion of a dipped oar. A tenor in the boat took up a lusty rowing chant and was answered by the other men in chorus, which seemed to lend an easy motion to their rowing.

"'Tis a fair passage you are getting this day, Father," confided the oarsman nearest to me. "Sometimes the anger of the sea shuts off the island for weeks at a time."

So we came pleasantly enough to Inis Deisceart, a brown jagged lump of rock which seemed so totally inhospitable that I was amazed to find that no less than forty souls resided there, trying to wrest their living from the dark waters which surrounded the island. Nestling among the grey granite boulders, which were strewn across the island, were several *clocháin*. These, my brother, are stone-built huts which are constructed without mortar and shaped like beehives. In these I found entire families resided. There were only a few better constructions among which was my church! Church! Forgive my bitterness for it was but a small oratory in which one man could scarcely stand. Yet it is consecrated for worship and dedicated to St Brendan whose reputation for voyaging in the west is legend.

I was later given to understand that few of my flock were native islanders. The inhabitants of these western islands usually dwell on an tOileán Mór, or the Great Island. It was during the recent famine years that many mainlanders came to the islands to escape the pestilence and hunger. Thus, where a few families dwelt, a whole village had sprung up. Such was the situation on Inis Deisceart.

The islanders gathered around me in curiosity as the boat came to shore. They were respectful and hands reached out to help me safely to dry land. Many a greeting was chorused and I replied in kind, finding that my dialect was readily understood by the majority. In spite of the courtesy with which I was received, I had the impression that the courtesy was for the cloth which I wore and behind that they watched me with veiled hostility and suspicion. There was respect but no welcome. As I moved among them I overheard one man say: "By my baptism, isn't he but a slip of a child to be a priest?" And another replied: "Yerra, he has scarce learnt to shave and yet he will show us the way to salvation." I stood hesitantly among them, my heart lacking resolution for the moment, wondering whether I should dare the Archbishop's fury and return to the mainland there and then. Some instinct made me brace my shoulders and ask if they knew where I was to stay.

Most of them turned away, muttering, suddenly finding important business to attend to about the island which necessitated their avoiding my company.

They all departed except for a young girl; she was no more than eighteen, I would say. Barefoot, as are most of the islanders, she was clad in a rag of a dress that had more holes in it than modesty would have allowed even in a city like Rome. Her figure would have rivalled the great marble statues of the masters in that city, so perfectly shaped was it. She was white skinned, her hair was flaming red, the setting sun kindling a furious fire in it as its bright rays slanted through the sky. Her eyes were reflective of the changing mood of the sea, seeming to change from quiet green to stormy grey with breath-taking ease. She carried herself proudly, her chin thrust forward.

"God and Mary to you, Father," she said.

"God, Mary and Patrick to you, child," I replied, my heart skipping a beat as I gazed at her untrammelled beauty. I may be a priest, my brother, but cannot a priest admire the beauty of God's creations?

"My name is Máire, Father," she replied. "I will show you to the priest's house."

11

Before I had time to give her thanks, she had turned and strode away among the rocks towards the oratory, which lay just beyond the village. A short distance from the oratory was my house.

House! By my faith, Brother Antonio, if you could only see it to compare it with those dwellings we shared in Rome! Still, this "house" is far better than the beehive huts of the natives. In fact, henceforth I shall call it by a more literal translation of the Irish word for it, which is *bothán* and is rendered as "cabin." It is a rectangular shell of roughly shaped stone, mortared with mud and washed with a yellow lime. The roof is thatched with rushes which rot easily in the heavy rains so that there is always a leak. Inside, the rafters are exposed. The interior walls are also lime washed and hung with a crucifix and a few religious paintings of cheap quality. There is just one room, the *seomra* as it is called. At one end is a bed, a chair or two, a cupboard and a washing basin. At the other end is a stone hearth, a great open chimney down which the light of day can be seen. Beside this stands an iron gallows-like construction with a swinging arm from which a cooking pot or kettle can be hung. This is my dwelling; I, who slept in the marble chambers of the Vatican, hung with their silken drapes, ceilings painted by the great masters of the Renaissance. Yet God calls and we must obey His summons.

It was strange, I do not think I was imagining when I tell you that as I entered that house I felt a passing coldness. It made me shiver. There is a saying about such a feeling. They say that someone has walked on your grave. My mind was uneasy as I stood on that cold threshold. But the feeling swiftly passed and I dismissed its cause as the dampness and gloomy atmosphere of the cabin.

"I will light a fire for you, Father," said the girl, Máire, as if she had read my thoughts.

"Is it long since there was a priest in this place, Máire?" I asked, watching her laying kindling in the hearth.

"Not since the start of the Great Hunger," she replied. The natives here refer to the famine years by that title.

I frowned.

"Where do you go to mass or confession?"

Máire shrugged as she lit the fire.

"If the weather is fair we row to the mainland. But mostly the weather prevents us."

I realised how badly these people stood in need of a priest. I thought of our mode of living in Rome; mass twice daily and two decades of the rosary on the toll of the Angelus bell three times a day. Yet these people go for months during the winter without the benefits of sacrament. I did learn afterwards that, because of their isolated station, the bishop had given dispensation to the people to make holy vows in matters of births, weddings and deaths until such occurrences could receive priestly blessing.

It took the girl some while before she was able to coax the kindling into flame and, when it was burning well, she laid the heavy sods of turf on it. Turf, or peat, is the substance which is burnt as fuel in these parts. It is slow burning and ideally suited for the stews and soups which are the people's main culinary art.

"There now, Father," she said, standing up and dusting her rag of a dress, "that should draw well but see to it that you feed it. Don't let it go out or you'll be feeling the cold. If you like, I'll come by each day and help you with the chores of the house until you are comfortably settled."

I told her that this would suit me greatly.

I spent an uneasy night in that place. I told myself that it would take a few days to get used to the new situation, the curious smells, sounds and sights of this alien environment. I resigned myself to my restlessness and the discomforture of the damp and cold.

In the morning Máire returned with a basket of food.

"I have taken it upon myself to collect this from the islanders," she said, setting it upon the table. "There is a small packet of tea, some sugar, a few gulls' eggs and potatoes. Later today, the fishermen might return with a good catch in which case there will be fish to be had."

Brother Antonio, this is the staple diet of these people. How

13

they exist by it, I do not know, but fish and potatoes, now and again augmented by the eggs of sea birds, are their main nourishment. Tea is the beverage that everyone drinks and one must learn to take this with goat's milk, there being no cows on the island but just a few goats. For stronger liquor, an islander named Seán Rua, or Red John, distils a spirit from potatoes called *poitín*. Potatoes! Each dish of the day consists of potatoes and these are always boiled and eaten with a little salt from the sea dried in the sun. There is a song that the islanders sing whose words I shall transcribe for you:

> *Prátaí ar maidin*
> *Prátaí um nóin,*
> *'s dá n-éireochainn i*
> *Meadhon oídche*
> *Prátaí a gheobhainn!*

> Potatoes at morning,
> Potatoes at noon,
> and if I were to rise
> at midnight
> potatoes I'd get!

Now may you know the full extent of my comfortless existence on this island.

It would be tedious work to recount the personal details of the various islanders whom I gradually came to know in the course of my pastoral duties. Among them Seán Rua seemed their chief spokesman and leader. In the main they were courteous but it was clear that they regarded me as a stranger, an outsider in their society. My only friendly contact was with the girl Máire who helped me in adapting to the spartan community by relieving me of many burdensome domestic chores.

"Máire," I said one day, "I do not recall meeting your parents."

"Nor will you," she replied, "for they are both dead."

I made a sympathetic reply and asked who looked after her.

She laughed gaily. "I look after myself."

"But with whom do you live then?"

"With Diarmuid Mac Maoláin."

"And who is he?"

"A fisherman," she replied, not understanding my question.

"I mean, what relation is he to you?"

"No relation," she responded. "He is just my man."

"Ah, your husband? Are you married to him?"

She chuckled.

"Och, no, Father. I like him well enough but to marry you must be in love and I do not like him well enough to serve him all my days."

I stared at her aghast.

"By my soul, child! You are living with Diarmuid Mac Maoláin as his wife and are not married to him? I must resolve this right away. You and Diarmuid must come to me this Saturday so that I may marry you."

She sniffed coldly.

"Did I not say that I do not like him well enough to marry? I'm content until I can find a better man."

My sensibilities were shocked.

"Holy Mary! You prefer to live with a man in carnal sin? Child, do you know what you are saying?"

She pouted. "By my baptism, child to you I am not! Why, you are scarce a man yet."

I coloured hotly. It is hard to be a priest and only twenty-three summers to give weight to one's authority.

"I am your father in God," I replied sternly.

"Priest you are ordained. It doesn't make you less of a man – or a boy for all that."

She laughed at my mortified expression and stalked away.

That afternoon I sought out Diarmuid Mac Maoláin. Imagine my astonishment when I came across a man who was elderly, with deep etched lines in his brown, weather beaten face, his tousled hair bleached white by the sun. I learnt that he was approaching sixty years in age but to my eye he looked ancient for here, where man is in constant battle with the inclement elements, nature prematurely ages a man. For all his ancient look, Mac Maoláin was tall, muscular and with narrow suspicious eyes. God's truth of it, brother! How he had managed to persuade such a comely young girl to share his bed, I cannot say. I will, however, make this comment. Mac Maoláin was a native to the island and owned his own *naomhóg*, cabin and nets. He was his own master and wealthy by the meagre standards of the island.

When I told him my business, he simply scowled.

"*Airiú*," he replied, using the term which the islanders have for "indeed" or "oh really?" "*Airiú*, Father. Marry Máire? It will take more than the two of us combined to put a tether on that one."

"Explain yourself, man," I demanded.

"Can you put a fence around the sea? Can you take the sharp west wind or spring and put it in a jar until summer? Máire is a wild thing, a sprite, a free spirit. I am an old man, Father. I merely thank God that she shares my house and, thanks be, my bed when the mood is on her."

I must have looked shocked.

"Do you not know how dire is the sin you commit?"

Mac Maoláin spat reflectively.

"I need no young boy to teach me the words of the Bible. I am a religious man but I am a man while you are a priest. I have a man's needs. I will accept this life which the girl offers and thanks be to God for it. Besides, I have said the words we were taught to say when no priest could reach the island because of the seas. Máire and I are vowed to each other in the eyes of the Blessed Virgin. We need no priest's blessing now."

I had, as I have mentioned, learnt of this dispensation.

"And did Máire say the words, too?" I insisted.

I saw the answer in his shifty glance.

"I said the words," he muttered.

"Unless the words are freely said by both people then it is no vow before God."

A red anger flushed his face. His blue eyes blazed suddenly as if in a battle fever. He took a step towards me, his great fisher-man's hands clenching. I confess, I took an involuntary step backwards before his fury.

"Before God and man, Máire is mine! She is wife to me and no one will interfere in that. No one, be he bishop, cardinal or boy-priest!"

It took me a moment to recover my composure. Young though I am, I was still his pastor.

"Máire and you are living in sin," I said evenly. "I shall have no more to do with the pair of you until you make a full confession of your transgression before God and declare that you intend to marry according to the writ of Holy Mother Church."

As I turned and walked away I heard his deep-throated laughter.

"We lived well enough before you came. We can live well enough now ... and after you have gone, we shall continue to live well enough."

I strode back to my cabin and sat a while in indignation, meditating on the low standards of morality in the island. I do not recall how long I sat in front of the fire. I lost all track of the passing of time. I simply became aware that it was dark and that the fire was smouldering. There was a fierce coldness about the cabin and the quiet was so intense that it almost hurt my ears. I shivered and made to reach forward to stoke the fire but, as I did so, I caught sight of a shadow at the far end of the room.

The figure was plainly that of a man, as much as I could see in the gloom.

"Who are you?" I demanded.

There was no reply but, to my horror, the shadow raised an arm. I could see in the faint light from the glowing embers a silver flicker of light on an open razor held in the man's hand. Then there was a swift motion of the arm, a strangled cry, before the figure staggered forward and slumped down.

For a moment it was as if some force held me to my chair. I pushed myself suddenly forward, my face breaking into a cold sweat.

"In the name of God...!" I cried, hurrying forward to where I had seen the figure fall.

Oh, Brother Antonio, believe me, what horror froze my blood in my veins when I discovered there was no body on the floor. There was no one in the cabin except myself. I turned with a stifled exclamation of disbelief and searched for matches, lit my tiny lamp and stared incredulously. There was no doubt about it. I was alone in the cabin.

Was I asleep, do you say? Perhaps. As I thought about it, I tried to convince myself that I had been subject to some vile nightmare. Yet I recalled the scene vividly as if aware of all my senses. I pondered the vision a long time before falling into a troubled sleep.

Can you imagine my surprise, Brother, when the next morning I was awakened from my slumber to find Máire boiling the kettle on the fire for my tea and preparing breakfast? I pushed myself up in my bed with a frown of displeasure.

"Máire!" I said sharply. "Did I not make myself clear to you and Diarmuid Mac Maoláin? I want to see you no more until you consent to marry in God's eyes."

She looked at me as if I had made some amusing quip.

"*Amaidí chainte*!" she replied. My jaw dropped. I am not sure how I should render this into English but suffice to indicate that she told me I was speaking rubbish.

"You are not a grey-haired old preacher so full of piety and age that you have forgotten how it is to feel young," she went on. "You are not that removed from this world that you do not feel the hot blood of youth coursing in your veins."

In disgust, I clambered out of bed and, standing in my night-shirt, ordered her to leave my cabin. To my outraged horror, she came forward towards me with a mocking smile and pressed her young body against mine.

"Why, Father," she sneered, "I feel your body trembling. There is man enough left behind that priest's robe for you to appreciate my needs."

God save me, Brother, but she was the devil sent to tempt me.

I closed my eyes and tried to shut my mind to the sensation of her soft warm body, from the smell of the wild summer fragrance in her soft hair.

"God help you, Máire!" I cried, suddenly finding the courage to push her roughly away.

She recovered her balance and stood in the middle of the cabin chuckling.

"God help you, Father," she mimicked my tones. "You were no more meant for the priesthood than I was meant to live my life on this God-forsaken island. Even if your mind does not accept the truth of what I say, your body admits it."

I was stunned by her boldness.

"What wickedness is this?" I gasped.

"None that I know of. All I know is what I saw in your eyes when they met mine on the day you arrived from the mainland. I saw that your body and soul desired me, as I want you, even though your priest's mind seeks to reject me."

I raised a hand to my brow in amazement. Was Christ tempted in this fashion, brother?

"Get out!" was all I could shout.

"How feebly your words are said, Father Máirtín," she whispered. "Yes, I will leave. But I shall return, and shall keep returning until you admit what is truth and what is sham."

I busied myself most of that day writing my first report on the parish to the bishop, determined to send it away to the mainland at the first opportunity. I tried to drive the image of that wilful girl from my mind. In the afternoon, I went to the oratory to baptise and bless five of the island's children born during the absence of a priest. That evening I went to visit Seán Rua in order to establish some confidence between the islanders and myself. After a glass or two of his *poitín*, Seán Rua unbent to confess that not only my age told against me but the fact that I was an *eachtrannach*, a stranger from another province, which made the islanders suspicious of me. Eventually, I returned to my cabin and prepared to retire.

At first I thought someone had opened the door, for the candle suddenly spluttered in my hand and the flames of the fire did a jig in the hearth. I felt a cold hand on my spine and shivered violently.

I turned towards the door fully expecting to see that it had blown open.

It was tight shut.

But there, there in the same gloomy corner, I could see the dark figure of a man, his back turned towards me. God look down on me! It was the same dream which I had before, yet I was not abed. How could this be dreaming? I was fully awake, a candle in my hand. Yet I was seeing this vision as clearly as I saw my own hearth and fire.

"Who are you?" I demanded. "In the name of God, I tell you to speak!"

I raised my candle high and felt a curious constriction in my throat as I saw that the image was clad in the black robes of a priest.

Then the head turned slightly in my direction and in the flickering light I beheld its face. Jesus, Mary and Joseph, pray for me! Never have I beheld such a vision of suffering. From a bony skull, over which the skin was stretched like a taut parchment, two black eyes gazed forth like open windows into hell. And in those terrible tormented eyes there gleamed something else – a hopeless longing; a muted cry for help.

"Who are you?" I managed to blurt again.

Then, as on the previous occasion, I saw the arm raised, saw the flicker on the open blade of the razor, saw the blade descend to the man's throat with a strange jerking motion. There was a strangled gasp and the figure staggered forward a pace before collapsing.

Still, as I watched, my candle held high, the image disappeared.

I tried to raise my hand in blessing and cry out the name of Our Saviour. What devil's vision was this? A priest committing suicide – the most unforgivable of all sins!

That night I spent in restless anxiety, aghast at what I had seen.

I was up early and trying to kindle the fire to boil the kettle when the latch lifted and in came Máire. I was in a quandary of emotions. I know I should have thrown out that brazen vixen there and then but, after my nightmare, I was emotionally weakened and exhausted. The girl behaved as though nothing had happened between us on the previous day and I was content to let the situation remain so. It was selfish of me, but I needed someone to confide to, someone to whom I could recount that awesome nightmare. She alone of the islanders would make a sympathetic audience.

"That's a strange tale," she conceded when I had done. "But, surely, there's an easy understanding of it. You are a stranger here and unused to the island. Unfamiliarity creates strange dreams."

"You mean that I was merely asleep and dreamt this spectre?" I asked her, almost hopefully. I found myself desiring the comfort in her voice. Oh, how weak this frail body of ours is; how weak its resolution.

She sat herself on my table and swung her long shapely legs, barely covered by her tattered dress.

"You say you saw the face of the image quite clearly? We usually put people we know into our dreams. Did you know the face?"

I shook my head thoughtfully, remembering that pleading, anguished countenance.

"It was no one that I recognised. No, of that I am sure. It was the face of a total stranger."

Máire shrugged.

"There are three kinds of things that come to us when we are asleep; dreams that are only strange stories that pass through the mind in sleep; nightmares that are nothing but fears of the night; and then the *aisling* which is the vision of things that have been. Yours was only a nightmare."

"How can I be sure?"

She smiled: "And you a priest not to know?"

"What do you mean?"

"Here on the island there is a powerful charm against nightmares."

"Charms!" I sneered in disgust.

"What are prayers but charms?" she countered. "The *ortha an tromluí* is handed down from generation to generation as a protection. Churchmen have been saying it for centuries, my boy-priest."

I glowered angrily at the girl.

"I will not have God taken into disrespect!" I thundered.

"I speak to the boy in the priest's coat, not to his God," she retorted.

Anger moved me and I made to catch hold of her to throw her out. I caught her around the upper arms and she slid off the table towards me, her body so close up against mine that I became aware of its soft contours. She was so close that her warm lips touched mine and – Angels preserve me! – I did not push her away until several long moments passed. Then I turned, my face hotly flushed, and rushed from the cabin.

What was it about this place, about these people, which was destroying my resolution in my vocation and the sacred vows that I had made to the Holy Mother Church? Was I but a weak man after all?

That evening, as I knelt in prayer, the ancient words of the *ortha an tromluí* came unbidden to my lips: "Anne, the mother of Mary, and Mary, the mother of Jesus, and Elisabeth, the mother of John the Baptist. These three between me and the nightmare from tonight until a year from tonight and tonight itself. *In nomine Patris et Filli et Spiritus Sancti. Amen.*"

And in spite of this the vision came again.

I awoke in the night to find the room in darkness save for the spluttering from the dying fire. It was ice-cold again and so I climbed out of bed to stoke the fire. It was then that I turned and saw the dark figure dressed in the priest's robes; saw the gaunt, anguished face with those terrible pleading eyes turned in my direction. I could not mistake that mute cry for help from those hell-tormented eyes. Then I saw the upraised hand; saw the glint on the open razor. I tried to cry out, tried to stop the downward motion of the arm ... then the vision vanished.

This was no nightmare, of that I was sure for here was I, standing in my nightshirt on the cold floor, fully awake and aware of my surroundings; aware of the cold; aware of the slow, ominous ticking of the clock on the shelf and the gentle roar of the sea outside.

When Máire came the next morning I found myself positively pleased to see her.

"It must be a dream," she said dismissively. "Didn't I tell you to say the *ortha an tromluí*?"

"God forgive me, I did say it," I confessed.

She glanced at me, a fleeting smile faltering in the corner of her dimpled mouth.

"So?" She did not speak what was obviously in her mind. Instead she pursed her lips gravely and sighed. "Then this is no nightmare. You must be seeing an *aisling*."

I shivered and crossed myself.

Brother Antonio, let me explain what this *aisling* is. It is the word we Irish have for a vision. Being an ancient Celtic people, we are much given to visions and vision-stories are a part of our old literature. Our beloved St Fursa, who founded monasteries in England before crossing to France where he died in the celebrated monastery he founded in Peronne in 649 *Anno Domini*, was the author of a great *aisling* tale, which is the first surviving such tale we have. Saints, scholars and poets have claimed to see an *aisling* and those who do are said to be the blessed of Christ.

As Máire was making the morning tea, I meditated on this.

If I was seeing an *aisling* of some past event, what did it portend? Had some poor priest taken his own life in the very cabin I now occupied? It was unthinkable that a priest could so neglect his vows as to commit such a mortal sin. Yet there it was. I had seen the vision and the vision was being shown me for a reason.

"Has anyone else seen such a vision on the island, Máire?" I asked, at length.

The girl shook her head vehemently.

"I would surely know if it were so."

"You have never heard it spoken of that a priest took his own life here?"

She shook her head.

"Tell me, Máire, who knows the history of this island well? Who would know if there is a memory of some ancient deed the like of which I have been witnessing?"

"You must consult the *seanchaí*," she said immediately. "If there is but a vague recollection of such a deed, then he would know."

I resolved to see the man at once.

Dael Mac an Bháird was the island's *seanchaí*, a sort of official storyteller who was the repository of all the history, genealogy, folklore and legend connected with the area. He was an old fellow who lived with his son in one of the *clocháin*, spending his days in the tutoring of his son in the store of knowledge he held. The old man felt his time was approaching and oral traditions must be passed on. I went up to his *clochán* and found him seated outside, it being a fine day. He watched me come up the hillside to where he sat and greeted me courteously.

"Come safely, Father."

"God bless all here," I replied and took a seat on the sod beside him.

"I hear you are the man to recount the history of the island?" I made no preamble.

"I am the *seanchaí*," he replied gravely. "And so was my father and his father before that and all the sons of the poet before them."

I must interject here, Brother Antonio, to tell you that the name Mac an Bháird means "son of the poet" and hence his allusion to the fact.

"Do you know the history of the priests of this island?" I asked.

He paused and reflected. "I do, by the faith."

"Did ever a priest take his own life here?"

The old man raised his eyebrows in surprise.

"God stay us from evil! Where did you hear such a thing? For a priest to take his own life is a most grievous sin."

"It is a terrible sin, yet did a priest ever do such a thing on this island?"

Mac an Bháird gazed long and thoughtfully at me and then heaved a deep sigh.

"There is such a tale, Father. I had it from my father and he from his and back many generations. Each *seanchaí* in turn has sworn never to tell anyone the tale other than the one who will fill his place."

I made an impatient gesture.

"I must know the tale."

The old man's eyes were troubled.

"I have sworn an oath only to tell the next *seanchaí* and no other."

"I absolve you from that oath."

He still hesitated and then I had a flash of inspiration.

"You may tell me in the nature of confession. By my soul, it shall go no further than the confessional."

Mac an Bháird considered and looked relieved.

"It happened long ago when Cromwell was the scourge of our people. It happened when the Irish were being cleared from their lands, pushed westward across the river Shannon where they were ordered to reside on pain of death. Any Irish found east of the river were killed or shipped to the Barbados to be sold for labour. Priests were killed whenever the English encountered them and there was a five pound reward for the head of any priest. A few lucky ones were able to follow their flocks to be sold in the American colonies."

I sighed impatiently. Who does not know that woeful history? The Irish folk memory of those savage days is as clear as ever it was.

"But what of this priest?" I pressed.

"He was a young priest, newly appointed to his flock. One night, so the tale goes, the English troopers rode down on his village, killing the old men and women and seizing the able-bodied and young children to take to the Barbados-bound ships. The young priest fled into the darkness. He did not stay with his people in this hour of peril. He deserted his flock and escaped alone to this island of Inis Deisceart where he thought no soldier would follow.

"*Airiú*! But his conscience followed him. He brooded on the desertion of his flock when they needed him. He pondered in his isolated melancholy until he could bear himself no longer. He was young. Perhaps that was his only sin."

"Is that the tale?"

"That is all I know," Mac an Bháird inclined his head.

I rose and gave a blessing on him and his house and departed.

When I returned to my cabin I found Diarmuid Mac Maoláin waiting for me. He stood in front of the fire, his big hands clenching and unclenching in agitation. He would not gaze fully into my face but I could see jealous anger spread as a mask across his features. His face was flushed, though anger was a small part of it for I smelt strong liquor on his breath.

"Do you think I am blind, Father?" were his first words, said without greeting or deference to my calling.

"I do not, Mac Maoláin," I replied gravely. "Why would you believe I do?"

Mac Maoláin made a gesture around the cabin.

"There is a woman's touch here and all the island knows it."

"No harm in it," I said defensively. "Máire does her Christian duty in looking to the needs of her priest. 'Tis a pity that others of my parish are not so obliging as to help in the care of God's servants."

Mac Maoláin stared at my bold front.

"So Máire is the model Christian now?" he sneered, after a hesitation. "Was it not the other day that you wanted to see no more of her until she consented to be married? Now I find that she comes here every day..."

"That I might guide her to the truth of God," I interrupted, the cold sweat breaking out on my face as I tried to still that small

voice whispering in my ear: "Thou shalt not bear false witness."
Oh Brother Antonio, I know above all people that false words are
not only evil in themselves but they infect the soul with evil. To
tell a falsehood is like the cut of a sabre for though the wound
may heal, the scar of it will remain.

It was then that Mac Maoláin raised his eyes to mine. I tried to
meet his gaze boldly, eye to eye, soul to soul, but it was I who let
my eyes drop before his.

"You are a young man, Father Máirtín," he said softly now,
his anger controlled. "You are a priest but a young man nevertheless. And there is a handsomeness which shapes your features
with an intelligent mind behind them. Who am I but a poor
untutored fisherman? You are a stranger, a representative of a
world that is strange but bewitching; a world which is alien but
beguiling. Máire is like a summer's honey bee ... she flits here and
there among the flowers, attracted first by one and then by
another; attracted to the beauty of one, then the colouring of
another. I can see in her eyes what is in her heart."

I tried to draw myself up and frown sternly.

"Man, are you forgetting that I am a priest? You are accusing
me of a most dreadful sin or the contemplation of a dreadful sin.
My marriage is with Holy Mother Church."

Mac Maoláin stared at me for a long time before he finally
spoke.

"*Airiú*, priests were not always celibate. Ask Dael Mac an
Bháird the storyteller. I have heard that once even the Popes
begat children. Because priests dress differently to other men and
say words before an altar, it does not destroy their manhood."

"I have heard enough, Mac Maoláin," I said angrily. "You
cannot realise what you are saying nor what it is that you are
accusing me of."

Mac Maoláin leant suddenly forward and grasped my arm in a
vice-like grip with an abruptness which caused my heart to
pound.

"I know what is in Máire's mind. I know her soul. But I do not
know what is in your soul, Father Máirtín. I have come here to

say that a cloud of gloom spread over this island when you set foot here; it hovers over the island still. Go away! Go away, for you are not wanted here."

I was livid with indignation.

"The cloud was here when I arrived on this bastion of heathendom!" I snapped. "The evil was here before my coming. Look into your own soul, Mac Maoláin. It is you who live in carnal sin, not I."

He swore a terrible curse and turned towards the door.

The vision came at dusk this time.

Again I saw the shadowy figure, saw the black mantle of his calling, saw the pleading white tormented face turned towards me, saw the upraised hand, the gleaming razor.

It was only after the vision vanished that the thought occurred to me; this *aisling* was being shown to me and no one else on the island. Why? It was because I, too, was a priest and could bless this wraith with holy sacrament and absolve the sin. In giving the matter careful thought, I realised the truth of it. I was dealing with a troubled earthbound spirit, an unquiet spirit seeking forgiveness for the desertion of his flock and that terrible act of self-destruction. Suddenly I became full of eagerness for the vision to re-appear so that I might perform this act of charity for a brother priest that his soul might finally rest in peace.

The following morning I arose early. I went down to the sea shore and started to walk along the sandy strand. I took with me my *Missal* to search its pages for an appropriate service of exorcism through which to absolve the earth-bound soul who haunted me. So engrossed was I in my meditative endeavours that I wandered quite a way from the village and did not stop on the strand until a clump of rocks barred my progress. I paused to consider whether I should climb around them or turn back to my cabin. Then I heard a cry of greeting which drove all other thoughts from my mind.

I turned my face seaward to see a white arm waving to me and I saw the red blaze of hair in the early morning light and knew it to be Máire.

I watched as she swum lazily towards the shore, her long white arms circling languorously in the blue waters.

"God save you," she called as she came near the shore and then, without shame, she rose from the frothy surf and came towards me, rose as naked as she had been on her birth.

God keep me from sin! *I am a man!* I am a man! My cheeks reddened yet I could not keep my eyes from drinking in the beauty of her body. I could see her examining me under lowered lashes and smiling demurely. I tried to clear my throat, tried to turn away from her, yet I could not. The sin of the flesh was beginning to make my body shake, my nerves tingle.

She stood there watching me as if aware of the tremendous struggle which coursed my body and soul. How well did she read my thoughts. She knew I would forsake all, send myself down into the bowels of hell, to touch her soft white body, to feel those warm red lips. She knew. Oh yes, she had always known.

"May I cover myself?" she asked coquettishly, nodding towards her tattered dress which lay discarded on some nearby rocks.

"No! Not yet!"

I could not believe that the voice which grunted from my throat was my own. I stood with the passion burning in my face.

She turned to me with a smile, a smile of triumph, took a step towards me and raised her arms as if in welcome. No word was spoken nor was any necessary. She had been right all along. I was a man!

Afterwards? The shame and horror of my deed drove me from her side without a word. With mortification heavy in my soul, I ran back to my cabin and threw myself on my knees, my arms held up in supplication for forgiveness. How I wished that I had never chanced along the sea shore; how I wished that I had never set foot on this island. But sin cannot be undone, only forgiven. Yet, Brother Antonio, how will I ever find the courage to confess this carnal sin? God knows and yet I find His terrible justice mild by comparison with the fears of my fellow brothers in Christ. How will they admonish me? You are my true friend, my brother in Christ; tell me what I must do, Brother Antonio. How can I redeem myself?

It must have been about noon when I was torn from my feverish prayers of penance by the thundering of a fist on my cabin door. What new affliction was this? Was it Diarmuid Mac Maoláin come seeking revenge? The thought of being revealed to the islanders made me hesitate before the door. Then the voice of Seán Rua sang out:

"God help us, Father! Are you in there?"

Trying to compose myself, I opened the door and stared at the circle of agitated faces which greeted me. There was Seán Rua, his face white, an expression of horror contorting his features.

"Come quickly, Father. Down to the strand."

"What is it?" I demanded as he seized my arm and began to propel me forward.

"God have mercy on us, 'tis Máire. She is dead on the strand."

I halted, rooted to the spot, my heart pumping wildly.

" I ... I don't understand."

"For the love you bear Christ, Father, come quickly now!" insisted Seán Rua. "Hasn't Máire been killed by Diarmuid Mac Maoláin?"

I was dragged forward like a man in a dream until we came to the spot near the rocks.

There lay Máire on the beach. She lay in that forlornly tattered dress of hers, as if sleeping on her side, one arm flung casually upwards, the other at her side. There was an ugly red welt across her skull. The instrument which made the wound was not hard to find for just beyond her lay a *sleaghán*. It is a special kind of spade with a wing at one side which the natives use for cutting the turf for their fires.

I knelt down beside her and felt for her pulse but it was obvious that she was gone from this world. God have mercy on her! I began to mutter the words of absolution.

When I had done, I stood up and looked round the gathered islanders.

"Where is Mac Maoláin?" I asked coldly. All feeling seemed to have departed. Perhaps it was the shock. I could not feel sorrow for poor Máire; I could not feel hate for Mac Maoláin nor could I feel guilt for myself. I was simply acting a part now. "Is there proof that he did this thing?"

Seán Rua shuffled forward.

"I was yonder on the hill and saw the whole thing, Father. Máire was sitting on the rocks there and I saw Mac Maoláin come up to her. He was coming from the turf field yonder," he jabbed a forefinger, "and carried his *sleaghán* with him. I heard their voices raised in angry tones. God help me, but then I saw him raise his *sleaghán* and strike a cruel blow."

He paused and there was a mumbling of amazement from those gathered.

"I cried out," continued the man, "and Mac Maoláin looked up and saw me. He dropped his *sleaghán* and ran along the strand towards the village."

"That's the truth of it, surely," intervened another man. "He came hurrying along the strand and launched his *naomhóg*. Didn't I ask him where he was off to in such a bother and didn't he reply not a word?"

I bit my lip.

"So he is heading for the mainland?" I sighed, making a natural assumption.

"Not he," responded the fisherman. "I saw him heading for the back of the island."

Seán Rua pointed to the greying skies against which black storm clouds were scurrying hither and thither.

"'Tis a bad time to be in those waters, God save him. Maybe he means to give himself to God."

"Give himself to God?" I asked bemused. "What do you mean?"

It was the old *seanchaí*, Dael Mac an Bháird, who answered.

"In ancient times, Father, when a man had committed a terrible sin, it was the custom for him to row his *naomhóg* to the back of the island where the Atlantic seas crash against the granite cliffs, where the shore is inhospitable. There the man

31

would wait for a coming storm. It was then up to God whether he drowned or survived. If he survived he was judged to have received God's forgiveness. It was the old justice."

I cannot tell you, Brother Antonio, of the thousands of thoughts which coursed my mind. Had Mac Maoláin seen Máire and me together? Was it that which caused him such overpowering anger that he struck the life from the girl and now was as good as committing suicide himself? In my strange emotional numbness I made my way back to my cabin just as the storm broke over the island. God's will or not, I knew well what the fate of that man would be, alone in his canvas boat among the Atlantic swells. I knew also that I shared his sin; more than shared it. Máire's death, Mac Maoláin's death, were both my responsibility.

The skies continued to darken and only the occasional lightning bolt illuminated the interior of my cabin as I sat there before the hearth watching the fire that Máire had kindled flicker and die into embers and then the embers themselves fade into dead ashes.

Strangely, I felt akin to Mac Maoláin, felt his agony as he sat in his tossing *naomhóg*. I felt the salt seas hurling the little canvas craft hither and thither amidst the black frothing fury ... hither and thither until – until it was rendered into pieces against the jagged granite cliffs; until it was sundered into a thousand pieces of matchwood; until the soul of Diarmuid Mac Maoláin was sent abruptly into the next world.

I shivered involuntarily. There again came that feeling which I had felt so often now, the sudden coldness on my spine. Even as I prepared myself for what was to come, as I turned to stare into the gloom, a terrible cold dread seized me. There stood the figure clad in the black robes of a priest. The flashing lightning at the window illuminated its pale, tormented, skull-like features – the dark pleading eyes turned towards me.

I tried to push the thoughts of Máire and Mac Maoláin from my mind. I had to help this troubled soul, to give the young priest rest. He had deserted his flock and in his brooding misery had taken his life. Yet surely his sin only lay in his youth and inexperience?

"In the name of Christ and all His saints," I cried, raising my crucifix to make the sign of the Blessed Cross. "Peace be upon your soul! In Christ's Holy Name, forgiveness for your deed. Depart now in peace!"

The transformation was amazing. The skull-like face filled out and momentarily I saw the fresh-faced features of a handsome young man. The expression on that countenance was one of peace and exaltation. For a moment the young man's face gazed at me in wordless gratitude.

Then it was gone. Oh my God! The face vanished but not the black-robed shadow.

I stared in bewilderment. A sudden searing flash of lightning across the island flickered on the upheld razor. I could see its wicked blade open, watch its swift downward stroke as impotently as I had watched it many times before.

Yet I had absolved the wretched spirit – had seen its departure with peace and joy!

There came another flash of lightning. I saw a new face staring back at me from the shadowy wraith. I could see the features as plainly as I saw the razor's descent, as plainly as I saw the vivid red welt across the throat just before the shadow fell and vanished from my sight.

I sprang backward screaming in terror, cold hands clutching at my palpitating heart.

We are all prisoners of consequences. Every deed must have a consequence to legitimise or cancel it and thus we must recompense the Creator for all our actions. I, who was not without grievous sin, did not have the power to absolve another without restitution.

The *aisling* was no longer a vision of the past. It was a vision of the future. It is my atonement for my terrible sin and I pray God will forgive me.

When I stared at the face of the *aisling* it was as if I were staring into a mirror. The pleading white face was now my own!

Aisling

Light a candle for the repose of my soul, my dear brother in Christ. Farewell.

II

Deathstone

"WHAT ON EARTH is that?" asked my wife Catherine. I heard the real estate agent shuffle his feet. "That?" He hesitated and then summoned enthusiasm. "That is what you might call a special feature of the property, madam. It's a menhir."

"A what?"

"A standing stone." The agent's voice contained almost an air of pride. It seemed to indicate that we should be impressed by the fact.

"You know ... one of those monuments that they used to erect in prehistoric times. You'll see plenty of them here in Ireland."

"But what is it doing in the middle of the garden?" demanded Catherine, clearly unimpressed by antiquity.

"Tinashan is an old house. That's what the name means in Irish – *Tigh-na-Sean* to give you the correct name. It was built on the site of an old prehistoric shrine, so they say. As you can see, the house is situated on top of the cliffs overlooking the Shannon estuary. Can you see Scattery's Island over there, sir ... oh!"

I could almost visualise the man biting his tongue and flushing with mortification. I smiled thinly.

"That's all right. I may be blind, Mr O'Brien, but I am capable of visualising landscapes in my mind's eye. Describe the place to me."

There was a contrite note as the agent resumed his speech: "The house is behind us. The garden sweeps down from a small stone patio to a lawn which stretches towards the top of the granite cliffs. They are about a hundred feet away. They fall two hundred feet into the Shannon. You have no need to worry on that score, sir. Before you get anywhere near the cliff top you'll find a stone boundary wall which encompasses the garden. There's also a barbed-wire fence strung along the edge of the cliff to keep back straying sheep or cattle."

"And where exactly is this menhir?" I asked.

It was Catherine who replied with a disdainful sniff.

"Slap in the middle of the lawn, Fergus."

"Does it have a story?" I was intrigued. I'd never heard of a monolith in a garden before.

"I suppose it does, sir. But I'm not a local man. I'm from Limerick. You'll have to ask one of the old men down at the village."

I felt Catherine's hand on my arm.

"Well, Fergus? Shall we take it?"

"It's a lovely spot, sir," chimed in the agent quickly. "We get a lot of artists and the like renting properties around here. I'm sure you'll be at home here, sir. Plenty of people to talk with."

"My husband does not want any disturbance." Catherine's voice was suddenly sharp. "We are looking for somewhere where we can be isolated. We want absolute peace and quiet. My husband, as you may know, is a composer. He's been ill for a while and he not only needs a place to work in peace but to build his strength back."

I frowned wondering why Catherine needed to emphasise my illness to the man. She had already told him I had been ill while we were in his office a while ago.

"Shall we take it, Fergus?" she asked me again.

"What do you think, Cathy?"

"I think it will do fine," she replied.

"Then we'll take it."

"A wise decision, sir," O'Brien said breezily. "Very wise. It's a beautiful spot and the scenery ... "

His voice cut short. He had embarrassed himself again. It's

amazing how often sighted people refer to things they see and instead of being natural about it try to disguise the fact for fear of giving offence to the unsighted.

"Will we be able to move in at the end of the week?" Catherine asked.

"You can do so as soon as we sign the agreements," the agent assured her.

"Where is this menhir?" I asked. I was still curious about the idea of some old megalith in the garden.

Catherine understood the direction I wanted.

"Straight in front of you, about fifty paces forward, Fergus."

Swinging my stick slightly before me I began to pace out, feeling the stone slabs change to springy lawn beneath my feet. At a count of forty-nine paces my stick struck something and I held out my hand. There it was. I could feel the rough texture, the abrasive touch of the weathered granite and its sharp edges.

Behind me I could hear the agent lower his voice, thinking perhaps that I could not hear him.

"I think your husband is amazing, Mrs Finucane. I've heard his music often on the radio but I never thought he was ... er, well, handicapped."

I groaned inwardly. People can be so god-damned patronising.

I ignored him and stood studying the menhir; feeling its contours with my hands in order to visualise it in my mind's eye. The sharp outlines were strange. For a moment I doubted my sense of touch for it seemed that there were faces carved on the stone. Several stone faces which merged into each other. I turned and called to Catherine.

"Come and look at this stone. Tell me what you see."

I heard her coming across the lawn towards me with the slightly heavier tread of the estate agent behind.

"What is it, Fergus?"

I swept my hands across the stone.

"Is there carving on it?"

"No. It's just an old grey granite stone, that's all. It's about three feet wide and seven feet tall."

"Are you sure there's no carving on it?"

"No. It's just rough and worn by weathering."

I bit my lip as I felt the strange face-like shapes under my fingertips. I had always been told that my imagination was good. I suppose I would not have taken to the arts had it not been. Yet I could swear that the contours were man moulded; that a myriad faces covered the granite monument.

"Come on, Fergus," Catherine linked her arm under mine. "Let's go with Mr O'Brien and get his forms filled or whatever we must do."

Three days later we moved into the house. It was a small Georgian mansion with perhaps too many rooms. On the ground floor she had chosen a study for me to work in and a firm from Limerick had delivered a baby grand piano. The windows opened to the sea and I could smell its salt tang and the soft balmy breeze of the summer evenings. Catherine said it was the ideal place for me to recover my strength and begin work again.

It was true when Catherine told the estate agent that I had been ill. That wasn't my only worry. At the age of forty-eight I could sense my career beginning to decline. I don't wish to cadge for sympathy but I have always been blind and it was an uphill struggle to work my way through the conservatoir. Yet I did so. Then I found it was almost impossible for a blind musician to obtain a job in an orchestra, which had been an ambition of mine. To get solo performances without a reputation was just as difficult. I spent years teaching piano to bored children while I fought to get my own compositions produced. I finally achieved success with a tone poem followed by a performance in my native Dublin of an operetta. Suddenly, I had won international acclaim and had a London agent. I moved to England then and spent fifteen years at the top of my profession. Performances, recordings and broadcasts followed from London to Moscow and New York.

I had married Catherine six years ago. I had then been forty-two and she only twenty years old. She was a very mature twenty and knew what she wanted in life. She was a music student and we met when I gave a lecture on my work at the Royal Academy of Music in London. Things just developed from there. I have often asked myself what would a beautiful young girl want with a man who was over twenty years her senior, and a blind man at that; but for some people age does not matter. The meeting of hearts and intellects is all that counts. I fell deeply in love with her. She became my life. I knew every contour of her sweetly chiselled features.

Indeed, in recent months I would not have known what to do without her. The trouble started eighteen months ago when my agent, Carlton Daniel, said he was finding it impossible to place my recent work. Critics were beginning to carp about it and it was becoming harder to get performances. Of course, I began to feel very depressed and each composition I gave Carlton was met by the same negative result. Then, I think it was eight or nine months ago, I began to get ill. Catherine said it was the result of my depression. I had awful migraines and peculiar stomach cramps. Hardly a week went by when I found myself spending a day or two in bed. Depression actually gave way to lethargy. My agent was blunt. I once heard him telling Catherine that he thought I had passed my creative peak. Everything was downhill.

Catherine insisted on nursing me herself and several times I overheard her arguing with my doctor about my treatment. It was Catherine who suggested that we leave London and return to my native Ireland; to the west coast, the rural remoteness of County Clare, miles from anyone; from anywhere. She would hire a house or cottage and nurse me back to health. The illness would go and I would work again. Then the critics would recant when I produced my magnum opus. Oh, she convinced me that I still had the magnum opus in me. I would show the critics and, most of all, I would show my agent Carlton Daniel. So enthusiastic was she that she enthused me and I became excited at the prospect. It took several days for us to get sorted out, for me to begin to find my way about the house.

I think it was on our third evening there that I was awakened and lay wondering what had caused me to be disturbed. I reached for my watch, lifted the glass face and felt for the hands. It was two o'clock. It was then I heard the sound. A strange humming. I raised myself from the pillows and listened, head to one side. The sound was difficult to describe. It was like a faraway singing, a chorus of suppressed keening like the wailing of souls in torment.

I turned and nudged Catherine.

I felt her stir and her sleepy voice demanded what was wrong.

"Do you hear that sound?"

"What sound?" she replied irritably.

"That singing."

She did not reply for a moment and then she said: "I don't hear a thing, Fergus. Are you feeling all right?"

"Damn it!" I snapped. "I've got good hearing. It's several people singing, some sort of lament."

She sighed deeply. "Go back to sleep. It's nothing."

I did not reply for the sound ceased abruptly. I lay back listening for a long time but it did not come again and I eventually fell asleep.

It was nearly a week later that Catherine went down to the village, to the post office, leaving me to get on with my work. I was sitting making notations on my Braille pad when I heard a sound outside the window and a dry rasping cough.

"Who's there?"

"Sorry to startle you. You are Fergus Finucane?"

The voice was full of the rich rolling sounds of the west of Ireland. It was a warm, friendly voice.

"Yes," I replied.

"I'm Fr Sheldon, the parish priest. May I come in a while?"

I suppressed a sigh and forced a smile.

"Come in and welcome," I said.

I heard him come through the kitchen door and enter the room. A firm hand sought mine.

"I know your music well, Mr Finucane. I try to get to Dublin or Cork whenever I see a work of yours is being performed. I am a great fan of your Song Cycle from the *Táin*."

I don't know why I invited him in. I was not really in the mood for a visitor. However, I offered him a drink, which he accepted, and suggested he find a chair, which he did.

"I'm afraid my wife and I are both atheists, Father," I said in order to forestall any invitations he might intend for us by way of increasing his flock attendance at church. I heard him sigh with resignation.

"I suppose I suspected as much. There is a certain pagan element that comes through your work, you know. It is a raw excitement which I am sure that no man happy in the promise of Christ's redemption would ever produce."

My face must have shown some astonishment for he chuckled.

"Anyway," he went on, "rest assured that I am not here to drum up business. This is merely a piece of socialising in order to increase my store of gossip. I gather your wife must be out."

"Yes. She went down to the village."

"Mr O'Brien told me of your coming. He mentioned that you showed some interest in the old standing stone in the garden."

"Do you know anything about it?"

"Mind if I smoke?" the priest countered. I shook my head and waited until I smelled the aromatic smoke drifting through the room.

"Well?" I pressed. "Is there a story? When I examined the stone I thought it was carved."

"Oh no, there is no carving on it at all. It is just one of those standing stones that proliferate in the area."

"But it has a story?" I insisted.

"Little to tell," began the priest, which is the Irish way of saying that an interesting story would follow. "Did O'Brien tell you that this house was built on the site of an old abbey church? The church was destroyed during the days of Cromwell, so it is told. Some English lord raised his house here during the time of the Penal Laws. The abbey was an old one. It was said that St Brendan the Navigator built it on the ruins of an old pagan temple."

"Ah," I said.

"There you have it. The standing stone is the only remnant to survive from the original pagan site, although it is said that the stones of the house came from the stones of the abbey which, in their turn, came from the pagan temple that stood here."

"But," I said, when he paused, "why was one standing stone left when everything else was destroyed? It must have some significance."

"There is a story," admitted Fr Sheldon. "The story was first written down by Sinlán Moccu Min, an Abbot of Bangor in Ulster, who died in the early seventh century. He is regarded as one of the earliest of Irish annalists. He wrote an account of the deeds of the ancient gods of Ireland, the Tuatha Dé Dannan. Do you remember the name of the god of healing and medicine?"

"Surely, Diancécht," I replied at once. I prided myself on my knowledge of Irish mythology.

"Diancécht is the right of it," agreed the priest. "He was a powerful god but, like all the Irish gods, subject to every human failing under the sun. When his son Miach proved himself the better physician, Diancécht fell into a rage and attacked him with a sword. The story goes that three times Miach healed himself. Then Diancécht struck his son a fourth blow, splitting his brain in two, and Miach was unable to heal this wound and died. When Diancécht recovered from his rage and realised what his jealousy had done he cursed the evil that was in all the race of man and vowed that he would find an instrument to expunge it from the face of the earth.

"As you know, Diancécht had a number of healing stones. Stones were a sacred object in ancient times which held the power of good and evil. The story goes that Diancécht, in his search for a stone that would heal evil, journeyed to the Land of Fomorii, the country of the evil ones themselves for only evil guarded evil. He returned with a stone called *Gallán na Mairbh*, the Deathstone, which subsumed all that was evil into it. He set it up in Ireland."

Fr Sheldon paused and I heard him relighting his pipe.

"And what has the tale to do with the menhir?"

"The stone is called *Gallán na Mairbh* and has been so far back as records show its existence. You'll find many an old storyteller who will claim that it is the very stone Diancécht set up after his visit to the Land of the Fomorii. But then, such tales are common. Every stone, every megalith, every hill and river takes its name from mythology in this country. Ah, gracious! Is that the time? I must be on my way."

I heard him rising to his feet. I was slightly disappointed.

"Is there no more to the story than that?" I asked.

"Surely that's enough?" came his amused response.

I felt his warm grasp on my hand.

"Delighted to have met you, Mr Finucane. Your music has given me a great deal of pleasure over the years. I hope you'll have a pleasant and rewarding stay in this house."

A short while later Catherine came in at the gate.

"Did I see a priest leaving here?" she asked.

"Fr Sheldon, the parish priest," I nodded.

"What did he want? I hope he didn't disturb you." I heard a slight aggressiveness in her voice. Of late she had been a little over-protective due to my illness.

"He was just telling me about the old standing stone." I smiled. "Apparently it subsumes all things evil to itself."

I heard her sniff.

"So long as he wasn't disturbing you. I don't want you being interrupted. We came here to get away from people."

I stretched out my hand to her.

"I don't know what I would do without you," I said. I meant it. These last months she had been a great comfort to me. She had taken it on herself to nurse me, encourage me when my agent thought my best creative period was over, and, indeed, had dismissed my doctor. In that she was proving correct for since we had come back to Ireland I had found my health greatly improving. I could forgive her protective attitude.

It was a week later that I again awoke to the sound of the strange chorus of sorrow and anguish. It rose and fell as if coming from a great distance. I could scarcely believe it, so clear did it now come to my ears. I turned in bed and felt for Catherine.

"Catherine! Can you hear this?" I whispered, putting out my hand.

The bed beside me was empty. The sheets cold.

"Catherine?" I exclaimed, puzzled.

There was no sound but the sibilant moaning of the strange chorus of the damned. I reached out, found my wristwatch, clicked back the lid and felt for the face. Two o'clock again. I threw back the sheets and felt for my stick. I made my way to the bathroom and called softly: "Catherine?"

She was not in the bathroom nor in the kitchen.

I stood listening to the rise and fall of the fearful, suppressed sighing. It seemed to be coming from outside the house, from the lawn that stretched down to the cliffs. I don't know how I knew but, suddenly and without question, I knew that the sound was emanating from the standing stone. I shivered violently. The stone was singing like a chorus of the damned!

Then I smiled. And me a musician who dealt in sound! Of course, it was the whispering of the wind over the strange contours of the stone that was producing the effect. I had heard several peculiar musical noises produced by the effect of wind over patterned surfaces. My imagination again!

I moved to the door, the better to listen to the remarkable effect.

As I stood there listening, the wind must have fallen away for out of the night air I suddenly heard voices. The sound of conversation came from the side of the house. The voices were low, intense, but with conspiratorial softness.

"It must be tomorrow, darling," said a male voice.

I froze at once. It was a voice I recognised. The voice of a man I thought was in London. Carlton Daniel, my agent.

"Why tomorrow?" It was a woman's voice.

"Because tomorrow evening there will be a programme devoted to his work on Radio Eireann. I tried to stop the broadcast. The presenter has interviewed a number of people bemoaning the fact that he hasn't written anything recently. If he hears that then he will know what we've been doing. He'll know you've been interfering with his mail and that I've been holding out on him."

"I don't like it!" I recognised Catherine's voice with a growing chill around my heart.

"We've waited long enough," Daniel's voice came. "Christ knows! Over these last six months you've fed him enough poison to kill a bull. He should have been dead long before this."

"We agreed that it had to be done slowly. How was I to know that he could build up an immunity to the stuff? And then that damned doctor in London began to suspect something was wrong. But now ... surely someone will question things if anything happens?"

"No," Daniel's voice was reassuring. The same warm reassurance he used to use for me when I was worried about some aspect of my work. "No one will suspect anything. He's blind. He wanders down to the end of the garden to sit in the sun for a while. He sits on the stone wall. When he gets up he makes a mistake in direction and instead of walking towards the house he walks away from it to the cliffs. By a curious misfortune an animal has broken the barbed-wire fencing. He stumbles through and falls to his death. It is quite simple really."

I shivered at the callousness of what I was hearing. I think it was only then that I appreciated that they were talking about me; about a plan to murder me! I had to reach out and hold on to the wall to prevent myself from falling.

"But how can we do it?" demanded Catherine. There was no remorse in her voice. It was simply practical.

"Tomorrow afternoon, about three o'clock, you will persuade Fergus to go with you to the bottom of the garden. I'll be there. As soon as I have made sure no one is about, I'll hit him on the head and throw him over. Then we'll telephone the police and report the accident exactly as I have told you."

"The police will want to know what you are doing here."

"I'm his agent, aren't I? I came over to discuss some work with him and it was when you called him to tell him that I had arrived that he got up and mistook his direction."

45

"Will it work, Carlton?"

"Of course, darling. It's the answer to everything."

"It will mean the end of a nightmare," Catherine sighed. "But I could have just left him."

"We've grown used to the good life, Catherine. Survival is not what we are after. Fergus Finucane has been one of the most talented composers of the century. His work is in great demand and I have had trouble stopping performances and pretending that Fergus is no longer writing anything. I can't do it for much longer."

"You said it was the only way to make him depressed and become a recluse in order to persuade people about his illness."

"That's right. After he's dead and I discover the bundle of recent compositions, which, of course, he never told me about, think of the money we will make. His death will increase the demand for his work. As his widow, my sweet, you will be rich. We will be able to live well for the rest of our lives."

I stood shaking as their horrifying scheme became known to me. God! What a fool I was. My wife and my agent! Two people I had utterly trusted and relied upon.

"Tomorrow at three o'clock," Catherine was saying.

There came a long pause and then the sound of gasping breath. I ground my teeth as I realised what they were doing.

"Let's go in your car, darling," I heard Catherine whisper voluptuously. "Fergus is dead to the world when he's asleep. He won't miss me for a long while yet."

I heard them move away.

I stood for a moment like ice. It took a great effort to move slowly back to bed. I lay there, eyes closed but fully awake. I was still awake when she slid quietly back between the sheets. I was a person unable to think. I understood what I had heard but I was simply incapable of formulating any action. I now realised what a rabbit must feel like when it crouches petrified before a snake that is about to strike.

Throughout the entire morning of the next day I sat in my study unmoving, answering Catherine's bright, cheerful tones with monosyllabic grunts. I wallowed in self-pity. At lunch-time Catherine came in and leant over me.

"Why, darling," she rebuked, "you haven't worked at all this morning."

"I'm not in the mood," I muttered.

She brought me some lunch but I could not eat it. I kept thinking of the migraines and stomach cramps that I had endured during the past six months. She had been poisoning me! It was not so hard to believe the evidence of my own ears.

I was still sitting brooding when she came in later in the afternoon.

"It's a beautiful afternoon, Fergus. Since you've not done any work why not come down the garden and sit with me a while on the old stone wall. The sun is really warm and the breeze off the estuary will do you a world of good after your illness."

"Is it three o'clock?" I found myself asking.

"Yes. Why?" I heard tension in her voice.

"Nothing."

I felt her hand under my arm coaxing me from my piano stool.

I made no effort to draw back. There was a terrible feeling in the pit of my stomach. I think I came to the conclusion at that moment that my life had been destroyed and that I would accept what fate had in store for me. My entire world was without purpose. What was the use of living when the only person I loved hated me enough to destroy me? I wanted to die. I felt a strange exhilaration in the experience. There was no point in life. I would walk with her willingly, walk down the garden. The sun was warm as we came out of the house. Catherine's soft touch guided me across the grass.

It was then that I heard the soft humming again. The soft moaning cry of sorrow and anguish. I halted.

"Is there a wind?" I asked with a frown. "I don't feel one."

"No." Her voice was a little on edge. "Why do you ask?"

"Don't you hear it?"

"Hear what?"

"The sound of the wind whispering over the standing stone."

"I can only hear the noise of the sea. There's no wind to speak of, just a sea breeze and that's not blustery at all."

We moved on down the lawn. I was mentally marking off the paces. Was Carlton Daniel waiting by the wall or would he attack me closer to the house? I did not care. I only wish they would do it quickly, painlessly!

The scream halted me in my tracks. It was the scream of a man. An awesome cry of fear and pain. Yet it was not my scream.

I felt Catherine tugging away from me.

"Carlton!" her cry was one of sheer terror.

I waited, half expecting the heavy blow to fall. Carlton Daniel must have been waiting by the standing stone; waiting to knock me out as I passed. But why had he screamed?

The cry of dread came again. I turned in its direction, the direction of the standing stone. It was then that I realised that the stone was positively vibrating with noise. It was no trick of the wind on its surface. The keening chorus of the damned was rising in exultation.

"God!" Catherine was screaming now. "God help me! Fergus! Help me!"

I felt her hand trying to catch on my sleeve only to be wrenched away.

"Catherine? What's happening?" I called.

Her voice was a shriek.

I moved forward, hands outstretched. I seemed to collide with the standing stone. Yet the stone was not gritty and hard as I had often felt it before. It was a squelching wet clay-like substance. Ice cold to the touch. My hands caught Catherine's spasmodically clutching hands. My mouth opened in horror. Was it my imagination or was she being sucked into the wet clay of the standing stone?

"Fergus! Help me!"

Her wail of fear came from a long way away.

I tried to pull her away but whatever was sucking her into the withdrawing ice-cold clay was far stronger than I was. The sounds of wailing rose, almost deafening me.

I reached up and my hand came into contact with Catherine's face. That beautiful face whose every contour I knew by touch. I felt the warmth of her flesh. I could feel her mouth now wide in soundless terror. The eyes were open and staring. Even as I felt, the flesh was growing cold and wet, mingling with the malleable clay. Then, as I stood there, I felt the wetness grow dry and hard. The surface under my hands became gritty and sharp, forming into the hard granite that was centuries old.

Abruptly, the noise of the keening was gone.

Scarcely daring to believe my senses I reached forward feeling the abrasive surface of the stone under my hands. It was there as I had felt it many times. I ran my finger tips over it, sensing the sandy touch of its surface, sensing the strange contours that seemed to me like countless faces all merging into the stone.

And now there were two new faces that had not been there before. I ran my hands over them to make sure. There was no doubt, for a blind man's touch is sharper than the keenest eye. I felt the agonised contours of the face of Carlton Daniel and, close by, I could feel the outline of Catherine's beseeching features.

III

My Lady of Hy-Brasil

ABOVE THE PLAINTIVE cries of the circling gulls, above the harsh whisper of the sibilant sea, and the angry smack of its whitefoamed lips on the tall granite rocks, I can hear the soft sweetness of her voice gently urging me to return to the island: urging me to return to Hy-Brasil. Though seven years is a long time to wait, wait it I must. I must return for she, too, is waiting for me; waiting somewhere out there in the cold, black Atlantic swell; waiting for me with a patience that eternity cannot destroy.

The whistle of the steamship *Naomh Eanna* shrilled as it edged near the black mound of the island. "That's Inisheer," smiled a sailor, brown of skin, blue of eyes, with sandy red hair blowing in the sea breeze. Inisheer, the smallest of the Aran Isles! The islands from where my grandfather migrated to New York and which had been such a magical place in my mind ever since I sat at his knee as a young boy and heard his tales about his own childhood there. I could scarcely believe that the cluster of dark humps ahead of the steamship were the islands; could not believe that I had finally made the pilgrimage which every Irish-American dreams of – a visit to his ancestral homeland.

The *Naomh Eanna*, named after the patron saint of the islands, so I was told, had dropped its anchor off Inisheer and a flotilla of small curious-shaped boats called curraghs – lath-ribbed, canvas-covered and tar-painted canoes, propelled by long, narrow bladed oars – came crowding out to the steamer. Passengers

51

and cargo for Inisheer had to be ferried to the island for its waters were too shallow for the steamer to approach it closely.

An animal, a cow, was hoisted from the for'ard hold of the ship in a sling; hauled limp and helpless over the ship's side and into the sea where it started to struggle fiercely in the water. Three men waited near by in a curragh. One of them grasped a rope around the head of the beast, and while the other two began to stroke at the water with their oars, the beast was pulled along, its legs threshing in a strange underwater dance, towards the shoreline.

Soon, all was offloaded for the few hundreds who inhabited the tiny island, and then it was on to Inishmaan, the middle island, before we finally steamed into Killeany Bay on the biggest of the Aran Isles – Inishmore. On steamer days, the friendly sailor told me, most of the island's thousand inhabitants turned out to greet the *Naomh Eanna* as she tied up at the pier at Kilronan, the chief town of the island. Ponies and traps and jaunting cars were in profusion and here and there, surprising me, were a few automobiles. Around me, as I came ashore, there rose the lilting sounds of Irish and hardly anywhere did I hear a world of English. I stood perplexed.

"Are you the American for Bungowla?" a soft voice enquired at my elbow.

I turned to face a middle-aged, rawboned man, sandy of hair like so many of the islanders.

"Yes," I replied.

"I am Peadar Flaherty. I have the trap here to take you to Bungowla."

Without a further word he picked up my suitcase and led the way through the milling crowd to a pony cart and motioned me to climb aboard.

"So Fr Connell wrote to you then?" I asked, stating the obvious since Flaherty had come to meet me. I had met Fr Connell in Boston during the previous year and he had offered to find me accommodation on the island should I finally make the decision to visit it on the long promised trip.

"He did so," replied the taciturn Flaherty.

"If it's any bother putting me up, I could stay in a hotel," I went on, desperately trying to make conversation.

Flaherty glanced at me almost pityingly.

"That you cannot do. There are no hotels on Inishmore. You are welcome to stay with us – indeed, where else could you stay if not in the cottage in which your grandfather was born? And are you not kin and cousin to me? Sure, I would be a poor sort of fellow to turn a cousin from my door."

He paused and frowned slightly.

"But it will be a simple place, I'm thinking, compared with what you are used to in America. There is no electricity in Bungowla ... only candle-light or gas lamp."

"Oh, that's okay," I said. "I'm used to roughing it."

I could have bitten my tongue for my unconscious discourtesy but Flaherty did not take offence.

"What I meant was that I'm a fisherman," I plunged on hurriedly. "I work on the trawlers out of Yarmouth; that's in the state of Maine."

"Is that so?"

I fell silent as Flaherty nudged the pony along the roadway; fell silent as I began to relax under the spell of the island, absorbing the scenery and sounds. The sea was everywhere; you heard it, smelt it, even tasted it from the brine that nestled on your lips. We trotted along the coastline of quiet coves and sandy beaches which would suddenly rise into sheer rock faces, cliffs as high as 250 feet, against which giant waves exploded with violence. Inshore the island was a maze of tiny fields, enclosed from the elements by low stone walls. Great slabs of limestone rock lay everywhere. I saw few cattle or sheep. Now and again we drove by tall stone monuments set beside the roadway which exhorted travellers to pray for the souls of men lost in the grey froth seas around the islands.

Bungowla was exactly as I had imagined it from my grandfather's stories, a small collection of whitewashed stone crofts shrouded in a pungent smell of burning peat and salt sea breezes.

The cottage to which Flaherty conducted me was no different to the rest except in my romantic imagination for was it not the place in which my grandfather had been born? Flaherty's wife came to greet me with three children of varying ages, each topped with her own gold-red hair, clutching at her skirt and peering shyly at me. Máire was a tall, gentle woman with solemn eyes and rosy cheeks who never seemed to stop working but always found the time to make another pot of tea.

For several days I basked in the hospitality of the Flahertys and was introduced to the warm friendship of the local islanders, especially to Phelim Conor Donn, an ancient man who was the village storyteller or *seanchaí* – as they called him. He could recall stories of my grandfather's childhood on Inishmore. As a fisherman myself, I felt at home among these people and could sympathise with the hardy folk who wrested their scanty living from a harsh, unfriendly sea. If there was a lesson of courage to be learnt, it could be learnt from folk such as these. They rose early, baked their own bread, cut their own hair, built their own houses, constructed their own boats, worked, drank, prayed and – finally – made their own coffins. They were a determined and stoic people, who lived close to nature; a people who saw the realities and meanings in the fierce, ever-changing elements; a people who had not yet lost their psychic reality as have city dwellers; a people who could still read the future in the brooding tempests and in whom nature and supernature met as one entity.

One morning, which dawned dark and ugly with rain sheeting across the island, I went into the kitchen having determined the previous evening to pay a trip to the Eerach Lighthouse that day. Máire Flaherty looked up from stirring porridge in a great iron pot.

"The day is angry with itself," she greeted, nodding to the grey skies beyond the tiny window.

"I wanted to go to the Eeragh Lighthouse," I said. "Is it still possible?"

"Eeragh, is it?" she frowned, as she ladled my breakfast into an earthenware bowl. "That's a strange place to be wanting to see."

"Is it possible to go today?" I asked again. "Will the weather be too bad?"

"Not for a trip to Eeragh," she said. "But my man will not be able to take you today. He is off down to Kilmurvy to buy Concannon's goat."

"No matter," I said, smiling. "If I could borrow Peadar's boat, I'll not trouble him to take me. I bought a chart of the waters around the island while I was in Galway City."

She pouted at me as if I were a fool.

"You mean that you'd go alone? That is a crazy notion. The waters round here are contrary when a fierce wind and sea are running."

"I'm not afraid." I could not help but sound patronising. After all, I was a trawler skipper of one of the best ships that ever sailed out of Yarmouth.

Maire Flaherty shook her head.

"A man who is not afraid of the sea will soon be drowned," she reflected, "for he will be going out on a day he shouldn't. But we islanders do be afraid of the sea, and we do only be drowned now and again."

Peadar Flaherty came in for his breakfast and I put forward my argument. His first reaction was similar to his wife's but I was adamant. It took all my persuasive powers, however, to convince Peadar to allow me to take his curragh, which was fitted with an outboard motor.

It was after lunch that I started the Yamaha outboard motor and nursed the curragh seaward. It was a light craft and easy to handle. In spite of the grey threatening day, the sea's long level – dim with rain – was fairly flat and the spray was like a gentle caress against my cheeks. Eeragh Island, on which the lighthouse was situated, was, according to my chart, one of a cluster of deserted islets called the Brannocks off western Inishmore. My grandfather had told me that there had been a light kept on Eeragh since 1857 in order to warn shipping putting into Galway City of the dangers of the rocks. It had been his first job to "keep the light" and hence my interest in it. A new lighthouse, manned by three keepers, rose tall and white on the rocks with a great 375,000 candlepower lamp shining for fifteen miles in any direction. The trip there was pleasant enough. There was no jetty on Eeragh and the place was merely a moonscape of rocks. I ran the curragh close inshore and jumped into the surf to push it beyond the reach of the waves.

"*Dia dhuit!*" a voice greeted me in Irish.

A moon-faced keeper stood near the jetty watching me curiously.

"Hello there," I replied, finishing my task.

The man's face registered surprise.

"Is it American you are?" he asked.

I nodded. "I wanted to see the lighthouse."

He gazed from me to the curragh and back again.

"Have you come over from Inishmore alone?"

I explained but he shook his head.

"The waters here are moody waters," he said, as if addressing some wayward child. "It is easy to fall foul of them." Then he shrugged. "Still, come up and see the place if you've a mind to but you should catch the tide within the half-hour or you'll not be getting off Eeragh this night."

It was four o'clock when I left the keepers, who kept shaking their heads and warning me of the changing moods of the waters. They watched me push off in the curragh to a chorus of "*Beannacht Dé ort!*" which I understood was an expression of farewell and good wishes. I pushed the curragh out into the surf and rowed a short distance before I started the outboard and began to ride the choppy swell towards the black hump of Inishmore.

I had not been out into the sea for more than a few minutes when the heavens suddenly ripped open, showing blinding white sky, and thunder growled menacingly overhead. The waves began to climb to incredible heights as the wind whipped up and the tiny curragh was tossed this way and that – sometimes the propeller of the outboard motor echoed the thunder with its shrill scream as a wave tossed it clear out of the sea.

Through the lashing spray I saw near by a dark headland and beyond that the gentle slope of a beach. I thanked God as I turned the boat and made towards it. I had been thinking that I was still some way from Inishmore but I must have been mistaken. Strangely, as I wrested to get the curragh close inshore, the skies seemed to clear, the rain ceased and the wind died away to a soft whisper. I ran the boat into the shallows and then hauled it up on the soft grey sand of the beach and stood peering around in surprise. As if by magic the bad weather had suddenly swept away and the sun was shining high overhead, shining down with an intensity of warmth which made me feel hot and uncomfortable as I pulled off my waterproofs.

I climbed out of the rocky cove in which I had landed and walked to the clifftop and looked around me. I discovered, to my astonishment, that I was not on Inishmore. I was on an island which was almost a complete round shape – some three or four miles in diameter containing a soft, undulating countryside, yet greener and more lush than the other islands. However, each field was marked out by the tell-tale stone walls and the place was as treeless as the other islands. Yet I could not help thinking that the vivid greens of the fields made it seem more like a painting that a true reflection of nature.

Dominating the landscape was a great grey stone house, almost castle-like in its structure and standing several stories high. It looked bleak and out of place among the low white-washed stone crofts, with their yellowing thatched roofs, which stood in isolated groups around the house. It gave an impression of some strange and unreal picture postcard.

I was aware of a thunder of horse's hoofs bearing down on me and turned to see a rider coming towards me like a maniac on a large white stallion. As he drew near, he hauled at the reins causing the great beast to rear on its hindquarters and lash at the air with its gigantic hooves, snorting in anger.

The rider, to my astonishment, was dressed in the brown habit of a monk. The sight of him, so incongruous astride his steed, brought a broad smile to my lips.

"*Fág an áit! Fág an áit!*" he cried, in a terrible voice that made me quiver with a sudden fear of him. "*Ó mo chroí amach ...* "

I halted his tirade of Irish by telling him that I neither understood nor spoke the language for I was an American, a visitor to the country.

He stared at me for a moment, his lips trying to form unfamiliar words, but then it seemed as if his eyes looked beyond me, over my shoulder, and widened a little. With one shaking thin hand he made the sign of the cross, suddenly kicked his steed and raced away.

A peal of merry, silvery laughter caused me to turn round.

A woman, no; a young girl, was sitting on a rock smiling at me. Never in all my years had I seen anyone so pretty as she. Her white heart-shaped face was surrounded by a tumble of golden red hair which shimmered in the bright rays of the sun and were tossed this way and that in the breeze. Deep sea-green eyes twinkled with a hint of mischief while her soft red lips carried a merry smile.

"You must forgive Brother Máirtín, stranger. He is a little demented but means no harm."

The voice carried a husky, rich seductive warmth.

My breath caught in my throat as I approached her.

"Good afternoon," I said. "Can you tell me where I am? I was running my boat before the storm and only just managed to beach her here."

The girl frowned, gazing at the sky.

"The storm?"

I grinned sheepishly, realising there was now hardly a cloud in the sky, so quickly had the bad weather abated.

"The weather changes quickly here," I conceded. "I was making my way to Inishmore when the weather overtook me."

"Ah, Inishmore is it? Then you are only a little way from your course. Inishmore lies two miles to the east," she pointed with a slim brown arm. "You are on the island of Hy-Brasil."

It was my turn to frown.

"You'll forgive me, but I did not realise there was a fourth large island in the Arans. Inisheer, Inishmaan and Inishmore I know of, but what did you say the name of this island was? I do not know it."

She pouted in mock displeasure.

"Hy-Brasil is the most beautiful island of them all."

It was a fact that I readily conceded for all its unreal quality.

"Hy-Brasil," continued the girl, climbing from her perch on the rocks, "is the last resting place of the O'Flahertys of Iar-Connacht."

"The last resting place?" I queried, smiling at her archaic phraseology.

"When we were forced from our ancestral lands on the mainland, in Iar-Connacht, we fled to Hy-Brasil to safety; we fled to our fortress there," she nodded towards the distant house. "In our tongue we call it *Dún na Sciath* – the fort of shields, for it was both refuge and shield to us in the days of terror."

She made it sound as if it had been only yesterday and as if she had been part of it.

"I gather your name is O'Flaherty?" I ventured.

She startled me by the way she suddenly drew herself up and by the momentary blaze in her eyes.

"I am *The* O'Flaherty now that my father is dead, *go ndéana Diabhal grásta*!" She crossed herself, at least I thought she did for it occurred to me afterwards that the act had been performed in reverse to how I was taught at church. The girl was watching me with a smile. "My name is Aideen O'Flaherty – I am called the Lady Aideen. Let me offer you the hospitality of my home."

It was a generous gesture, most grandly made and I accepted.

We walked along the dirt track which led through the fields towards the great house. Here and there men and women working in the fields rose to watch us pass by. They seemed stiff and rather odd, almost more like waxworks than real people, staring with unblinking hollow eyes.

"Do you get many strangers here?" I asked at last. "The people stare at me as if I had just dropped from outer space."

"From where?" laughed the girl.

"As if I just flew down from the moon," I amplified.

The girl gave a gleeful peal of laughter.

"What a strange saying. But take no notice of these people," her voice hardened slightly. "They are but peasants and their curiosity borders on ill manners."

Watching her face suddenly set in grim lines I had a passing thought – that I would hate to displease this girl and win her enmity for I sensed a hardness that was neither charitable nor forgiving.

The interior of the house was more impressive than its stately exterior. Long tapestries and oil portraits bedecked the walls. Among them scowled a gallery of O'Flahertys from bygone ages, frowning down on the accoutrements of war – swords, battle-axes, spears and shields. The furniture, too, was straight out of an antique store. In one large hall a fire crackled welcomingly in a fireplace that was almost the size of an apartment room. A meal was laid out on a big table before this fireplace and, curiously, two places were laid yet there was no sign of other guests nor, indeed, of the person who had set the places.

The time seemed to fly by; I chatted happily with the girl, ranging on many subjects, mainly about the Irish, their language, literature and folklore, on which she was more than well informed. I found myself growing strangely attracted to her – as if I were basking in the pangs of first love. Even her quaint archaic speech, which I attributed to her first language being Irish, held an attractive quality to it. Time sped like a strange dream and only the darkening of the sky made me rise regretfully.

"I must be getting back to Inishmore."

"Oh no; no, please ... you must stay."

I was aware that there was something slightly different about her manner; perhaps it was the way she carried herself, the way she smiled at me. Her prettiness had gone; now she seemed more voluptuous, even seductive. Her lips were more red, more full than before, pouting in a lascivious grossness. A red tongue flickered nervously over small white teeth.

"I cannot," I replied. "The family with whom I am staying on

Inishmore will be anxious if I do not return tonight."

She blinked her eyes and, to my consternation, I perceived they held tears in them.

"Please stay. It is so lonely, so utterly lonely here on this island and I do so like talking with you."

Automatically, I reached forward a hand to take hers in a reassuring gesture.

"I'll come back," I assured her. "I'll come back to explore the island tomorrow, if that is convenient."

She blinked and a tear dropped onto the back of my hand like a scalding hot raindrop.

The girl sniffed and forced a smile.

"Yes," she said. "Yes, I know you will come back now."

There was a curious intonation in her voice.

As the door of the great house shut behind me, after my brief farewell, it was as if I had entered another world entirely.

The sky had darkened into blackness, the wind was howling and sending sheets of rain across the island. I could hardly see my hand in front of me. I put my head down and began to propel myself through the wind and rain towards the cove where I had left the curragh. By the time I had gone a hundred yards, I was beginning to regret that I had declined the girl's invitation to stay. The house had been so warm, so comfortable, a refuge against the elements – wasn't that what the girl had said it was – a refuge? Yet something inside of me, some curious anxiety, made me push on. It was a cold, wild night. I did not fancy the journey back across the roaring seas to Inishmore but that feeling of anxiety, of disquiet, could not be denied and forced my footsteps forward.

There was a loud crack of thunder and a white blinding flash as the sky split asunder. The rain intensified, beating down like a myriad of tiny pellets against my skin. I became aware of a strange smell, the smell of brine and ... I suddenly heaved, for it was an awful smell of rotting fish, a bitter sweet stench of corruption that made me almost choke on my own bile.

My perplexity gave way to a growing unease as I found myself slipping across seaweed strewn rocks with little dank pools which I had no recollection of crossing a few hours previously when the hot sun was burning down on the summer island. Nowhere in the gloom could I perceive a landscape remotely like that which I had seen that afternoon. Instead I felt the awesome presence of the sea all around me, as if I were struggling over low lying rocks which its waves threatened to engulf at any moment. Apart from the howling of the wind and the surging roar of the sea I could not even hear the lament of a sea bird nor the friendly croaking of a frog. Grey-black slimy wilderness, from which granite and limestone rocks thrust themselves aggressively into the air, surrounded me. And that awful fetid stench of corruption ever assailing my nostrils.

I had lost all sense of direction. I no longer knew where the curragh was beached.

Then I heard it – a plaintive cry, a sadness filling the air with a doleful wailing which caused even the howling wind and splatter of rain to fall silent. It was a sobbing, a human cry of despair rung from the depths of a soul in torment.

I turned towards the sound.

A figure hunched in the darkness.

"Is there something the matter?" I cried.

The figure started. It was vaguely familiar. Around it flapped a robe.

"Go from here," a voice suddenly hissed. "Go away from here, stranger. Can you not see that this is a doomed spot? Or you, too, will be reduced to such as I."

It was the demented monk – what had the girl called him? – Brother Máirtín.

"It's all right," I said, pacifying. "Perhaps I can be of some help?"

"Stranger, leave here or you will not be able to help yourself. I came to this island thinking I could help, I came here thinking I was protected being a man of God ... I was but a man full of the corruption of man, misled by the superficial beauties of this place, by the superficial beauties of the girl ... the Lady of Hy-Brasil. ... It was all an evil facade. Now I am forsaken by my God!"

I sighed. The poor man was utterly demented.

It was then I suddenly felt the sea washing at my ankles and looked down in bewilderment.

The monk saw my glance and gave a deep wail of despair which froze my very blood.

"It is too late! Oh God protect you! Too late! We shall return to the depths of corruption from whence we came!"

A blinding flash of lightning abruptly lit the scene before me. It was as if the entire island were disappearing beneath the waves. Only a small outcrop of rock, seaweed strewn, rose above the waves. A fear came upon me such as I had never known.

Then I heard a voice echoing clearly in that nightmare gloom.

"You must stay now ... must stay. It will make me so happy ... I have been alone here far too long."

I looked up fully expecting to see the young Lady Aideen in the light of the flashing storm. Instead I saw an old woman hobbling through the rain towards me, skeletal arms outstretched, claw-like hands towards me, a leering smile on a skull face whose teeth seemed oddly protruding and sharp white. It was a caricature of a woman and yet – yet her voice was an echo of my Lady Aideen's.

"Stay with me ... stay with me ... "

Seawater suddenly swirled around my legs causing me to stagger and almost lose my balance. I felt a thud in the back of my legs, turned and saw the curragh floating by. With a cry I turned and hauled myself aboard, falling a-tumble into the bottom, gasping from the exertion.

"Oh God protect you!" came the wail of the monk which was overshadowed by a feminine scream of rage that seemed to end in a gurgle and kiss of the harsh sea.

I raised myself to stare around.

I was in the midst of a dark tempestuous sea with the dark shape of Inishmore not far away. I crawled to the stern and lowered the outboard motor and, after a couple of attempts, succeeded in starting it. The little boat smacked and bobbed its way over the waves towards the shoreline and, wet and exhausted, I rounded the headland into the tiny cove where the fisherfolk of Bungowla beached their curraghs. A tall man was standing on the foreshore holding aloft a storm lantern.

"Man, man," cried the voice of Peadar Flaherty, "is it yourself, safe and well?"

I hardly had the strength to beach the boat and he bent forward to help me. When we had beached the curragh, Flaherty gripped me by the hand and stared with concern into my face.

"Where have you been? We thought you were drowned for sure, and was I not cursing myself for the fool I was to let you go out in the curragh alone? Why, we have sent for the Kilronan lifeboat already. Och, man, where have you been?"

I gently tried to reassure him and apologise for the worry I had caused. My own fears had evaporated and I was beginning to rationalise the last few minutes of my leaving the island as a product of panic-strewn imagination.

"When the storm came up," I said, "I put in at one of the islands."

Flaherty frowned.

"Islands? You managed to get ashore on the Brannocks? Sure, but that was a dangerous thing to do."

"No, no," I smiled. "It was one of the most pleasant islands I have ever seen. The people were ... ?"

"People?" Flaherty was puzzled. "People? Oh, do you mean you stayed with the keepers on Eerach?"

"No, this was a pleasant little island which was very green and fertile and had a great house and a village on it. I met a woman, a lady, who said she was The O'Flaherty. You must know it."

"*Dia linn!*" Flaherty started back and crossed himself. "What are you saying man?"

Again I felt a growing unease.

"Oh, come now," I insisted. "You must surely know who I mean. Why ... " I remembered abruptly. "She told me the island was called Hy-Brasil."

"*Dia idir sinn agus an anachain!*" cried the islander, his face white. "God between us and all evil!"

"What ... what is it?" I cried, fearful of the expression on his face.

He was silent for a while, trying to overcome the emotions in him.

"Do you still carry a chart of these water?" he eventually said, his voice trembling a little.

I felt in my pocket and nodded.

"Look, then, look for the island of Hy-Brasil," his voice rose a tone.

In the yellow glow of his storm lantern I spread the chart and looked vainly for my island.

"Why ... it's not marked at all," I said, desperately trying to fight back my fears.

"It will not be. It does not exist."

"Nonsense!" I forced a laugh. "I landed there, I talked with ..."

"Wherever you landed," Flaherty's voice was intense, "it was not Hy-Brasil! There is no such island. Speak no more of it."

And with that he turned and strode off towards the village.

The next morning, following a strange dream in which I heard my Lady Aideen calling me, calling me back to the island, I went down to the kitchen for breakfast. I had already booked with Flaherty to go fishing with him off the Brannocks but Máire Flaherty apologised for his absence. "*Tá stodam air ... tá taghdanna ann* ... He is in a bad mood ... he is subject to moods," she said by way of explanation. It turned out that Phelim Conor Donn, the old village storyteller, was going fishing that day and offered me a place in his curragh. We pulled for the Brannocks. I suppose I already knew what I would find. However, I took my sightings from the lighthouse of Eeragh to make sure. Where my island had stood on the afternoon before there was a large expanse of grey foaming sea above which the gulls wheeled and cried fretfully.

Phelim Conor Donn pulled a face.

"Do you hear them cry?" he asked, jerking his tousled grey head skywards. "Sure, you'd be thinking they were cries of souls in torment."

I peered into the black depths of the waters.

"Phelim," I said abruptly, "have you ever heard of an island called Hy-Brasil?"

The old man stared and slowly crossed himself.

"Now that's a story barely told outside of Inishmore," he observed curiously. "How would you be hearing it?"

"Oh, just something my grandfather said once," I lied. "Tell me the story."

The old man heaved a sigh.

"Well, it was said that Hy-Brasil was once the most beautiful island of the Aran Isles – more green, more lush than any other. And that once its mistress was the equal of its beauty – my Lady Aideen, chieftain of the O'Flahertys of Iar-Connacht. You will have noticed that many bear the name Flaherty in these parts for these were the clan lands of Flaherty."

He paused as I nodded and then went on:

"It was said that my Lady Aideen was so beautiful that she could charm the birds from the trees by the sweet sound of her own voice. Even a wolf would stop its baying when she began to sing. But her beauty hid a black soul. Aye, she was self-willed and skilled in the black arts and able to conjure demons to her bidding. Many a young man lost their hearts and their very souls to her. There was the tale of Angus Óg Dara of Clanricade who left his wife and children to follow her to her accursed island and who was never seen again. Then another, Brother Máirtín of Loch Dearg, who thought she was but a woman and he was a man of God; but it turned out that she was more than a woman and he was but a man.

"It was said that she consorted with the devil so that she might have earthly power and, in return, promised him a rich harvest of souls of young men who were enticed to her island. God have mercy on all the poor souls who followed her siren call to Hy-Brasil," he crossed himself again.

"Well, the story goes that my Lady Aideen's evil reputation grew to the extent where even the Pope in Rome and his cardinals sent their emissaries to do battle with her in the name of God and to try to set free those souls she had enslaved. She defied them.

Aye, she worked an awesome spell for her own protection which forced the entire island to sink beneath the waves of the cold Atlantic."

The old man shivered slightly.

"But, it is said, the spell was such that the island rises ... rises up, lush and green, once in every seven years; rises up with its fiendish inhabitants to prey on the blood and souls of the living."

I shuddered violently at the intensity in his voice and stared into the choppy swell.

Phelim Conor Donn smiled.

"Aye, aye ... I know the legend well. But have no fear, *a mhic*. Only if a man lands on the island at the time of its rising and is marked by the Lady Aideen can she eventually call him back to the island to become her vassal in the service of the dead for all eternity."

My mouth gaped in horror.

"Only if he is marked by her?" I echoed. "What mark?"

The old man smiled.

"It is said that if one of her tears falls on the skin of a man, he must become her slave for all time."

I felt the stinging tear, scalding on my hand, and stared down at the blood red blotch which now lay there. Her mark! I could hear her voice, soft and mocking: "I know you will come back *now*!"

My cry was taken up by the circling gulls above who cried like souls in torment above the black waters.

And above the plaintive cries of the circling gulls, who cried like souls in torment above the black waters, above the harsh whisper of the sibilant sea and the angry smack of its white-foamed lips on the tall granite rocks, I can hear her soft sweet voice gently urging me to return to the island: urging me to return to Hy-Brasil. Though seven years is a long time to wait, wait it I must. I must return for she, too, is waiting for me; waiting somewhere out there in the cold black Atlantic swell; my lady of Hy-Brasil is waiting for me with a patience that eternity cannot destroy.

IV

The Samhain Feis

KATY FANTONI BEGAN to wonder whether she had made a mistake almost as soon as she left the eastern suburbs of Dublin, taking the western road by the small airport at Rathcoole. Yet she had to get away from the stuffy city, away from the Victorian disapproval of Aunt Fand and her thin-lipped glances of reproach. She needed peace; a place to relax and work out her problem without the narrow-minded condemnation of her only relative.

It had been the local shopkeeper, a kindly woman, who had suggested that Katy might like to stay in the holiday cottage which she owned up in the Slieve Aughty Mountains in County Clare. At first the idea of spending a week in a remote country area was attractive to Katy, especially with the alternative being a week with Aunt Fand. But now, as she drove the hire-car through Kildare, misgivings began to tumble through her mind. After all, what was she going to do in a remote cottage in an alien countryside except brood ... brood about Mario and her busted marriage?

She glanced into the driving mirror and caught sight of her seven-year-old son, Mike, sitting quietly on the back seat playing with his teddy bear. Was it fair to him, she wondered? He had been restless staying in Aunt Fand's house but, in her eagerness to escape Aunt Fand, had she precipitated them into a worse situation? It was to be a whole week in the isolated country cottage. She tried to dispel the disquiet from her mind with a shake of her fair hair. No, she refused to turn back now. Something urged her onwards, perhaps pride. She had already earned the disfavour of Aunt Fand; no need to give her another example of what the old woman saw as her niece's fecklessness.

Katy Fantoni – or rather, Katy Byrne, as she was then – had been born in Dublin but, when she was five years old, her parents had emigrated to America and she had grown up in the Jamaica Bay area of Brooklyn. There was nothing special about her childhood; it was a common story of most immigrant Irish families. Not long after she had graduated from high school and secured a job in an advertising agency, however, her parents were killed in an automobile accident. Then she had met Mario Fantoni. Mario managed a chain of diners, owned by his father, Salvatore Fantoni, on Long Island. It was whispered that Salvatore Fantoni was "connected" ... a euphemism for membership in the Mafia. Katy Byrne's agency was owned by Gentile Alunno and it was doing a campaign for the Fantoni diners. That was how they met.

Mario was young, handsome and good company. Katy was young, attractive and very much alone with an emotional vacuum since the death of her parents. To both Katy and Mario, with their Catholic backgrounds, marriage was the next step. Mama and Papa Fantoni were not exactly happy that Mario was not marrying "Italian," for they were Sicilians of an archaic type. But they consoled themselves with the fact that Katy Byrne was a good Catholic.

So Katy and Mario were married. Mama and Papa Fantoni bought them a house in Glen Cove, overlooking Long Island Sound. It was a large house and with it came Lise, a good-natured though coarse-looking Calabrian, who was the housekeeper. A year later they had a son, Mike. Katy mentally prepared herself to settle down to an indolent life. After all, working for his father, Mario Fantoni had no financial worries.

The honeymoon did not last long. As soon as Katy became noticeably pregnant she began to learn some unpleasant truths about Mario. Mama and Papa Fantoni had brought him up in some old-fashioned Sicilian philosophies where wives were concerned. Even after Mike was born Katy was expected to stay home, act as hostess at a moment's notice when Mario decided to invite his friends to drop in, and not to develop any friendships of her own. Mario was always out on "business dates" and it soon came to Katy's knowledge that his business colleagues were all about twenty years old, came in a variety of colourings and just one gender – female! When she contemplated her seven years with Mario, Katy did not really understand how the marriage had survived that period. She supposed it was unconscious pressure from her Catholic upbringing. Or maybe she had been waiting for Mario to mature, waiting for him to change …

Then Mario went off on a West Coast tour "strictly for business" … and Katy was not long in discovering that the business sessions were taking place in Las Vegas night spots and motels and that his travelling companion was some TV starlet. That was when her Irish blood finally boiled over and she hopped a plane for Dublin with little Mike in tow, telling Lise that she would return in a couple of weeks – probably!

Katy Byrne Fantoni had one surviving relative and that was Aunt Fand in Dublin. She was the elder sister of Katy's mother, and while they had exchanged cards from time to time, Katy had not seen her since she was five years old. She had thought to find in Aunt Fand some of her mother's caring nature, her broadmindedness and concern. Instead Aunt Fand was a bigot as only a spinster of fanatical religious disposition can be. Ostentatious piety was a substitute for Christian charity. Her narrowness was demonstrated by her enthusiastic support of Archbishop Lefevre, who refused the introduction of the modern vernacular Mass in his churches as being impious and adhered strictly to the sixteenth-century Latin Mass. Aunt Fand's ideas on divorce were more extreme than those of the Pope. She was parochial and narrow and threw up her hands in horror when Katy began to speak of her problems with Mario and hinted she was contemplating a legal separation. Aunt Fand was hardly the person to confide in.

After the first week living in Aunt Fand's house in the small Dublin suburb of Kimmage, Katy was feeling stifled and oppressed. Even young Mike asked her one bedtime whether Aunt Fand was their wicked stepmother. Katy had taken the boy to see Disney's *Cinderella* a few days before.

Katy felt that she just had to escape in order to think quietly and rationally about her situation.

It was when she was in the local grocery store and fell to talking with Mrs MacMahon, the owner, that she mentioned she would like to get away for a few days to the west of Ireland. Mrs MacMahon promptly suggested that Katy might like to stay in a holiday cottage which she owned in County Clare.

Katy hesitated out of a certain respect for Aunt Fand's hospitality before agreeing.

"It's up in the Slieve Aughty Mountains," smiled Mrs MacMahon. "Near Lough Atorick. All you have to do is take the main road from Dublin to Portumna, drive past Lough Derg, turn south on the Ennis Road; turn off at Gorteeny for Derrygoolin, and then ask for Flaherty's farmstead. Ned Flaherty keeps the keys of the cottage and he'll let you in. There's a trackway from his farm which winds up into the mountains and you'll find the cottage by the lakeside about ten miles further on."

Ned Flaherty was a man of indeterminate age. He had snow-white hair, a shrewd weatherworn face and sparkling deep blue eyes, almost violet in colour. Humour never seemed to be far from his features.

When Katy drove up to the farmstead, found him and handed over Mrs MacMahon's scribbled note giving her permission to stay at the cottage, Flaherty was clearly astonished. He looked from Katy Fantoni to young Mike in surprise.

"'Tis late for tourists," he said in his slow, rolling County Clare drawl.

"I'm not really a tourist," Katy replied. "I just want a few days of quiet in a remote spot."

He frowned. "And you an American?" he pondered. "Well,

peace and quiet you'll be getting up at the croft and that's no lie."

He turned into the farmhouse and reappeared with a bunch of keys. "I'd best come and show you the croft."

He climbed into the car beside her and directed her up a track, a single unpaved trackway that twisted itself into the mountains. It was obvious that this track was rarely used. Now and then they had to halt and push their way through sheep who stood indifferent to the angry blasts of the car horn. As they climbed upwards the scenery became spectacular. Katy had always believed that Ireland was at its best in the golds, russets and muted greens of autumn. The gorse-strewn mountains were speckled in pale yellow.

Suddenly they came round the shoulder of a mountain on to a high plateau, a small valley with a large lake in its centre. By the lakeside stood a quaint thatched cottage with thick grey stone walls.

"Mrs MacMahon's croft," gestured the old farmer with a jerk of his head.

She halted the car before the cottage, or croft as Flaherty called it, and the dismay must have registered on her face.

The croft was fronted with a garden, bordered by a low stone wall of the same grey granite as the house. The garden had become overgrown and wild.

"It's a lonely spot, right enough," Flaherty said, observing her expression. "No gas, no electricity, nor a telephone."

Her spirits fell. "What shall I do for light and heat?"

"There's oil lamps, a fire, and plenty of turf, and there'll be a primus stove as well for the cooking. I'll show you."

She sighed as she climbed out of the car and followed him to the cottage door. Little Mike was running after them in ecstasy.

"Look, Mommy! Look! Can I play here? Is it ours?"

Well, it was certainly a beautiful spot. "Isolated" was hardly the word for it, though. It seemed a million miles from anywhere. Flaherty seemed to read her mind.

"No one has lived here for many years. In winter, when it rains, the road gets cut off. The old croft was deserted until Mrs

MacMahon from Dublin bought it. She only comes for a fortnight in summer and then lets it from time to time. I've never known it to be occupied so late in the year, though."

Katy turned and gazed about her as he fiddled with the keys.

The sun shone on the lake which reflected the pale blue of the sky. It seemed pleasant and inviting. To the side of the croft the mountain rose to a black jagged peak, looking more like a hill from this elevation on the high plateau. It was strewn with granite boulders, poking up in grotesque shapes through the black earth. It was a strange landscape, almost out of a fantasy world.

Flaherty caught her gaze.

"That's *Reilig na hIfreann*," he said.

"What does that mean?"

"The Cemetery of Hell."

Katy grinned.

"I see the likeness. The granite boulders do look a bit like tombstones."

They left little Mike racing around the garden, finding curious things to do.

"Keep in the garden, Mike," she admonished him as Flaherty conducted her inside. The door opened immediately into a large room which was apparently a combined kitchen, dining and living room. Two doors led off this large central room with its big open fireplace. One door led into a small bedroom which Katy immediately designated for Mike, while the other led into a large bedroom which she took for herself. It was primitive but it was quaint. She knew many New York matrons who would pay a fortune to stay in such a place.

Flaherty proved to be a treasure. He laid a turf fire and lit it, showing her how to build it so that it would remain alight through the night. He showed her how the primus stove worked and how to light the oil-lamps. The water was drawn by a pump which emptied into a big china sink. They managed to find a kettle and some tea-bags and brew a cup of milkless, unsweetened tea.

74

"I'll have to collect some groceries from the village," Kay reflected.

Flaherty nodded.

"At least you have a car," he smiled. "In the old days one had to walk the twelve miles to the village and return the same way carrying the shopping."

"No wonder the place became deserted."

They finally climbed back into the hire-car and drove back down the mountain road. Once again Flaherty shook his head as he gazed at them.

"I've never known the croft to be let so late in the year," he said. "'Tis almost the *Samhain Feis*." The words were pronounced "Sowan Fesh."

Katy gazed at him with a smile of puzzlement. "What's that?"

"Hallowe'en. We still call it by its old name in these parts."

Young Mike piped up from the back seat: "Mommy! Mommy! Are we going to have a Hallowe'en party with pumpkin masks and candles and games?"

"We'll see." Katy smiled at him in the driving mirror. "Do they have any local Hallowe'en celebrations in the village, Mr Flaherty?"

Flaherty gave her a curious glance. "The *Samhain Feis* is not a time to celebrate," he replied in an almost surly manner.

"I thought everyone celebrated Hallowe'en," Katy said with raised brows. "In the States it's a great time for the kids."

Flaherty sighed deeply.

"Samhain, which you call Hallowe'en, is an ancient festival celebrated among the pagan Irish centuries before the coming of Christianity."

"Tell me about it," said Katy. "I'm interested, truly."

"*Samhain* was one of the four great religious festivals among the pagan Irish. It started on the evening of October 31 and continued on November 1. It marked the end of one pastoral year and the beginning of the next. The name is derived from the words *Samred*, meaning summer, and *fuin*, meaning the end. Hence it was 'end of summer,' for *Samhain* was the first day of

Gemred, the winter. It was the time when, according to the druids, the Otherworld became visible to mankind and when spiritual forces were loosed upon the human race."

Katy chuckled. "So that is the origin of the Hallowe'en idea? The night when evil marches across the world, when spirits and ghosts set out to wreak their vengeance on the living?"

Flaherty simply stared, obviously not sharing her merriment.

"Christianity was unable to suppress many of the old beliefs. A great many pagan beliefs and superstitions and even ceremonies were adopted by the early Christians. *Samhain* was renamed All Saints' or All Hallows' Day so that the evening before became Hallowe'en."

Katy smiled. "You have quite a wealth of folkloric knowledge, Mr Flaherty."

"When you live up in these mountains, the folk memory becomes an extension of our own experience."

Within two days Katy had settled in the area and even grown used to the primitive living conditions of the croft. As for little Mike, he loved playing in the garden. Ned Flaherty seemed to take them under his personal protection and was always calling by for a brew of tea. He was a natural storyteller and had an amazing wealth of knowledge on many subjects. The English he spoke was slow and sedate and apparently Irish was his first language. In fact, Irish seemed to be quite widely spoken among the remote mountain folk.

It was on the third day that Katy suddenly realised that she had not once thought about Mario. Mario! It was high time that she sorted that mess out. After all, it was her whole reason for being in Ireland. But she had been so engrossed with learning to live in primitive style, with listening to Flaherty's stories and walking amidst the wild countryside, that the problem of Mario seemed remote and almost nothing to do with her.

It was surprising. She could not even blame the distraction on little Mike, for the boy was no burden at all. He loved playing by himself and, indeed, invented an imaginary playmate with whom he seemed quite content.

One day when Katy was cleaning the kitchen he came running into the croft to tell her about his playmate.

"He's called Seán Rua, Mommy. That means Red John," added the little boy proudly.

Katy frowned, peering out of the window. "And where is this Red John?" she demanded.

Mike pointed to the garden gate. "There he is."

Kay could see nothing except a bird perched on the gate post, a bird which looked like a raven, although the sun made its black feathers glow with a curious coppery colour.

It was at that point that Katy realised the situation. She had had an imaginary friend when she was Mike's age; it was a phase all children went through.

"I see." She smiled and ruffled the boy's fair hair. "Well, you run off and play for a while because I'm going to fix your supper."

Dutifully, little Mike trotted off.

The next morning Mike was eager to play with his "friend" and so Katy left him with strict orders not to move out of the cottage garden while she went to pick up a few necessary provisions from the village. As she drove by Flaherty's farmstead she saw the old man sitting on a stone bridge which spanned a gushing mountain stream. He was gazing moodily up at the darkening rain-laden skies while whittling a stick. He smiled when he saw her, and waved, so she halted the car and wound down the window.

"Settling in?" he asked.

"No problems," she replied with a smile.

"And where is the *garsún*?"

Katy frowned. "The gosoon?" she echoed.

"The boy. Isn't he with you?"

"Ah, no. He's having a game around the cottage. He's invented an imaginary friend to play with. He calls him Seán Rua."

"*Nár lige Dia!*" whispered Flaherty, suddenly making the sign of the Cross.

Katy gazed at his troubled face in surprise. "What's wrong?" she demanded.

"Nothing," muttered Flaherty. "Will you be out long?"

"I'm just going down to the village to buy a few things."

The old man peered at the sky. "You realise that it is the *Samhain Feis* tonight?"

Katy couldn't quite grasp the abrupt change of topic.

Flaherty stood up, nodded to her and walked briskly towards his tractor.

When Katy returned to the croft she found Flaherty sitting on the stone wall of the garden, whittling his stick and watching little Mike as he attempted to dam a stream which ran through the overgrown wilderness. Katy thought that the old man was being a little overprotective.

"You shouldn't have bothered to watch over Mike," she said as she unloaded the car. "He wouldn't have come to any harm in the garden."

"Ah," shrugged the old man, "it's turned into a nice afternoon. The rain clouds have blown clear of the mountain and it's nice enough to sit in the sun."

Katy nodded absently as little Mike came running up. She had promised to bring him some sweets. As she handed him a toffee he said, "Mommy, may I have one for Seán Rua?" Inwardly she groaned. She would have to watch that. Imaginary friends were all right until two of everything was demanded. Just this once, she thought, as she handed Mike another toffee. He took them both and ran to the far side of the garden where he appeared to be in conversation with someone.

Flaherty, watching him, plucked at his lower lip thoughtfully.

"Strange that the *garsún* picked on that name," he mused. "There is an old tale hereabouts ... "

"The whole place is riddled with old tales," Katy interrupted as she heaved her shopping bags to the cottage.

Flaherty followed.

"One of the beliefs of the *Samhain Feis* is that on the stroke of midnight the fairy hills split wide open and from each fairy hill there emerges a spectral host ... goblins, imps, bogeymen, demons, phantoms and the like. They spill out to take revenge on the living. The local people stay indoors on that night of the *Samhain Feis*."

Katy smiled tolerantly at him as she started to unpack. "What has that got to do with the name Mike chose for his playmate?"

"Of all the goblins and imps who appear at the *Samhain Feis*, there is a small red-haired imp called the *Taibhse Dearg*."

"The Tavesher Derug?" Katy tried to repeat the name. "What's that?"

"The Red Bogeyman," replied Flaherty solemnly. "Round these parts we call him Red John. It is said he eats the souls of children."

Katy glanced at the old man, not sure whether he was joking with her. Flaherty's face was grave.

"Tonight is the *Samhain Feis*, Mrs Fantoni. Do you have a crucifix in the croft?"

Katy's jaw dropped a little. Then, trying to suppress a smile, she pointed above the cottage door where an ornate crucifix hung.

Flaherty nodded approvingly. "That's a good place to hang it," he said. "But would you take notice of an old man? Mix a paste of oatmeal and salt and put it on your child's head before he goes to bed tonight."

Katy could scarce keep from laughing. "What would that do, Mr Flaherty, except make a mess for me to clean up?"

"It will keep the boy from harm," he replied solemnly. Then the old man wished her a "good night" and walked off towards his tractor.

Katy watched it trundle down the mountain path and suddenly realised how removed she had become from the superstitions of her Irish roots. The years in New York had taught her some sophistication. Oatmeal and salt indeed! Crucifixes! Goblins! Imps! The *Samhain Feis*!

A wild croaking made her peer upwards.

A flock of birds was wheeling around the roof of the cottage, their wings beating in the crisp air. She came out into the garden to stare upwards, attracted by their lamenting cacaphony. She knew enough of birds to recognise ravens by their appearance, although the lowering sun seemed to make their feathers flicker with a coppery glow. Three times she watched them circle overhead and then fly upwards towards the distant peaks of the mountains.

She turned into the croft again and continued to sort her groceries.

Katy had just finished cooking supper when she noticed the chill in the air and realised that the sun was already disappearing over the mountain tops. It was nearly time to light the lamps.

She looked through the window and saw young Mike standing at the garden gate. She gazed in surprise for he was with another small boy, a boy with bright coppery hair which flickered with a thousand little pinpricks of light in the rays of the setting sun. Katy hurried to the door and opened it.

Was she cracking up? Mike was standing by the gate alone. Katy peered round. There was no one about.

"Mike!" she called "Time to come in now."

Mike turned and waved at the empty air and then trotted towards her.

"It's been a lovely day, Mommy." He smiled.

"Mike." Katy hesitated, feeling foolish. "Were you with a small red-haired boy just a moment ago?"

"Of course," came his prompt reply. "I was with Seán Rua."

Katy shuddered slightly. Perhaps she was cracking up?

"Seán Rua wants me to go out and play with him tonight because it's the *Samhain Feis*."

Katy pulled herself together. "Well, Mr Fantoni Junior," she replied, "I am sure that young Seán Rua's parents will have him tucked up in bed tonight and that is where you are going to be."

Little Mike's lips dropped. "Aw, Mom!"

"No buts or complaints, it's bed for you at your usual time, young man."

Mike had finally settled to sleep in his room and Katy had put some more turf on the fire, then sat in the old carved chair before it, warming her feet and sipping a cup of hot chocolate. It was so peaceful, just sitting there with the music of the ticking clock on the mantelshelf and the crackle of the fire in the hearth.

She supposed it was at that moment that she made up her mind finally about Mario Fantoni. It was ridiculous pretending that a relationship still existed. Separation or divorce was the only solution. Everything swam into crystal clarity. She set down her cup and sighed.

Abruptly she became aware that a curious thing had happened. A deathly silence pervaded the cottage. The loud ticking of the clock had stopped. The silence made her glance up in astonishment. It was one minute to midnight. She turned her eyes to the fire whose flames roared and crackled away ... without any sound at all. God! Had she gone deaf?

Her heart began to beat wildly.

Then she heard a sibilant whispering which was incomprehensible at first but which grew in volume like the keening of a wind. It grew louder until she could hear the clear, melodic voice of a child.

"Mi-ike ... ! Mi-ike ... ! Come and play with me ... come and play ... "

She turned her head to see where the whispering came from.

The creak of a door caused her to start.

Across the room, the door of Mike's bedroom was swinging slowly open.

A shadow moved there.

Little Mike came stumbling forward, barefoot, clad in his striped pyjamas. His eyes were blurry and blinking from his sleep.

"Mi-ike! Mi-ike ... come and play!"

She tried to stand up and found a great weight pressing her back in her chair. She tried to call out to Mike but her throat was suddenly constricted.

A sharp rasp of a bolt being drawn caused her to jerk her gaze over her shoulder towards the door of the cottage. She gazed fearfully as she saw the bolts being drawn back of their own volition! First one iron bolt and then the other was drawn aside, then the handle moved and the cottage door swung inwards.

The whispering voice grew louder.

"Mi-ike!"

Little Mike's eyes were wide open now and he was smiling.

"Seán Rua!" he cried. "I knew you would come for me. I want to play, truly I do."

Katy struggled to free herself from her strange paralysis while Mike, ignoring her, went trotting trustingly towards the door.

Katy turned her frantic gaze after him.

Just beyond the cottage door she could see the shadowy outline of a little boy.

Then a great chanting chorus filled the air and the earth seemed to quiver and shake under the cottage. It rocked as if there was an earthquake.

Through the open door she could see the outline of the oddly shaped peak which Flaherty had called *Reilig na Ifreann* – Hell's Cemetery.

Even as she watched, the earth seemed to spring apart as if opening a jagged tear down the side of the mountain. A pulsating red light shone forth into the night. The chanting grew exhilarated, increasing in volume until Katy felt her eardrums would burst with the vibration.

She saw Mike's little figure run through the doorway, saw the shadowy figure behind awaiting him with outstretched hand.

The light from the open hillside seemed to glow on the figure's red coppery hair, causing it to dance as if it were on fire. And the light from the cottage fell on to its face.

Oh God! That face!

Malevolent green eyes stared unblinking at her from slanted, almond shapes. The face was deathly white and its contours were sharp. The eyebrows also rose upwards. The cheekbones were sharp and jutting and the ears were pointed, standing almost at right angles to the head. It was an elfin head.

For a moment the face of the creature – what else was it? – stared at Katy and then, slowly, a malicious smile crossed those bizarre features.

Little Mike ran straight up to it, their hands grasped each other, and then the two tiny figures turned and ran towards the opening in the mountainside.

Katy's wildly beating heart increased its tempo until she could stand its beat no longer and fell into a merciful world of blackness.

She awoke still sitting in the chair, twisted uncomfortably before the dead fire. The oil lamp was spluttering and smelling on the table behind her. The room was terribly cold and the grey half-light of dawn seeped through the small windows of the croft.

She raised her itching eyes to the monotonously ticking clock. It was seven-thirty. She eased herself up, stretched, and stared at the dead embers of the fire.

Then she remembered.

Her eyes swung to the door of the croft. It was closed. The bolts were in place and nothing seemed out of order. She sprang from her chair and turned towards Mike's room. The door was closed. She hesitated before it, scared of what she might find on the other side.

Summoning her courage, she turned the doorknob and peered in.

Mike's tousled fair head lay on the pillow, a hand to his mouth, thumb inserted between his lips. His breathing was deep and regular.

Katy could have wept with relief.

She turned back into the main room, shivering.

So it had been some grotesque nightmare after all? She must have fallen asleep in front of the fire and had the strangest dream! She supposed it was a mixture of fears; fears about Mike, her own fears ... and all restated through Flaherty's folk tales. She shook her head in disgust and set to building a fire. She had just set the primus stove going when she heard the sound of Flaherty's tractor halting outside.

"I was just passing," the old man said when she opened the door. "I thought I'd call by ... "

"I'm making tea." Katy smiled as she gestured him to enter.

His bright eyes gazed keenly at her.

"You seem tired," he observed.

"I fell asleep in front of the fire last night," she confessed, "and had a rather nasty nightmare."

He pursed his lips thoughtfully. "How's the *garsún?*"

"Mike? He's sleeping."

"Ah."

Katy glanced at the old man pityingly. She felt confident now in the morning light. "Well, your *Samhain Feis* is over. Did anyone get their souls eaten last night?"

Flaherty sniffed. "'Tis not a thing to joke about. But, true, the *Samhain Feis* is over for another year, *búiochas le Dia* … thanks be to God," he added piously.

"Mommy!"

Katy turned as Mike came stumbling from his bedroom, yawning and rubbing the sleep from his eyes. "Mommy, I'm hungry!"

Flaherty slapped his thigh and laughed. "Now that's the sign of a healthy lad. Here, *a mhic,*" he called to the boy, "I've a little something for you."

He reached into his coat pocket and handed little Mike a length of wood, the same wood piece that Katy had seen the old man whittling so often. It had been transformed into a beautiful ornate whistle.

"'Tis called a *feadóg stáin*, a penny-whistle," smiled Flaherty.

Mike held the whistle up and gave a few tentative blasts.

"*Go raibh maith agat,*" he said solemnly to the old man.

Flaherty chuckled. "*An-mhaith! Is ró-mhaith uait é sin!*" He clapped the boy on the shoulder and turned to Katy. "I see you're making the boy fluent in Irish."

Katy frowned. "Not me. I don't know a word of the language. Where did you pick that up, Mike?"

"From my friend," smiled Mike, retiring to a corner to practise on the whistle.

Flaherty apparently did not hear, nor did he see the troubled look which passed across Katy's face. He sipped appreciatively at his tea.

"I shall miss the *garsún* and yourself when you leave."

Katy turned back to him and smiled. "That's a nice thing to say. We'll be going back to Dublin in a day or so and then straight back to New York."

The old man gazed shrewdly at her. "And the problem you came her to think about? Is it resolved?"

Katy smiled, a little tightly. "In my mind it is."

Flaherty sighed. "Then perhaps you'll come back here one day."

"Perhaps."

A week later the cab dropped Katy and Mike at the house in Glen Cove. Mario was home and he was drunk and angry at Katy's "disappearance." Almost before she stepped into the living-room he started to scream abuse at her for taking *his* son out of the country without permission. He accused her of attempting to kidnap young Mike. Katy tried to keep calm; tried to keep her temper in check. In the end she let it all out: how she was sick of Mario's countless girlfriends, his drunken boorish behaviour, his attitude towards her and, finally, how she was utterly sick of him and their relationship. She wanted a separation pending a divorce.

After his initial shock Mario grinned derisively. "You try to divorce me and I'll countersue," he sneered. "What's more, I'll make sure that enough mud is thrown at you to ensure the courts give me custody of Mike so that you'll never see him again. No one walks out on me, baby!"

Katy stared at him aghast.

There was no use asking if he meant it. She could see by the triumphant leer in his eyes that he meant every word and was capable of carrying his threat through. She knew exactly how much power the Fantonis could wield. He would take Mike from her not because he cared for Mike but in order to spite her. That was when she picked up a china ornament and threw it straight into Mario's grinning, triumphant face. He dodged aside easily and called her a string of foul names.

"I wish you were dead!" she snarled in reply. "I hope you rot in hell!"

She turned on her heel and found little Mike standing in the open doorway behind her. He was staring at his father with a curious expression on his face. There was a look of such malevolence in his eyes that it made Katy pause and shiver. Mario, too, saw the expression.

"Hey, kid, wipe that look off your goddamn face and show your old man some respect! Don't stare at me like that!"

Mike said nothing but continued to stare at his father.

Mario became really angry. "Hey, what stories have you been filling the kid's head with about me, you bitch?" he snarled at Katy. "Have you been feeding the kid with tales about me?"

"He only has to see the way you behave to know what kind of person you are," replied Katy evenly. "There's no need for tales."

Mario was staring at the boy's hair.

"Have you been dying the kid's hair?"

Katy frowned, not understanding what he meant at first. Then she glanced at Mike's hair. The fair tousled curls were much darker than usual, a deeper brown, almost chestnut. She blinked. Maybe it was the lighting in the room. The hair seemed to verge on copper in colour.

"Quit staring at me, kid!" shouted Mario, suddenly lunging towards the boy.

Katy did not know how it happened, but as Mario moved forward he somehow tripped and fell on his face.

She glowered down at him.

"You drunken bum!" she said through clenched teeth. "When you've sobered up, we'll talk about that divorce."

"I'll see you in hell first!" swore Mario from the floor.

Katy grabbed little Mike and hurried upstairs.

It was early the next morning when Lise, the housekeeper, woke Katy from a deep sleep. Her face was pale and she was in a state of agitation.

"*Dio! Dio! Signore Fantoni è morto!*"

Katy rubbed the sleep from her eyes and stared at the woman who was waving her arms, repeating the words in her broad Calabrian accent.

"What is it?" demanded Katy. "Is it Mike? Oh God, has something happened to Mike?"

"No, no." The woman shook her head between her sobs. "It is Signore Fantoni … "

"What's the matter?"

Lise was shivering hopelessly and pointed to the corridor.

Since their relationship became uneasy Katy and Mario had separate bedrooms. Mario's bedroom lay across the corridor opposite.

Katy threw on a dressing-gown and strode to Mario's door with Lise sobbing in her wake.

The first thing Katy noticed was the blood. It was everywhere, staining the room streaky red. Mario lay on his back on the bed amidst the jumble of bedclothes. His eyes were wide and staring as if in fear.

Katy raised a hand to her mouth and felt nausea well from her stomach.

It looked as if part of Mario's throat had been torn out.

Behind her Lise breathed, *"Animale! Lupo mannaro!"*

Katy paused a moment longer, drew herself together, and pushed Lise from the room before her. Outside, in the corridor, she felt shivery and faint.

"Call the police, Lise," she said. "Get a hold on yourself and get the police." Her voice was sharp and near hysteria.

Lise turned away.

"Mike!" Katy suddenly cried. "We must keep him away from this. Where is he?"

Lise turned back, sniffing as she tried to control herself. "He was playing when I started to make Signore Fantoni his breakfast. Just playing on the lawn, signora."

Katy ran to her bedroom window and gazed down on the lawn below.

Sure enough, there was little Mike playing; running round and round in circles on the lawn, the sun glinting on his coppery hair. Katy caught her breath. His *coppery* hair!

Almost as if he heard her sharp intake of breath, he stopped and gazed up at the bedroom window.

Katy's heart began to pump wildly and she clutched for the window-sill.

It was little Mike's face right enough, yet the features were somehow distorted, sharper. The eyes were almost almond shaped. The ears were pointed and stood out at right angles. The face was malignant, elfin. He stared up and his green sparkling eyes gazed into Katy's. Then he smiled. A shy, mischievous smile. And she noticed there was blood on his lips.

V

The Mongfind

"IT'S A UNIQUE house," commented the fat man from the Building Preservation Society, gesturing round the tiny parlour of the seventeenth century farmhouse.

"Ireland is full of historic buildings," I replied with feigned boredom. "What precisely is it about this one which has necessitated me driving all the way from Dublin? My chief didn't exactly make the situation clear."

I was not going to tell this red-faced enthusiast that my position in the Manuscripts Department of the National Library of Ireland was so lowly that the director had simply ordered me to drive down to Ballyporeen in County Tipperary and meet the representative of the Building Preservation Society on a matter which might interest the department, but without feeling the necessity of explaining what that matter was.

The fat man, Doherty by name, had conducted me from the hotel at Ballyporeen – an unimposing little village known only as the birthplace of the great-grandfather of American president Ronald Reagan – up to the foothills of the Knockmealdown Mountains where he showed me the ruins of the old farmstead.

"It hasn't been occupied in centuries," he confided, as if the crumbling nature of the edifice needed explanation. "It has a reputation locally."

"A reputation?" I smiled patronisingly.

"Indeed so. The locals say that it is haunted."

He quivered in ecstatic pleasure but I responded to his theatrics with a chuckle.

"I never knew an old house which wasn't said to be haunted," I replied with heavy sarcasm. "Why should this one interest me?"

"As I have said, the house seems to have been deserted for a long time. There is no record of anyone attempting to live here since the mid-eighteenth century after the Whiteboys attempted to burn it down. They were a sort of guerrilla resistance to the excessive exactions of rents and tithes from absentee English landlords, a sort of secret peasant organisation who ... "

"I know my Irish history, Mr Doherty," I interrupted.

"Well, after 1762 it was not occupied. The place is marked on the old maps as Te-na-Groynought which is obviously English phonetics for an Irish name."

I frowned and asked him to write it down. He did so, but the name became no clearer. He was watching my puzzlement with obvious enjoyment.

"I think I might be able to clarify it," he said, writing down alongside the phonetics the Irish: *Teach na Gráinneacht*.

"Ah, *Teach na Gráinneacht*," I said. "The House of Ugliness?"

"That's one translation," he confirmed. "I would prefer, however, The House of Detestable Horror."

"Confirming your theory that the place is haunted," I smiled.

"It's no theory. It's local folklore," he protested. "People from these parts talk about the Mongfind."

I pursed my lips cynically.

"And who, or what, might the Mongfind be?"

"One of the banshee ... a supernatural creature who lives on blood," replied the fat man, closing his eyes in shivering pleasure. "There are references to such a creature in pre-Christian Irish mythology though nothing is known of its origins or what it looks like ... unless one takes the name as a description."

"The name?"

"*Mong*, as you know, means 'hair' or 'mane' while the word *find* is probably a corruption of the word *fionn* meaning 'white.'

So we have the name 'White Hair' or 'White Mane.'"

I gave a sigh of exasperation.

"None of which brings me any closer to the reason as to why I have come all this way from Dublin."

The fat man apologised nervously.

"Because of the historic value of the house," he began pompously, "the Building Preservation Society for the county, of which I am secretary, raised enough money to purchase it. Our purpose is to restore it and open it as a folk museum. As you can see from the excavations, we have been hard at work all summer."

There were certainly signs of enthusiasts at work about the place and in the small parlour there were a camp table, storm lanterns and pieces of camping equipment.

I waited patiently. The man would obviously get to the point in his own good time.

Doherty turned and pointed to the large stone fireplace.

"That is the original; we have managed to date it back to late Tudor."

The fireplace was certainly worthy of preservation. Its grey flagstones were in good condition and the rusting iron hooks for hanging pots and the roasting spit would need very little treatment to bring them into excellent order. The great chimney-breast also had a fascinating feature with what was obviously the original cupboards, with their wood dark and warping, still in place on either side of it.

"It was while we were working on the fireplace that we came to a loose flagstone, took it up to check and found a small iron box beneath it."

He turned to the table with the air of a conjuror about to produce a rabbit and removed a dustsheet. The iron box was rusty and obviously quite old.

"One of the archaeology students from Cork who was helping us at the time opened it. The box was fairly airtight and inside was a decaying leather pouch. Inside this were several sheets of paper in a remarkable state of preservation. The text was written in English and dated at the top of the first folio to 1658. Well, seventeenth century English is not our provenance which is why I telephoned the National Library to ask them to send down an expert."

Everything made sense now. My master's degree was in seventeenth century manuscripts.

I went to the table and opened the box carefully. Sure enough, inside was a worn leather pouch, a typical container for its day. Inside this were several folios of tough rag-paper. The old hand-made paper had certainly survived extremely well and the writing, while fading, was still legible. I glanced at the opening paragraphs. They looked promising. I looked round and dropped into a chair at the table.

Doherty coughed. "Are you proposing to read the manuscript now?" he asked in surprise.

"If you've no objection."

"Well, if you don't mind, I must get back to Ballyporeen to transact some business. I should be back in an hour or so."

I nodded absently, keen to get into the manuscript.

"That's no problem. I'll just sit here and read this and then I'll be able to give you a brief report on its value when you return."

At the door he hesitated and came fussing back.

"It's a grey day and dark in here. You'd best have this storm lantern alight."

So saying, he struck a match, trimmed the wick and left me to the sudden pungent odour of burning paraffin.

I hardly noticed his going as I carefully spread the sheets of paper on the table before me. Whoever had written the manuscript had been able to afford good material. The rag paper was hardly decayed. However, a quick observation showed that the hand that wrote it was not that of a learned man; the letters were often ill-formed and quite child-like. In some places the letters were open and curiously looped, in other places they were close together and constricted. I smiled; a psychiatrist would be greatly entertained trying to make an analysis of this handwriting. Even bearing in mind the lack of conformity in spelling in seventeenth century English, the words were often spelt in a bizarre fashion. Having noted these preliminary observations, I sat back to read.

* * *

Writ at Te-na-Groynought, near Ballyporeen, May 20, in the Year of Our Lord 1658.

I have taken up the quill to recount the strange and confounding experiences which befell me in the barony of Ballyporeen, in the troublesome country of Ireland, only with the utmost reluctance. I have set about this awesome task not from vanity in my own abilities but 'tis the only means wherein I may confess all to record, for I must tell someone, if only this inanimate paper, or go mad.

I am but a poor soldier whose rough tongue has, by good fortune, received a brief instruction in lettering from the charity of the local *dominus* of my native village of Sizewell, in the county of Suffolk, England. I know well that my hand is not sufficiently tutored nor skilled to attempt to narrate my experiences in a way which would commend them to any of literary disposition. Nor do I have theological understanding by which to discourse on the significance of the events which bechanced me. I will content myself only in a rough soldier's report. Perhaps the finder of my transcriptions might, for charity's sake, forward them to the learned editor of the *Public Intelligencer* and he, in kindness, might render my unsightly scrawl to an essay more worthy of public knowledge.

Tom Sindercombe is my name and I be formerly a private soldier in the regiment of Colonel Lawrence, the governor of the town of Wexford. I was twenty years of age when I left my master's farm at Sizewell and volunteered to bear arms for Parliament. I was four-and-twenty years of age when I sailed on the frigate *Revenge* which brought General Fleetwood to be commander-in-chief of the English Army in Ireland. That was in September, in the year 1652, when we landed at the port of Wexford where I did find myself enlisted in Colonel Lawrence's dragoons.

Ireland was then but recently conquered but do not think that life was easy for the soldiery. There were many skirmishes and engagements still to be fought with the stubborn remnants of the Irish armies. Entire tribes of Irish had taken to their bogs and mountain fastnesses to ride forth and do battle in unsoldierly ways. We honest Englishmen knew not from which dark valley, or from behind which bush, the Irish hordes would descend on us with pistol and sword. Yet God and the Lord Protector was on our side. At the very time I landed in Ireland the Physician-General of the Army, Sir William Petty, had computed that we had already wasted some 504,000 Irish by sword, banishment and pestilence during our campaign.

Not long after I arrived in Ireland there came the order that the Popish natives were to be driven out of the country almost entirely, pushed back beyond the vast reaches of the river Shannon into the wild province of Connacht and the county of Clare. Fortresses were to be erected to hold the Irish barbarians in these confines and here they, men, women and children, would have to transplant themselves from the rest of the country before May 1, 1654. If, after that date, they were found on the eastern side of the Shannon, they would suffer death. Their lands, farms, their towns and villages, thus confiscated, would be given to the English soldiery in the stead of their army pay. Thus a new England would arise in Ireland and thus would that rebellious nation be placed so that it would never again be burdensome to English rule

Naturally, the announcement of this great plan for settling the country was greeted with signs of ferocity by the natives. Ambushes and murders of English soldiers and settlers increased. The Tories, as we called the Irish bandits, deriving the word from a native source *toiridh,* universally applied to cut-throats, grew many.

To facilitate the scheme of transplanting the Irish from those areas designated to be settled by the English, the Government decided to round up entire villages and place the populace on board ship for trans-shipment to the American colonies for use as labour on the plantations. Barbados was a favoured destination as well as other islands of the West Indies. My Lord Broghill, a prominent Government leader at Dublin, was very much concerned in such schemes and I recall in one week alone we seized and transported 1,000 Irish wenches to provide wives for a like number of English soldiers who were thus encouraged to take ship for the New World to sustain the population of the colonies. At the same time we seized 2,000 Irish boys of ages varying from twelve to fourteen years for shipment to the colonies to be brought up in English habits.

For the rest of the native breed, the army paid £5 for the head of any Irish rebel brought in to the local commander. For the most part the soldiery regarded "Irish" and "rebel" as synonymous and a head can make no plea of defence once severed from a body. I have seen many soldiers grow rich on such bounty. A favourite sport of the soldiery was hunting out Popish priests, some we hung and some we burnt for the idol worshipping barbarians that they were. Sometimes, though seldom, our officers would intervene and the priests would be marked for transportation where their Popery would be sweated out of them by labour in the plantations. The authorities tried to encourage this later course by announcing a bounty for each priest captured.

To make the situation plain, any Englishman encountering an Irish man, woman or child east of the river Shannon, unless they could produce a written form of protection from the Government, became the absolute arbiter of their fate: immediate death, transportation or simple arrest until the authorities determined their future. Yet, even under these conditions, there remained many who persistently refused to transplant westward into Connacht and County Clare. The highways were littered with entire families of Irish hanged on every available gibbet and tree as a warning and encouragement to their fellows. In every hedgerow one would find decapitated corpses, for the soldiery preferred to claim the £5 bounty on rebels rather than apprehend them. Even so, the task of removing the Irish from the land was like trying to remove lice from one's body after a hard campaign in the boglands.

I have digressed a little from my main narrative only to provide some consideration of the conditions appertaining in the country lest a future generation misunderstand the reasons for my subsequent actions.

The spring of the year 1655 witnessed several companies of our regiment scouring the Galtee Mountains, just south of the town of Tipperary, in search of a band of Tories who had recently attacked our garrison at Cahir. Our captain had detached a sergeant and two troopers, myself being one of that band, and ordered us to scout the valleys to the south where the Knockmealdown Mountains began to climb skywards. It was as breath-taking a countryside as one would wish to see, with high granite peaks covered with green and purple, here and there speckled softly yellow with gorse. I recall that I was fondly contemplating the fact that my term of service would be up within a few months and that I, too, would be apportioned a farmstead as pay and a farmstead in such a countryside as this could be a profitable venture. Yet, I supposed, by the time the officers and the non-commissioned officers claimed their shares, the land left for poor privates such as I would be barren and infecundous indeed. Such were my thoughts when we neared the hamlet of Ballyporeen where great forests skirted the lower reaches of the mountains.

The first indication of danger I had was the bang of a musket so close that I smelt the acrid stench of powder. Our sergeant flung up his hands, gave but a single groan and fell to the ground. I turned my horse, drawing my sword at the same time and saw our enemies behind some trees. Another musket exploded and the ball came dangerously near my face. My companion had also drawn his sword, for our pistols were holstered and unloaded. Together we rode down on those skulking cowards. There were four of them; Tories, I supposed. Even now I see their images. They were dressed in an assortment of rags and goatskins, so I presumed the animal skin to be. They were brutish fellows with matted, flattened hair, so long that it seemed to naturally join the hair of the goatskin and conceal so entirely their faces that one might easily have taken the skin as their own and confound those viperous villains at first sight with the animals whose spoil served as their clothing. There was no disavowing the hatred and malice which gleamed from their wolf-like eyes through the mat of their hair. They were animals intent on the kill.

One sprang forward and levelled his pistol at my companion. The ball took him in the face just as I cut the man down. His companions, crying wildly in their Irish gibberish, ran towards me, one of them gripping my bridle while another, striking up at my swordarm with a great wooden cudgel, caused my fingers to be rendered nerveless and in horror I saw my sword fall useless to the ground. Then I was being dragged from my mount and fell heavily among them. The man with the cudgel raised it once again and a deep blackness overtook my entire sensibilities.

I have a vague recollection that I came to some while later. I recall intense cold and darkness. I lay shivering with a fierce pain splitting my skull. I only recall feeling that death would be a merciful end to my predicament. Then I was plunged into blackness again.

The second time I recovered consciousness I could register that I had been stripped and left for dead, my head caked in my own blood from the cudgel's blow. It was night now and the moon was full and standing high beyond the tall whispering trees. In the distance I heard the plaintive cry of a wolf. I tried to move but all feeling had deserted me. Then I sought to call to my companions, lest they, too, had survived, but my tongue cleaved to the roof of my mouth, so dry was my throat. I could only groan softly in my pain and coldness.

I heard the snapping of a twig. I could not turn my head in the direction of the sound and could only lay like a helpless babe, trying to still my rasping breath in case it be one of the Tories returning to make sure of the deed. A dark shadow appeared above me: a face, whose features were indistinguishable in the gloom, bent down to mine and I felt a hand on my breast, feeling for my heartbeat. The hand then touched my head, causing a thousand spear points to dig deep in my brain. I groaned aloud. If

I could have screamed with the pain I would have done so.

The figure gave a long shivering sigh just as the distant wolf howled again. A man's voice spoke sharply: "*Mactíre! Fan socair!*"

I write as I afterwards learnt the words for, in truth, at that time I knew nothing of the babbling verbiage which passed among the Irish.

I do confess that at the sound of the voice my hopes sank and I resigned me to death. I had fallen once more into the hands of my enemies.

The figure bent over me again and I felt strong and sturdy hands under my back and legs. As easy as you might lift a new-born infant, the man had raised me from the ground and placed me in the back of a cart. I could not see much but discovered afterwards that it was a small cart drawn by an ass, which the natives here use as a beast of all work. I remember the jerk and creak as the cart lurched forward and then I descended into my black pit of insensibility once more.

I awoke in the warmth and comfort of a bed, lying under coverlets of duck down that made me recall my childhood on a farm in my native Suffolk. I recall the smell that greeted me as I awoke, the smoky smell of burning peat. There was a silence broken only by the sharp crackle of a fire.

I groaned and tried to clear my constricted throat. Then into my line of vision came a woman's concerned face. It was a homely face, well into middle age; a pale face surrounded by hair the colour of jet, partially covered by the folds of a red shawl. Large grey eyes twinkled at me as the woman smiled.

I coughed again and said: "Am I still alive?"

At this a shadow passed across the woman's face and she glanced over her shoulder as if to address someone who stood behind her and whom I could not see.

"*Is Sasanach é!*" she whispered.

At the sound of her Irish remembrance came back to me and with it the horror of my predicament. It was obvious that I had been rescued by natives who had mistaken me for one of their own and once my identity was discovered I would be despatched without a moment's thought. I tried to struggle up but I was weak. The woman leant across and pressed me firmly back into the bed as if I had been a child.

"*Éist*! *Éist*! Hush ... " she hesitated for the right words and to my surprise began to speak an English of sorts. "No harm to you ... no harm. I worked at a big house in Dublin. There I learnt your tongue. That was before I married my man."

"Are you going to kill me?" I demanded sullenly.

The image of a tall, dour man appeared behind the woman and stared down at me.

"*Céard dúirt sé*?" he demanded.

The woman turned and spoke rapidly to him at which he laughed and shook his head.

"*An saighdúir tusa*?"

"My man asks, are you a soldier?" interpreted the woman.

I sighed and resigned myself.

"Aye. Attacked and near murdered by Tory vermin. My companions are already dead."

The woman repeated my words as the man gazed down at me. There seemed no hate nor malice in his face. His delivery was rapid.

"My man says that he is Donal O'Derrick. He is a farmer, not a soldier. All he asks is to be left alone to farm his land as his father, his father's father and the generations gone, farmed it before him. What is the war to him? He had no part with its making, no part with its continuance. No harm to you. You are welcome to remain until you recover from your hurt and then you may depart in peace."

With that I must have passed out again for I remember no more.

The days passed and my strength began to return to me. O'Derrick and his wife, Finuala, as I learnt her name, nursed and fed me until I was able to place my feet over the edge of my bed and try a few faltering steps. I could not fault their hospitality and kindness. They called me Ralph in the simple belief that they had heard all English soldiers were named so, or, as they pronounced it, Ráif.

The O'Derrick farmstead was on the edge of the vast forests which covered the lower slopes of the Knockmealdon Mountains, far enough away from the village of Ballyporeen to discourage visitors; indeed, far enough away for our troops to have missed it when rounding up those recalcitrants who refused to transplant. Neither Irish Tories nor English troopers came this way. Yet it was a pleasant farmstead, the sort of land that I dreamt of some day owning ever since I was a young boy labouring on the squire's farm at Sizewell.

There were several barns in addition to the farmhouse and O'Derrick kept herds of shaggy Irish cattle on the upper slopes of the mountain while his lower fields produced a goodly abundance of maize and grain. His goats supplied him with additional milk and cheese; hens gave eggs and there were rabbits in plenty. A man might live out his life on such a farm in freedom from the poverty that I had witnessed in other parts of this Godforsaken country.

One day, when O'Derrick was in the fields and I was resting before the fire, I asked Finuala O'Derrick if they knew of the Transplantation Order. She shrugged and said that she had heard of it vaguely but knew it could not apply to her husband and herself. They were farmers and knew nothing of war; they had no part in the troubles and kept themselves to themselves. When I asserted that it applied to all the Irish Nation, she frowned in disbelief and asked me what great sin the Irish had committed against the English to be treated in such a manner.

I explained that the Irish had rebelled against lawful English rule and caused a great effusion of English blood which the Lord Protector Cromwell, with God's aid, sought revenge for, scattering the wretched Irish armies.

"But why should Englishmen rule in Ireland in the first place?" she asked, puzzled.

I laughed at this piece of colossal ignorance and patted her gently on the hand.

"We have come to bring you civilisation, the English language and the true religion of Christ."

She shook her head in bewilderment.

"Poor, poor Ráif," she replied, speaking as if it were I who was the ignorant one. "The Irish stand in need of no such instruction. We are an old and proud people. It was our monks and scholars who first took the word of Christ to the English and turned them from their pagan gods. Our saints and scholars spread the Gospel throughout Europe when the tribes of Angles, Saxons, Goths, Huns and Vandals had all but extinguished it. Our scholarship and literature were eagerly patronised by the monarchs of the world."

I stood up in my disgust. How could an Englishman learn anything from such ignorance?

The next day, my argument forgotten, I was feeling better and therefore eager to be out in the warm sunshine, feeling the gentle fragrant breeze on my pale body. I was now all but healed from my experience.

I went for a walk among O'Derrick's lower fields and came upon the farmer busy at work. All my boyhood memories came tumbling back. Soon I, too, was hard at work alongside the Irishman; working and weeding, digging and hoeing at the crop, as eager as he was to wrest the wealth from the fertile soil. At the end of the day both O'Derrick and I bathed in the cold mountain stream near the farm. Common work had made us momentarily brethren. So it continued for a week or two. I gave myself willingly to working the farm alongside O'Derrick. And in my day-dreams, I dreamt that the farmstead was mine. Then I grew depressed at the thought that someday soon, when the O'Derricks were transplanted to Connacht, a thin-faced officer or heavy jowled sergeant would move into this beautiful spot and claim the land as their own. It greatly troubled me. The very thought of it began to gnaw like a maggot at the back of my mind.

One evening, as I sat outside the farmhouse watching the sun lowering itself in the western gap between the Knockmealdown

Mountains on one side and the Galtee Mountains on the other, Finuala O'Derrick came to call me for the evening meal.

"You know you will have to leave this land soon," I told her.

"Never," she replied vehemently.

God, how the Irish clung leech-like to their soil!

"It is the law," I replied. "The Lord Protector has ordained it so."

"*Is treise tuath ná tighearna!*" she shot back at me in her own tongue, then, hesitating, she sought translation. "A people is stronger than a lord."

"Strong or no, you will still have to go."

"Son Ráif," she said softly, "for in these days you have been with us you have somehow taken the place of the son we were never blessed with; son, I would have you know this, this land is in our blood. For thousands upon thousands of years, our ancestors have worked these fields. From the mists of time when the Dé Dannans wrested the land from the dark gods of the Fomorii, this land has been ours. For countless generations we have lived here, close to nature, part of nature; watching the seasons come and go; seeing nature and supernature co-join as one great entity. The land is ours, we are the land. We cannot be separated. The land holds the blood and bones of the countless beings we once were; it holds the breath of life of the countless beings we will become. Listen, Ráif! Listen!"

I found myself fascinated by the strange animation in her face. Found myself unwillingly listening to the gentle sigh of the breeze down the mountain, the sibilant whispering of a million tongues among the leaves of the tall dark forest around us.

"Do you not hear them, Ráif? Do you not hear the voices of our ancestors and our children unborn? We will never give this land up; we may die upon it, but our rich warm blood will only fertilise its soil. The heart of this land is us; is timeless. It is from this soil that the old gods first drew breath. Lugh the Mighty, Bel the Creator and the ever present Mórrígú, the goddess of death and battle. The land is filled with a countless host, spirits of the earth, trees, springs and streams; all of these are our allies and when you seek to destroy us, and drive us from the land, you must also destroy them. How can you destroy what is eternal?"

I stared at her a little with open mouth. In my native Suffolk, such meandering protestations would have resulted in the woman being hauled before the Witchfinder-General and a fire would have consumed her black soul before another sun rose. It was true, I meditated, that these idol-worshipping Papists were every bit as heathen as our army chaplains had told us.

It was O'Derrick who interrupted my revelry by calling from inside:

"*Tá mé stiúgtha leis an ocras!*"

The woman shrugged.

"My man is hungry," she said and made to rise.

It was at that moment that the most unearthly wail split the evening gloom. Never had I heard a cry like it. It was a shrilling unhuman screech of despair. Once, twice and a third time its bloodcurdling tones cleaved through the quiet dusk and then subsided.

Finuala O'Derrick had half risen, her face ashen, her mouth working silently. Slowly she raised a trembling hand and blessed herself. I still had not accustomed myself to open displays of Papistry.

O'Derrick appeared at the doorway, his face troubled. He gave a nervous cough and muttered: "*Mactíre! Mactíre!*" This was one of the few words I had learnt and knew its meaning to be "wolf" for there are countless wolves among these forests and anyone bringing the head of such a beast to the stockades could claim a bounty. O'Derrick's woman shook her head.

"*An bhean sídhe!*" she whispered.

O'Derrick snorted and spoke in rapid tones.

"What is it?" I demanded.

Finuala O'Derrick gazed fearfully at me.

"What is it?" I repeated again.

"It is the *bean sídhe!*"

"Banshee?" I tried to repeat the word as she had said it. "What animal is that?"

"The *bean sídhe* is the woman of the fairies whose shrieks and moans portend a death."

I tried hard to keep my face from splitting into a grin of derision.

Abruptly there came a rustling sound in a nearby tree and a large black bird went winging up into the heavens and was lost to sight. The effect of this simple occurrence was marked. Both man and woman let out a low moan and peered affrighted at each other. I gathered that it symbolised some black omen in their superstitious minds.

"Be warned, son Ráif," whispered Finuala O'Derrick. "Before another sun has set there will be death in this house."

She turned abruptly and followed her husband inside the house.

For a while I sat outside, laughing to myself about the simple ignorance of these natives. God be praised for making England a Protestant Nation if Popery bred such ignorance. Then I paused and frowned. The woman had gazed on me with a curious expression as she pronounced her prophecy. "Before another sun has set there will be death in this house." Was it a warning? A warning for me? Were they planning to kill me after all and, in her own way, the woman was giving me a chance to escape? I thought about this prospect for some time. Then the thought of that pleasant farmstead began to fill my mind, displacing my fears. It was not right that the farm which I so coveted should be given to some rude mechanic from the crowded streets of London when I was country born and bred and best suited to working the rich land. Yet how could I claim it as mine?

I retired to bed that night and found myself tossing in sleepless agitation. I had decided to sleep lightly in case the woman's words had been a warning and her husband meant to kill me. In that I was quite prepared and secreted a knife about my person for my defence. My wounds were now healed and I was recovered and strong. But, above all, the worm of envy gnawed inside my mind. At dawn I finally dozed, dozed and dreamt the farmstead was mine and mine alone.

I came to with a start, cursing myself for my lack of vigilance. Yet I need not have been afeared. Although the sun was well up, nothing seemed amiss. O'Derrick was chopping wood outside while the woman was busy cutting freshly baked bread in the parlour.

I rose and went out to bathe in the icy waters of the mountain stream.

I had bathed and was about to dress myself, for I preferred to plunge my entire body naked into the waters, when the resolution came upon me. All my anxieties suddenly clarified and I knew what had to be done. Perhaps it was the sight of O'Derrick gathering wood, his back towards me, a little distance from the stream. Something seemed to take possession of my actions, ordering my limbs to obey and quietening the nervous beat of my heart. I slipped quietly from the water and trod, with naked feet, over the ground towards the farmer. My eyes had caught sight of the billhook which hung on a nearby fence, sharpened ready for the morning's work, its silver thin blade sparkling in the cold morning sun. My hand reached out. My lips were set firmly. I came up behind him, quite close.

"O'Derrick," I whispered.

He rose, arms filled with wood, and started to turn.

My hand holding the billhook was flung back.

I saw his eyes dart towards it, glazing with surprise and fear.

With one powerful motion, I struck. He had no time to cry out as the billhook cleaved the air. I felt but the slightest resistance to my downward sweep. He staggered forward a step, wood spilling from his hands. His head left his body cleanly from the blow I had dealt. Blood gushed in all directions like a fountain. The head, the eyes still wide with surprise, dropped against a pile of wood. The headless body seemed to hesitate, move a few steps, and then it collapsed in a bloodied heap.

I stood there a moment, chest heaving.

I had seen too many Irish fall in similar fashion to the sharpened swords of my comrades in arms to spare a thought for remorse or regret. What matter that O'Derrick had rescued me from the perils of the forest after I had been attacked? He was still a mere Irishman and therefore his death was of no consequence.

Aware of my situation, I turned swiftly for the house, the billhook still in my hand.

I lifted the latch slowly and eased into the parlour. Finuala O'Derrick was bending over the fire, stirring the contents of a large iron pot which simmered on the flames.

Something made her feel my presence for she glanced up with a startled expression, her eyes grew round with horror as she saw my naked body, splashed bright with the red blood of her man. They travelled slowly to the weapon in my hand.

"Ah, Ráif! Ráif! So was it you that the *bean sídhe* warned of?"

I made no reply but moved forward, the billhook raised.

She backed a pace as if to elude me. Her eyes blazed with a bright hatred.

"Be warned, Ráif! The land is us, we are the land. You cannot separate us. The land encompasses the blood and bones of the countless beings we once were; it holds the breath of life of the countless beings we will become. Listen, Ráif! Listen! The land is filled with a countless host. Do you not hear them whispering? Spirits of the earth, the trees, the springs and the streams, all of these are our allies and when you seek to destroy us, you must also destroy them. How will you destroy what is eternal?"

Anger in me, I swung back the billhook.

She opened her mouth and started a piercing shriek.

The billhook descended, driving as a knife through butter. Perhaps it was my frenzied imagination but, as the head flew from the body, I fancied that the woman's shrieking wail of terror continued, continued for a full half minute after it lay in a pool of red blood on the wooden floor of the parlour. It took a while before I could collect my shattered nerves and gaze down on it.

The head lay resting on the floor, mouth still agape, the lips twisted back over the gums with the teeth showing long and yellow. The tongue twisted obscenely between them. Still the eyes were open; they gazed at me with bright grey malevolence. But it was not those awful features that caused my bile to rise and my blood to run ice-cold. It was the hair. The hair ... at my very moment of striking, that raven-black hair of Finuala O'Derrick's had turned snow white, standing straight out from its roots by some impulse I cannot explain. The face of the homely woman had been transformed into that of a harridan.

For a time I stood there staring from head to body, from body to head, and then I turned, in a desire to cleanse myself of the deed, and ran out of the farmhouse to the mountain stream and plunged myself into the cold waters.

It was half an hour later when I dressed myself, put on a pair of O'Derrick's stout leather boots, and went outside to the edge of the forest. There I dug a hole. Returning to the house I dragged the headless body of the woman to the forest's edge and deposited it into the ground. Then I made a similar journey with O'Derrick's body, before filling in the earth.

I gathered O'Derrick's head and stuffed it into a sack which I placed on the cart. I then went into the parlour to collect the woman's head, picking it up by that long straight white hair. I was about to take it to the cart when I heard a noise. Was someone coming through the forest? Now, of all the times to choose, was someone approaching the farmhouse? I hesitated, turned and thrust the head into a cupboard which stood on the right hand side of the old fireplace and closed the doors upon it.

Agitated, I peered around for a weapon and to my delight espied an old fowling piece. Yet there was no powder nor ball to load the ancient weapon with. I prayed that whoever was approaching would not be able to tell that I had no means of firing the weapon. Cocking the piece, and resting it in the crook of my arm, I went out to the porch.

I heard the sound of someone thrusting their way through the bushes and raised the weapon offensively.

Just as I was about to cry out a command, the bushes swayed back and the intruder emerged.

It was O'Derrick's untethered ass.

I wept for the relief I felt. This was the very beast I wanted.

Putting aside the flintlock, I caught the little creature by the bridle and soon had him harnessed to the cart. When it was done I took the bloodied sack, returned to the parlour and opened the door of the cupboard. There stood that frightful white-maned head, standing upright as if still on its body. It was staring straight at me. Then, even as I looked, its eyes narrowed and its mouth distended, splitting into a malicious smile.

I started back; a the cry of terror sprang from my lips.

The head remained in position with the new expression graven on its bloodless features.

It was some time before I reasoned that there must have chanced some strange muscular contraction at the very moment I opened the cupboard. This muscular change had caused the expression on the face to change as if it had still been alive. I have heard many such tales from my comrades wandering a battlefield after the slaughter. Indeed, I can vouch myself that I heard a dead man belch a good two days after he was killed. I cursed my delicate sensibilities. With firm resolve, I reached forward, seized the white-maned head and thrust it into the sack.

I was firm in the resolution of my plan.

It took me nearly all day to reach Clonmel in O'Derrick's aging cart and, God be praised, I saw no antagonists on the lonely road to that town. Clonmel was the nearest garrison town and I had nearly reached its protective walls when I was accosted by a troop of horse, the sergeant initially believing me to be Irish, for such my apparel proclaimed me. I soon convinced him to the contrary and had him bring me to the saturnine major in command.

"Two months you have been missing, Sindercombe," he admonished. "What have you to offer in defence? The penalty for desertion is death."

"I did not desert, sir!" I protested, flushing in indignation. And I fell to telling him about the attack of the Tories on the slopes of Knockmealdon. Then I said that I, badly wounded as my scars bore mute testimony, was taken by the Tories to a farmhouse and kept captive by one of their number. This Tory and his wife had kept me in virtual slavery until that very morning when I managed to pry loose my shackles, kill them both, and return straightaway to the army.

The major grunted with scepticism.

"You can offer proof of this tale?"

I thrust out the sack.

"Behold, sir, I have brought in the heads of the Irish rebels who held me captive."

At that moment I became aware of a man standing in the shadows of the room behind me. He came forward now and peered over my shoulder into the bag. I recognised him immediately as General Fleetwood, our commander-in-chief.

"You know me, soldier?" he asked with a smile, observing as my face betrayed recognition.

"I came to this country on the *Revenge* at the same time that you were brought hither."

He nodded absently.

"You have done well, soldier. This was a deed of bravery. We must reward you well."

"Lord General," murmured the major in protest, "the reward is already fixed; five pounds for the head of each Irish rebel."

Fleetwood gestured him to silence.

"This is a deed of great gallantry. Alone and unaided, this soldier overcame these Irish rebels in their own lair. What reward would you consider worthy, soldier?"

I hesitated, hardly daring to believe my luck.

"Lord General," I ventured, "I leave the army in one month and am to be allocated a tract of land as payment for eight years' service under the colours."

General Fleetwood gazed at me in question.

"Lord General," I hurried on, stumbling over my words in my eagerness. "Let the farmstead that I am given be that of these Irish rebels wherein I was made to act as slave these last weeks."

Fleetwood chuckled.

"A just retribution on these barbarians! A good reward. What say you, Major?"

The major frowned.

"But we have no survey nor valuation to guide us to whether the property is too valuable to award to a simple private," he protested.

Fleetwood frowned.

"Do you think Irish rebels would have hold of some grand mansion, major? I have made up my mind. Make out the deeds immediately, so I may sign them. This man deserves his reward."

The major shrugged indifferently.

"As my Lord General wills it."

Thus it was that I, Tom Sindercombe, was discharged from the army one month later at Clonmel and presented with the title deed of the O'Derrick farmstead.

As soon as I was able, I rode swiftly back to the slopes of Knockmealdown. The farmstead was just as I had left it and I began work immediately to tidy things up. One of the first things I noticed was that the tall grasses and gorse had grown swiftly over the graves of the O'Derricks. Already it was difficult to discern that there had been any commotion of the earth.

The fields were right for the harvesting and I was able to call upon the help of a former corporal of foot, Fletcher Hopkins, who farmed a few miles across the mountain. The earth was dark and fruitful; the livestock of the O'Derricks, having survived a month of wild living, provided me with an excellent basis for my farm stock. Two whole years sped by and each year the harvest was more bountiful than before; the cows came into calve, the chickens produced wondrously well, even the nanny-goat gave birth and, by selling surplus stock, I soon had three horses, a stallion and a mare and one good plough-horse, a shire brought specially from England. The fruit of my toil gave me money to save and I became respected by my fellow settlers in the barony of Ballyporeen. Indeed, by my second Christmas, Reverend John Smith, the pastor of our community, invited me to serve on the parish council of elders. From lowly state I had risen to become a gentleman.

In the spring of that second year, I took ship from Wexford

and arrived in Bristol one fine, pleasant morning. I arranged with a local merchant for certain purchases to be made and shipped back to Ireland. Then I took a stagecoach to London and thence on towards my native Suffolk. Never had I thought to see the like. As I rode into my native Sizewell, former neighbours who had never given me time of day, touched their caps respectfully and out came the squire and parson both to greet me as if I were their equal. I boasted of my deeds, embroidering them not a little and told of my new-found wealth, my lands and possessions. I had a purpose to my visit which was to find me a comely wife to share my toils and provide me with an heir to my wealth. She I soon found in the pretty person of Miss Lucy Hawkins, the daughter of Japeth Hawkins who farmed ten acres outside the village. I made my overtures and within three months was shipping back to Wexford with my lovely bride.

All that ever I had wanted in life was now mine.

It was mid-afternoon when my wife first caught sight of her future home. The day was an unhappy one for it had been raining most of the time on our journey from Clonmel. We had an escort for part of the way because the Tory cut-throats still managed to conceal themselves in the shadows of the mountains and ride out to attack our settlers and burn our farmsteads and raid our garrison towns. We had left our escorting troop of horse at the crossroads where the track divides towards Ballyporeen on the one hand and up to the farmstead on the other. Our wagon creaked up the mountain path, through the dark forests until it came to the brow of the hill which looked down upon the fields and farm. I was quite relieved to see it once again, standing as I had left it, and praised God for the solicitude and kindliness of my neighbours who had been watchful on my behalf. As chance would have it, at the moment we reached the brow of the hill and looked down upon it, a cloud chased across the sky causing a dark shadow to flit over the farmstead.

Poor Lucy shivered.

"Oh Tom!" she cried in her dismay, "it looks such a dismal place."

"Nonsense!" I replied with spirit. "'Tis not at its best in this gloomy light. Wait for the sun to return and you'll see it to be a beautiful spot."

I was about to stir the horses into motion when I suddenly heard the sound of horses' hooves galloping at a rapid rate on the road behind. Lucy heard them too for she turned and looked back with a frown.

"Who can it be who rides so hard, Tom?"

"One of the soldiers, perhaps," I hazarded. "Or ... "

A Tory? I left my second thought unspoken but I reached for the pistol in my belt and checked its charge and powder.

We waited for some moments listening to the sound of approaching hooves thundering on the roadway, expecting any minute to see horse and rider appear. Then, just when the steed must surely come into view, the sound ceased abruptly. We looked at each other in uncertainty.

"Where has he gone?" Lucy asked perplexed.

I climbed down and trotted back to the point in the road where I could command a view of the other side of the hill. The road rolled down before me. There was no sign of a horse or rider in sight, nothing as far as I could see back across the broad slope of the hills. I tugged at my lip and shrugged. The rider must have left the roadway and gone off over the shoulder of the hill toward Fletcher Hopkins' farmstead. I ventured the explanation as I climbed back into the wagon. Neither of us gave the matter any more thought.

That evening, after the fire had been set and was roaring up the parlour chimney and food had been set on the table, Lucy expressed herself to be far happier with her new home and bade me forgive her for her early misgivings. The sun had come out briefly, dispelling the gloom, and now it was lowering beyond the valley and twilight was swiftly creeping over the mountains.

"Hark!" smiled Lucy happily. "Listen to the birds calling to one another. Why, if I close my eyes I might imagine myself back in the marshes of Sizewell in our own county of Suffolk. I can almost feel the cool sea breezes."

I smiled indulgently. "We are not near the sea here, Lucy."
She frowned abruptly.

"Yet those are sea birds that I hear right enough," she insisted.

I went to the door, bathed red in the glowing evening sun, and stood listening. Lucy was right. Once brought up in the low marshes on the coast of Suffolk, one can never forget the knowledge acquired. I could hear the cry of a curlew very clearly while, as if in answer, came the fretful call of a golden plover. I gazed in astonishment at the surrounding woods. Then to confound me further there was a third cry ... that of the solitary whimbrel. All three were sea birds and when not haunting the coastline would seek out mud flats or large lakes where they could use their webbed feet and bills to gather food. Such birds did not frequent wooded mountains. They sought open country such as provided by low lying bogs and lakes. While one such bird losing its course was an interesting phenomenon, three differing species doing so and joining together was astounding. There was the curlew who usually flew in large flocks, here was the whimbrel who seldom flocked and was a solitary creature and then came the golden plover who also preferred to flock with its own kind. Here they were, wheeling all together around the top of the farmstead, crying to each other in weird, plaintive sorrow. As I stood and watched them, they flew three times around the chimney stack and then, with an abruptness, flew upwards into the twilight and disappeared.

The following Sunday, after services at Pastor John Smith's stone church, we invited our neighbours back to eat and drink with us so that all might get to know Lucy. Here it was that Lucy mischievously astounded me by announcing that she was with child and would present Tom Sindercombe with an heir before next spring. I was delighted, as were my neighbours, and we celebrated well into that night, even though Parson Smith had cause to rebuke us for it was Sunday. But Smith was not an austere preacher and he eventually condoned our celebration of the new life by joining us in more than one flagon of home-made beer.

113

It was on the following morning that an incident occurred which greatly upset Lucy.

She went to open a window to drain the odour of smoke and ale from the parlour and stopped, hand to mouth, with a gasp.

On the sill of the window was the bloodied body of a black bird.

Lucy's gasp drew me to her side and I bent down to pick up the creature. It was a crow, the type most people refer to as a raven. It seemed to have flown against the window-pane and dashed out its life on the thick glass.

"'Tis a bad omen, Tom," frowned Lucy on recovering her wits. "That's what 'tis said among our folk. For a bird to dash itself to death against one's windows is a portent of death."

"Nonsense!" I chided. "Besides, you are in Ireland now, a land where we colonists will forge our own customs. We will leave aside the old superstitions."

It was some days before the depression left Lucy, for she was still steeped in her native folklore whereas I, Tom Sindercombe, had seen service in the army for eight years and learnt enough to reject signs and omens as delusions and fables. Eventually she became her old self and grew to help me as I busied myself with the early summer chores about the farm.

One day I was working on the lower meadow where I had a goodly crop of corn growing. It was the very field in which I had first worked with O'Derrick, though I only bring this memory up in retrospect for now I scarcely remembered those Irish vermin. I had not thought of them since I claimed the farm as my own three years ago. I was working very hard now to prepare the land and contemplating expansion for I had heard that Fletcher Hopkins was thinking of selling out and returning to England. I did not glance up from my work until I saw the sun sinking below the far mountain tops.

I hurried through the copse which separated the lower fields from the open meadows around the farmstead and, bursting through the wood, halted abruptly in surprise. In the evening light I saw a tall white column of smoke rising from the chimney.

I halted, mouth agape and rubbed my eyes. The smoke did not continue up into the heavens, dispersing in the wind, but it curved like a bow, a curious arc, which returned to a spot on the ground near the old woodpile, close by the mountain stream.

What witchery was this? How could smoke curl in such a fashion and return to earth in the same columned shape as when it left the chimney?

My pulse suddenly quickened as I perceived a figure bestirring itself within the smoke. A dark shadow moved as the smoke billowed around it. My blood turned to ice as it moved forward. I could see by its skirts and outline that it was a female figure. As my eyes grew wide, the figure suddenly stepped away from the smoke.

Imagine my relief; imagine the palliation to my nerves as, laughingly, my own gentle Lucy stepped out of that peculiar smoke column and waved up towards me.

With a cry, I hurried down the hill, across the rough ground towards the farmhouse. My frenzied mind was imagining all sorts of possibilities. Lucy might have had some accident with a cooking pan and taken the burning pan out into the yard, whereupon the smoke from it had risen to meet the smoke from the chimney, thus causing the smoke to cojoin so that I observed this bizarre optical effect.

Yet when I reached the yard, both smoke and Lucy had disappeared.

Frowning, I pushed into the parlour.

Lucy gazed up at me in astonishment.

"What ails you, Tom?" she asked, carrying a platter of meat to the table.

I stared at her.

"'Twas the very question I was about to ask you," said I. "What was the smoke out in the yard?"

She looked bewildered. "Smoke in the yard? I know nothing of that." She went to the window and peered out. "I can see no smoke."

"It's gone now," I replied lamely. "You must have seen it. You were standing in it."

Her eyes widened: "Standing in it? What do you mean?"

I sensed an awesome feeling of unease.

"Were you not out in the yard just now as I came over the hill?" I asked softly.

"Not I, Tom. I have not ventured from the parlour these last few hours. I was too busy with the cooking."

Her voice was clear and adamant.

Something made me decide not to press the matter and I extricated myself from the situation by saying that the chimney must have been momentarily blocked and that I must have imagined I saw her shadow there. How could I say that I had seen her as clearly as I was seeing her now? It worried me. Was she lying or was I seeing hallucinations?

It was the following day as we sat outside watching the sun go down and drinking a glass of ale, an event which had become a custom with us, that Lucy turned to me with a frown.

"Tom, what were the people like who lived here before we came?"

I stared at her for a moment, a coldness in me wondering what had prompted that question.

"How should I know?" I shrugged defensively.

She sighed. "I just wondered what the natives were like in general. Do you know that I have been in this country for some time and never seen a native Irish man, woman or child? Where have they all gone?"

Here I felt on safer ground.

"By order of the Lord Protector, they have all gone to hell or to Connacht. They have been moved west of the river Shannon to allow honest English settlers to take over the towns and farms and civilise this Godforsaken country."

"It must be hard for them, hard to be driven from the land they and their ancestors worked. Is it right that we do this thing to them, Tom? How would we feel if the French came and drove us all into the shire of York and gave our farms and holdings to French folk?"

I chuckled at her gentle logic.

"It is not the same thing at all, Lucy. The Irish cannot count as people. They are uncultured savages. I have seen enough of them to know that they are murderous cut-throats, every one. An Englishman cannot move through the country unarmed."

Lucy, gentle soul, was not convinced.

"Yet isn't that how we would behave towards anyone who invaded England?"

"It is not the same," I insisted. "We tried to bring them civilisation, tried to teach them our language, our religion and values, yet they prefer to hang onto their barbarian gibberish and Papish customs. They are animals and must be treated as such."

"All the same, Tom," insisted Lucy, "as we sit here in the evenings, sipping our ale before going to bed, I cannot help but wonder whether an Irish girl and her husband also sat in this spot, watching the sun, sipping their ale, and wondering about those who worked the land before them."

"You cannot be sentimental over savages, Lucy," I admonished. "Just because this is a land close to England, do not think its inhabitants have risen above the wild savagery of those natives our New World colonists have encountered. Your Irish native lives the life of the savage and retains the idol worshipping superstitions and practices of ancient times. They live in utter ignorance of our just laws, our manners, our customs and our language. They are incredibly ferocious, brutally obstinate but crafty and unforgiving of strangers. Better our Lord Protector's plan to utterly obliterate them from the earth than feel them worthy of sentiment."

We fell silent for a while and then Lucy asked: "Is your cut healed, Tom? You should have told me that you had cut yourself. You must be more careful."

"I don't understand. I have not cut myself."

She sighed prettily with exasperation.

"There was blood on the parlour floor this morning. Did you cut yourself shaving?"

"I have not cut myself," I repeated disdainfully. "Perhaps it was spilt blood from the beef I butchered last night."

She bit her lip, hesitated and then nodded and stood up. "I think I will turn in now, the sun is already down ... oh!"

I glanced up. She was staring towards the woodpile.

"What is it?"

"I saw an old woman across the yard by the woodpile, Tom. She had bright snow-white hair standing out all over her head."

I leapt to my feet and grabbed for my pistol which I always kept in readiness.

"Tories, mayhap?" the words were snatched from my lips. "Where is she?"

"Gone now," replied Lucy, anxiety in her voice. "But she was there, I swear it."

"I'll check. Get inside the house and bar the door."

She obeyed me without a word while I set off at a run towards the woodpile. I searched the area for a full quarter of an hour without finding a sign of any intruders, let alone an old woman with a shock of white hair. Finally I returned to the farm and called softly for Lucy to unbar the door.

"There is no one about," I reassured her. "I will keep vigil tonight just in case there are bands of cut-throats on the prowl."

I did not mention that I had recently heard that old Parson Dicks' homestead near Mitchelstown had been razed to the ground by a pack of Tories who had escaped up into the Galtee Mountains. Some of their raids were getting more audacious. Within the last week a Popish priest, about to be hung in the square at Clonmel, was rescued in broad daylight by a group of Tories and carried off in triumph to their mountain lair. I had determined to follow the example of my fellow farmers in purchasing and training a pack of Wolf Hounds, a local breed of ferocious dog, to act as sentinels.

I was still standing in the doorway when the most unearthly wail split the evening gloom, a shrieking cry which rose in crescendo.

Once, twice and a third time came that blood-chilling screech.

Lucy cried out and grasped my hand.

"What is it, Tom?" she demanded fearfully.

I had heard that cry before; I tried to dredge the memory from my mind. Indeed, I had heard that self-same cry at this very door three years before.

"It's only a wolf," I said. "It will not harm us if we bar the door."

So saying, I proceeded to fasten the bolts and send Lucy off to bed.

For some time I sat awake, my pistol at the ready. In my mind the words of Finuala O'Derrick began to echo. "The *bean sídhe*, the woman of the fairies whose shrieks and moans portend a death!" What superstitious nonsense was this? Yet her words echoed loudly. "Be warned, son Ráif. Before another sun has set there will be death in this house."

It was broad daylight when I started awake and found Lucy already stirring in the parlour. I had fallen asleep in my chair with my pistol in my lap.

"Before another sun has set there will be death in this house." The words of Finuala O'Derrick were the first I seemed to hear.

I started up and peered wildly around me.

"Poor Tom," Lucy came forward smiling. "You have spent an uncomfortable night for nothing. No bandits attacked. It is morning and all is well."

She kissed me on the forehead and turned to prepare breakfast.

I tried to drive the wraith of Finuala O'Derrick from my mind's eye. I had done so successfully for three years. Why had her fiendish image come back to haunt me now? I could see that awful staring head with its shock of white hair, hair smitten white as I had severed it from her body with one blow of the curved bladed axe. It was than I realised what was preying on my mind. Lucy claimed that the old woman she saw on the previous evening had bright snow-white hair, hair that stood out all over her head ... just as, just as ... I cursed myself for a superstitious fool. I was becoming as bad as the natives! I shook the image savagely from my mind and turned to where Lucy was standing before the fireplace.

"I have to cut the shrubs and weeds in the middle meadow today," I said, trying to sound bright and cheerful. "Will you bring me down a flagon of ale and some bread at midday?"

She smiled gaily.

"Of course, but do you have some breakfast now. I'll ..." She turned towards the cupboard by the fireplace which acted as our larder, and her mouth became a round "O". "Tom, look!"

I followed her gaze. Oh God be my companion against evil! The blood froze in my veins. Never after that moment would it resume its regular ebb and flow, for my heart beat like a thousand drums rumbling in discord.

Blood was seeping from the cupboard. Blood, rich and red, was dribbling down its wooden doors and oozing softly, drop by drop on to the floor beneath.

"What on earth could it be?" frowned Lucy, making towards the cupboard with a hand outstretched.

At that moment I knew. *I knew!* It was the cupboard wherein I had placed the freshly severed head of Finuala O'Derrick; that terrible head whose hair had turned white before my eyes. It waited for me now; waited in that dark cupboard behind those closed doors, its blood still oozing ... still dropping steadily, blood drop by blood drop ....

"No!" my voice was a scream. "Don't open the cupboard, Lucy!"

It was too late. Lucy had reached forward and swung open the cupboard door.

She turned with amazement to my white, strained face.

"Whatever is the matter, Tom?" she demanded. "'Tis only the leg of beef we placed in here last evening. I foolishly did not provide a dish deep enough to hold the seeping blood and 'tis spilt. That's all it is."

I collapsed onto a chair. Concerned, Lucy fetched me a tankard of cool ale and watched me drain it like a man dying of thirst. At last I felt my heart resume pumping as near normal as it could and I was able to look up and meet her worried gaze.

"I am not feeling too well," I said foolishly. "I must be working too hard."

She nodded: "In that I would agree. Why not rest for a few days?"

I half-nodded but I did not want to remain in the gloom of the house. I wanted to get out among the fields and bathe in the sun.

"I shall finish the clearing of the scrub and weeds from the middle meadow," I resolved. "I'll be finished in a day. Tomorrow we will take the cart into Clonmel and see the town. Perhaps you can make a few purchases?"

She smiled happily.

"I would like that, Tom."

Feeling a little more cheerful, I went outside and honed my billhook to sharpen its rusty blade. Then I wandered down to the middle meadow in which I hoped to plant a crop of root vegetables. The potato plant from the New World was becoming a favourite food and fetched good prices. The morning swiftly passed as I progressed across the field, my axe scything the tough scrub and bushes before me, hand flashing to and fro in easy rhythms.

"Tom!" I heard Lucy's happy call behind me. "Tom, 'tis lunch time."

There was just one clump of bushes to finish.

"A moment, dear!" I cried, sweeping back my hand for the stroke.

My arm went suddenly light. There was a terrible scream.

I stood there, my eyes going first to my hand. I still grasped the wooden handle of the billhook but of the sharpened metal axe-head, there was no sign. It had parted company from the handle. Slowly, fearfully, I turned.

Lucy stood a little way behind me, unsteady on her feet, still clasping the tray with ale and bread and cheese before her. There was a smile of uncertainty on her pretty features.

The wickedly shining axe-head lay at her feet.

In relief I returned my gaze to her face. Oh God! The horror of it! Even as I watched her head seemed to wobble and fall forward onto the tray she held. That terrible headless body staggered forward a few paces towards me as if it were offering me the severed member. Then the body crumpled up and collapsed to the ground.

I do not know how long I stood there gazing down. I only know that some time later I found myself unwillingly listening to the gentle sighing breeze from across the mountain, the sibilant whispering of a million tongues among the leaves of the tall dark forest which hemmed the field in its embrace. Then I heard *her* voice!

"Do you not hear them, Ráif? Do you not hear the voices of our ancestors and our children yet unborn? We will never give this land up; we may die upon it, but our rich warm blood but fertilises the soil .... Listen, Ráif! Listen! The land is filled with a countless host. Do you not hear them whispering? Spirits of the earth, the trees, the springs and the streams, all of these are our allies and when you seek to destroy us, you must also destroy them! How will you destroy what is eternal?"

Hands to my ears to stop that frightful voice, to drown the sounds of the screams which rose in my throat, I ran headlong for the house.

I reached the parlour and paused, my breath rasping. Then I found my eyes being drawn unwillingly towards the cupboard. The stains of blood were still there and as I looked dark red liquid began to ooze slowly through the seams of the wood, drip-dropping on the floor below.

Her voice was quite clear now; clear and cold.

"Be warned, Ráif! The land is us, we are the land. You cannot separate us. The land encompasses the blood and bones of the countless beings we once were; it holds the breath of life of the countless beings we will become. Listen, Ráif! Listen! Do you not hear the voices of our ancestors and our children yet unborn? We will never give this land up; we may die upon it, but our rich warm blood but fertilises the soil ... Listen, Ráif! Listen! The land is filled with a countless host. Do you not hear them whispering?

Spirits of the earth, the trees, the springs and the streams, all of these are our allies and when you seek to destroy us, you must destroy them! How will you destroy what is eternal?"

In some odd way her voice calmed me. I knew what it was that I must do.

I cannot fight the unnumbered generations of the dead nor those that are yet to be born. I cannot fight the ancient gods of these people. They demand sacrifice for my crime, for all the crimes against these people whom they jealously protect. I must ameliorate them.

So it is that I have taken up the quill, though I be unused to book learning, and placed before me the paper which I had been saving to record the births of our children, Lucy's and mine, and sought to set down this sorry and terrible history that others might learn from my blindness, my avarice and stupidity. When 'tis done, I shall place these papers in a box underneath the hearth stone where our few treasures are kept. Here, some time, I trust some sympathetic soul will find them and pray for me in purgatory.

Aye, for what of me? Lucy's innocent blood will not placate the nameless gods that beset me seeking vengeance. Only my blood will erase my deed. There is a strong tree which stands by poor Lucy's shattered body; a strong tree with a stout branch. I have a new hemp rope. It is *their* due. My atonement. God of this world and the next, pray be merciful to me.

Tom Sindercombe

* * *

I must have sat there for some time in the old farmhouse parlour engrossed in that fascinating manuscript whose contents moved me so deeply.

Tom Sindercombe, sometime soldier in Cromwell's army in Ireland, had clearly been a prisoner of his time and its prejudices. The English soldiery had been taught to treat the Irish as less than human. Sindercombe had found an Irish couple who had showed him human kindness and yet his prejudice and avarice had made him slaughter them like animals. Deep within him, Tom Sindercombe had known that his deed was vile and wrong. The realisation began to grow slowly in his mind. He began to imagine all manner of signs and omens. Then came the appalling tragedy in which his young wife had been accidentally killed in a manner which Sindercombe saw as similar to the way he had murdered the O'Derricks. Now his mind was completely turned. In desperation he wrote down his wild fantasy and then ... then presumably he went out and hanged himself.

I sighed; it would be quite a task to check the records to see if there was a reference to the suicide of Tom Sindercombe in these parts in 1658.

Only one thing slightly puzzled me, as I sat staring at those yellowing sheets. Sindercombe must have gleaned quite a knowledge of Irish folkloric customs and beliefs for each omen he had put into his narrative, without comment, were accurate superstitions. The sound of galloping hooves, the dead bird, the curious smoke, the *doppelgänger* of his wife, Lucy, and the wail of the *bean sídhe* are all well-known portents of death in Irish country places. Yet how did Sindercombe gain such knowledge in the place and time in which he lived?

I sat a while puzzling over the problem.

At sometime during this contemplation I became aware of a soft drip-dripping, like water oozing from a tap. Frowning, I turned to seek for its source.

I do not know what it was that prompted my eyes to turn towards the old warped cupboard by the fireplace. It was shadowy in that corner and at first I dismissed it as my imagination, set afire by what I had recently read; yet, peering closely, I saw a dark stain on the old wooden doors.

I rose from my chair and moved forward in curiosity.

Yes, the wood was much darker around the seams of that ancient cupboard. I reached out a tentative finger and drew it over the stain. It felt wet and sticky. I stared at my finger in disbelief. It was stained red, as if with blood.

I jerked back, my heart thundering a frenzied tattoo.

Then I laughed. How stupid people were to allow their imaginations to be fed by some long dead hand. There was a logical explanation to everything.

I abruptly reached forward and threw open the cupboard. There stood a frightful corpseless head, standing upright as if still attached to its body. It was surrounded by a thick white mane of hair, hair which stood out stiff and snow white all around it. The eyes were wide and staring malevolently at me. Then, even as I looked, the eyes abruptly narrowed and its mouth distended, splitting into a malicious smile. An evil, throaty chuckle filled the air. I swear it! I swear that the sound came from that terrible head.

With a cry of animal fear, I turned, knocking the storm lantern from the table so that it smashed and the burning oil began to roar with eager tongues at the wooden floor. Screaming insanely, I pushed my way to the door and ran out into the daylight, out towards the green fields ...

VI

The Pooka

WHEN JANE AND I separated after ten years of marriage it was not an amicable severance. What are those often misquoted lines from Congreve?

Heav'n has no rage like love to hatred turn'd
Nor hell a fury like a woman scorn'd.

I have known many people whose marriages have been dissolved and who have gone their differing ways while remaining the best of friends; people who have come to the end of their relationship, mutually recognising that the ending was inevitable. They have had the foresight to see that it was better to quit while they respected one another, rather than cling to the situation as it deteriorated to a stage where all feeling was destroyed, where the coin flipped from love to hatred.

Regretfully, that was not the way it ended for us.

Jane had been my secretary before our marriage. I was just starting out in a small advertising agency as a junior accountant in those days. Now I am financial director of the same company, which is still a small but prosperous agency.

In fact, it was Jane's second marriage. She had previously been the wife of a young account executive named Garry Pennington, who had worked in our company.

I can recall Garry Pennington well; he was one of those typical brash young men, two years out of university with a second-class degree and on the way to their first million; work hard and play hard. You know the sort. The type you see shrieking down Park Lane in his BMW sports coupé, clad in a Savile Row three-piece suit, on the way to dine at the Hilton Hotel's roof-garden restaurant on an expense account. The only language Pennington understood was how much he could make out of the company for the minimal amount of effort.

Jane was hardly his type. She had joined the company as a secretary. She was not exactly beautiful, more winsome, with a mystical type of attractiveness that caused heads to turn. She had fair skin, freckles, grey eyes and raven-black hair. The type of features which cause you to hear a strumming harp, sea breaking on a granite shoreline, and visualise billowing mists over thrusting mountains. It was no surprise to me to learn that her parents had been Irish and that her first name was really Sinéad. She preferred to use the English equivalent of Jane because it saved trouble with insular English attitudes.

Jane and Garry Pennington were like chalk and cheese, but there is a universal rule that like poles repel and unlike poles attract. Within six months of Jane's joining the company, they were married. Young love, perhaps, with all the bewildering pain it entails. They were more or less the same age, about twenty-two. During their courtship, it became a little repugnant to me to see them mooning about the office, holding hands during the coffee breaks and snatching the sly kiss behind an office door. No, I am not prudish. At the time, I was only twenty-four myself. No, the truth of the matter was that I was jealous. I had fallen in love with Jane and I had come to detest Pennington's self-assured, flamboyant attitude.

They had a Catholic wedding – Jane was devoutly Catholic – and the office staff were invited. In fact, only the office staff comprised Jane's guests, for apparently she had no family in England, nor any who made the journey from Ireland to attend. Only Pennington's family attended in force.

I recall that it was not long after they returned from their honeymoon in Ireland that Pennington began to speak slightingly about Jane and once called her "a superstitious bog-Irish gypsy."

I was moved to impotent fury on Jane's behalf.

It was only two months after the wedding that it happened.

Garry Pennington was speeding down Park Lane one fine day when his brakes failed and he went straight into the back of an articulated lorry. His death was instantaneous. Jane became a widow.

Old Greyson, our managing director, who was a bit of a sentimentalist, persuaded Jane to stay on with the company and, soon after, when I was promoted, she became my secretary. As the months went by and Jane began to recover, we started to discover that we had many interests in common. Literature. Theatre. Concerts. We began to go out together now and again and then more frequently. To cut a long story short, eighteen months later, we married. As a widow who had not lost her faith, Jane insisted on a Catholic wedding again. Personally, I am an atheist but, so long as it pleased her, I did not mind.

We spent a three-week honeymoon in Ireland, visiting the south-west of the country, where, Jane said, her people had come from. She took a great delight in showing me the area, which quelled my misgivings, the spark of jealousy aroused in me because I was following in the footsteps of Garry Pennington. It was an uncharitable thought.

It was while we were on our honeymoon that we acquired our good-luck charm which Jane called "the Pooka." We came to a village called Adrigole, on the Beara peninsula; it was a small port with a sandy beach. Jane asked me to halt a little way from the village in order that she might show me the vista across Bantry Bay towards the dim, rugged outline of the Sheep's Head peninsula. I couldn't think why Jane chose that particular spot, for there were far better scenic parking areas farther along the road. Besides, this spot was near a group of dirty caravans whose occupants, by dress and manners, proclaimed them to be travelers, or "tinkers," as the Irish call them.

We had just left the car and walked to a point to gaze at the grey level of the sea when an old woman came up. She was dirty and had a high, whining voice. She started for me with out-stretched hands.

"Ah, lovely sir, may the Lord bless you. Would you not have a coin to spare for luck? I can give you a blessing, sir, a blessing for you ... "

I shook her beseeching hand roughly away with a muttered exclamation.

"You'll get nothing from me, you old beggar!" I snapped. "Go away or I'll find a policeman."

I have always had an irritation about beggars.

The old woman's voice rose several octaves and she started to shout at me in what I presumed was Irish. Jane afterward told me the words.

"*Fágaim mallacht ort! Fuighleacht mallacht ort!*"

Her voice halted abruptly and I turned to see Jane placating the crone by handing her some money.

I frowned my disapproval.

"Jane! We can't waste money by giving it away to these sort of people. They are leeches on society. They ought to be made to go out and work, every last one of them."

She turned with a wistful smile.

"Isn't it better to ensure good luck than a curse?"

"Nonsense!" I replied brusquely, climbing into the car. "People have no need to beg in this day and age. They are lazy, idle people."

The old woman fumbled with something in the folds of her shawl and pressed it into Jane's hands.

"*Go raibh maith agat, a cailín ghil mo chroí. Coinnigh é agus go gcuire sé an t-ádh ort!*"

Then the old woman turned to me and spat on the roadside.

"Keep and cherish her well, my fine *ógánach!* Woe is your lot if you treat her as you treat me!" With that she went scuttling away towards the caravans and disappeared.

"What the hell was that about?" I demanded as Jane climbed into the car. "What was she gabbling about?"

"She was giving me something for luck, that's all," replied Jane.

I chuckled. "Well, I bet the old witch wasn't giving me anything for luck."

Jane's lip drooped. "She cursed you."

"I'll bet! What was it she called me? An ogre?"

"*Ógánach*," corrected Jane. "It means 'young gentleman,' that's all."

She held a small object in her hands and I stared down at it. It was a small green stone carving. Connemara marble, as I afterward discovered. It was a small, elfin creature, a tiny figurine with a jaunty pointed cap and shoes and a mischievous smile.

"What's that?" I asked.

"It's called a *púca*;" she pronounced it Pooka, and Pooka it became from that time on. "It's a hobgoblin, an imp."

I laughed. "I thought hobgoblins were evil. Well, I'm not superstitious. We'll make it our good-luck charm."

And so "the Pooka" took pride of place on our mantelshelf.

Our marriage started out as a good one. It took me three years before I began to feel dissatisfied. As we grow older and extend the limits of our experience, so we change and develop. Just as we outgrow a suit of clothes, we outgrow our friends and acquaintances. Each man's road in life is marked by the milestones of his discarded likes and dislikes. Wasn't it Saint-Exupéry who said, "To live is to be slowly born?" I suppose I am trying to rationalise my subsequent conduct, because people will find it odd. After all, I had an attractive, loving wife. We hardly ever quarrelled. More important, we were great friends, having interests in common. I had a comfortable home and a secure job. So why was I dissatisfied?

To be truthful, I can't quite rationalise that aspect. I needed excitement. The idea of doing something "forbidden" made life less tedious and dull. Yet, why did I need excitement when I had most things that the average man would envy? I can't explain it, except that there is pleasure to be derived from being in a ship being blown about in a storm, an excitement to be derived from the danger. That's why horror movies are so popular. People crave excitement in their lives. Mine came from having casual affairs purely for sexual excitement. Jane had now left the agency and did part-time typing at home, so there was the office romance to offer passing satisfaction; business encounters – models were always hanging around the agency for work. For years my life became that of a "cheat". Oh, I was very careful not to let Jane suspect anything or to hurt her in any way. After all, I would always go back to Jane. She was my wife.

Then I met Elizabeth.

She was tall, blonde, with a mischievous laugh and a ready sense of fun. She was an executive of a market-research company who were used by our advertising agency. I met her by virtue of mutual business. We had a business lunch one day which was so delightful that I did not get back to the office until 3.45 p.m. It was not the hangdog, "love at first sight" emotion that I had had for Jane; it was a sparkling warmth of feeling which flowed through me when I heard Elizabeth's voice or saw her face.

Two days later I asked Elizabeth to have a pub lunch with me, pretending that there was a query which I wanted to clear up. She accepted, although, when she arrived at the pub, it was obvious that she had seen through my ruse. To my astonishment, she was not coy or indignant. It was the first of several such assignations. Then came evening rendezvous, and then, well, there were several days when I pretended to Jane that I had to go away on business.

Beth, as I called her, was the complete woman. She was not as intellectual nor as mystical as Jane, but Beth's earthy approach was a welcome change. Her sexual appetite was as bold and demanding as mine and she was not afraid to argue when she thought my point of view was wrong. My affair with Beth went on for more than a year. That in itself was unusual and gave me cause to re-examine my lifestyle. Gradually I came to the conclusion that I was in love with Beth; not just "in love," but "loved" her. She was the perfect partner, because there was no homely wistful complacency. With her, life was a constant excitement. The excitement was not drawn from the fact that our relationship was illicit; it was drawn from the fact that Beth was an exciting woman. It was as simple as that. Eventually, only one course of action was feasible. I determined to separate from Jane and live with Beth until such time as I secured a divorce and could marry her.

Telling Jane was an experience that I never wish to go through again.

I have heard of people going "berserk" and now I saw it. Gone was the mystic, brooding melancholia which seemed to hang over her most of the time. Instead, her face was filled with a resistless fury, a frenzy of emotions through which she screamed and shouted at me as she had never done before. Her eyes were wide and staring. Some people talk about the Irish temper; I was seeing it for the first time. Finally I shrugged and turned for the door.

"I'll come back for my things when you've calmed down," I said. "Your behavior doesn't alter the fact that I'm leaving."

"I'll never give you a divorce!" she screamed.

"You don't have to," I sneered. "I'm not bound by your Catholicism. If you won't agree to a divorce now, I'll just wait two years and get it myself. You better understand that it is all over between us."

"Curse you!" she shrilled as I slammed the door.

I waited three days before I went back for my bags. To avoid a repeat of the terrible scene, I took John Graham, my solicitor, along. John was a mutual friend as well. Jane let us into the house, demure and self-assured as ever she had been. She was subdued; all sign of her vile temper had gone. John Graham stood nervously by, obviously ill at ease, and declined the drink Jane offered.

"I am sorry that it has to end this way," I said to Jane.

She stared at me; her gaze seemed to be focused behind me, rather than on me.

"I have packed your suitcases with your clothes and personal possessions. If you think there is anything else to which you are entitled, you'd best draw up a list and give it to John to bring round."

I sighed.

"That'll be for the best, I suppose."

She did not appear to have heard me. There was an awkward silence.

"I hope things work out for you, Jane," I said hesitantly.

She stared at me blankly.

John Graham coughed and looked pointedly at me.

"I'll instruct John about the financial arrangements," I pressed. "You won't have to worry."

After another awkward pause, John and I left carrying three large suitcases and a box of my books.

It was a week later that I unpacked the box of books in Beth's bedroom. The transition to life with Beth had not been traumatic. It was a wild, fascinating adventure, totally different from my previous ten years of staid domesticity. Beth had a vast assortment of bohemian friends. We seldom ate in and we were still in the first, excited flush of unbridled love. Then, a week after I moved in, Beth had to go on an overnight business trip for her company, leaving me before the television set with a frozen dinner and her tabby cat to look after. The Friday-evening television programs were terrible, and so I hunted around for a good book. That was when I decided to unpack my books and see if there was something which took my fancy to read.

On top of the books, wrapped in white tissue paper, was the little Connemara-marble figurine – the Pooka, with his elfin hat and coat and mischievous smile.

Frowning, I dialed Jane's telephone number.

She answered immediately, her soft, breathless voice, her familiarity causing me to feel discomfort.

"Jane, I … er, I was just unpacking my books and I found the Pooka there." I left the question unspoken.

"You were the one who felt it a symbol of luck," she replied, her voice completely indifferent.

"It was given to you, though," I pointed out.

"It was meant for you," she answered.

There was an awkward pause.

"Are you keeping well?" I felt foolish asking the question.

"Perfectly. John Graham has been round a couple of times to inform me about the financial arrangements."

"Don't hesitate to ask if there is anything –"

"Good-bye," her voice sliced coldly through mine. There came a metallic click as she replaced her receiver.

For a while, I stared at the grinning imp and then, with a sigh, put it on the mantelshelf of the bedroom fireplace. It was a good-luck piece; after all, it had seen me climb from a junior account-ant to financial director; had seen me meet Beth, who had brought me more happiness than I had known.

The next morning, dashing to pick Beth up from Heathrow airport, I cut myself rather badly while shaving, spoiled one of my best shirts and arrived late and cursing at the terminal. But Beth was waiting, waved gaily and came across with a grin.

"My word!" she exclaimed. "You look as if you've been in the wars. Don't say Tabby scratched you?"

I sniffed. "As a matter of fact, your cat and I got along extremely well. We simply ignored each other," I explained ruefully and asked her whether she wanted to go straight home or stop off for a meal.

"Home," she smiled. "I'm tired."

We drove from the airport on to the M4 Motorway, which is the quickest route into London, for Beth's apartment is in Chel-sea. I had driven the M4 route more often than I could remember. The motorway was fairly clear of traffic, which was unusual at this time of day. I was cruising at 70 mph in the centre lane and coming up to the Chiswick turnoff. Suddenly the wheel was wrenched from my hand, spinning madly.

Beth screamed as the car lurched across the road, cannoned against the centre-section crash barrier, and bounced back on to the carriageway, slewing around in a complete circle. I struggled hard with the wheel and, finally, face pouring with cold sweat, brought the vehicle to a halt on the hard shoulder before collaps-ing over the wheel shaking with fright. I had never been so close to death before.

The next thing I knew was the arrival of a police patrol. The officer was polite and considerate. There had been a bad patch of oil on the centre lane, which caused the car to skid. I climbed out of the vehicle and stood with the policeman gazing at the dented offside wing. It would be a panel-beating job as well as a paint-spray job. I shook my head in disgust. Finally, I felt well enough to drive on to the apartment.

Beth, who was nowhere near as shocked as I was, poured us stiff whiskies before we stripped and went under a hot shower together. An hour later in bed the fright of the near accident was dispelled.

"What the hell is that?" demanded Beth suddenly. She sat up in bed and pointed to the mantelshelf.

I squinted and grinned. "That, my love, is the Pooka," I replied.

"The *what?*"

"My good-luck charm. I picked it up in Ireland years ago."

Beth sniffed. "It doesn't look lucky to me. It looks positively fiendish."

I chuckled. "It's brought me good luck."

"You should have had it with you this morning," she replied, reaching for a cigarette.

"We were lucky to come out of that skid alive," I said defensively. "Damned lucky."

"Doubtless thanks to your goblin friend." Beth grimaced before dropping the subject.

The following day was Sunday and we went to a film show before ending up in an exotic Mexican restaurant where I indulged in a large plate of chili con carne. I should not have done so. I awoke in the early hours and only just managed to make it to the bathroom before vomiting.

"Damned restaurant!" muttered Beth as she helped me. "You've got food poisoning."

She went on to say something about five hours passing since the time of the meal and sickness at such a time being indicative of food poisoning. I was past caring. I was wishing for death! It was pure misery. But, at last, I was able to fall asleep. In the morning I awoke sore and exhausted but feeling better. Beth telephoned my office and explained that I was going to spend the day in bed. She also reported the restaurant to the health authorities.

That evening I was feeling much better. Beth prepared a fairly simple meal and then started to call her cat for its plate of food. The cat was usually on the balcony of the apartment. It was not an adventurous animal and hardly ever stirred from the place. That evening, it was nowhere to be found.

Beth turned to me with a frown: "Have you seen Tabby?" she asked.

I confessed that I had been too busy wrapped in my own misery to notice the activities of her feline friend.

We ate our meal, watched some television and while I went for a shower, Beth called the cat again, with no better response than before.

"Where ever can it be?" she frowned as she came to bed.

"Even a cat has to go on the tiles once in a while," I murmured sleepily.

She dug me sharply with her elbow. "He's been doctored, idiot!"

"Then, he's probably developed into a peeping tom," I quipped, ducking as she went to hit me with her pillow.

We thought no more of the animal until the next morning. The caretaker of the building rang the bell with a morose face, and a cardboard box tucked under one arm.

"Excuse me, miss," he said as Beth opened the door, "would this be your animal?" He removed the lid from the cardboard box and held it out. The caretaker was clearly no animal lover, or respectful of the feelings of anyone who was.

Beth's cat lay squashed and bloody in the box.

"Found it outside the front door. Seems to me like it was run over by a car."

Beth was upset. She had kept the animal for four years and grown quite attached to it; you know how some people can be about cats. I can take them or leave them; independent, willful creatures.

Although the cat's death had upset her, Beth decided to go in to work to take her mind off the matter. I was restless. I telephoned old Greyson, my managing director, and told him I still felt queasy. He sounded preoccupied, and while he told me to take the day off, he seemed anxious that I return to the office as soon as possible.

I wandered about the apartment for a while and then decided to give Beth a surprise. I took out the vacuum cleaner, duster and brush and began to give the place a thorough cleaning. I was dusting the mantelshelf in the bedroom – lifting the objects to dust – when I found myself picking up the Pooka. The little green imp was grinning away.

I stared hard at it.

There was a strange hint of malevolency on its features which I could swear I had never seen before. Mischief – yes; but the grin was more pronounced than I had previously observed. I wondered why I had ever doubted the expression on the face of the creature; it was positively malignant, its tiny features were filled with maliciousness and animosity.

"Come on," I muttered, replacing it. "You're supposed to bring me luck, remember?"

I turned. I know it sounds foolish, but as I turned I tripped over the lead of the vacuum cleaner and went sprawling across the floor, banging my head against the leg of a chair.

As I ruefully picked myself up, I caught sight of the figurine. Was it my imagination or was the damned thing grinning more broadly than it had been before?

Nonsense! I cursed myself for a fool. Ten years with Jane was making me believe that an inanimate object was capable of feeling. Jane, for all her intellectual qualities, still had that superstitious quality that is common to the Celts.

Well, the days passed and it seemed that our run of bad luck was over. Well, of course, I never really believed in bad luck, but it is strange, isn't it, how bad things never happen in single events?

Life resumed its normal state. I returned to the agency to find that Greyson was worried about a "cash-flow" problem, as he called it. He wanted me to devote myself to gathering all unpaid accounts. Beth and I began to go out and visit friends, mainly Beth's friends. Unlike Jane, Beth had numerous acquaintances in the artistic world. Her circle was far more cosmopolitan than the one in which I had previously mixed. One evening, we went to a party held by some artist and one of the guests was a clairvoyant who went by the grandiose title of Count Elhanan Roscovski. The count was supposed to be famous; not that I would know, because I always regarded clairvoyants as charlatans, peddlers of gobbledegook. When I was introduced to Count Roscovski I held out my hand with an expression of amused cynicism.

As he touched my hand, a strange thing happened. He jerked as if he had touched a live electric wire. His bright black eyes stared wildly into mine. His lips moved slowly.

"*An rud a scríobhann an púca léigheann sé féin é!*"

At first I thought he was speaking in some Slavonic language, but I suddenly picked out the word *púca* and frowned.

"What did you say?" I demanded, as the other guests crowded round in interest.

The count just stood rigidly before me, eyes staring into mine.

"*An rud a scríobhann an púca léigheann sé féin é!*"

I frowned at him suspiciously.

"Is that Irish that you are speaking? What does it mean?"

It was as if he had not heard me at all.

I turned to Beth and whispered: "Beth, just write down the words – put down the phonetics if you can. This character has obviously gone into his act but I'm curious."

Beth fumbled with her bag, sought an address book and pencil just as Roscovski said the sentence for a third time. Then he added:

"*Chughat an púca!*"

His eyes closed and he staggered forward as if he would pitch upon his face. Several hands caught the man and he looked around him, bewildered.

"I feel unwell," he said, a trifle plaintively. "I must go home."

Our host was genial. "What were you saying to this gentleman, Count? You were speaking in a strange tongue."

Roscovski gazed at me perplexed and a little flustered. "I do not know. I do not remember."

"Oh, come on!" I cried. "You don't know what you said a moment ago?"

Roscovski shrugged. "I don't feel well. I must have had a … a sensation. I must go home."

He made to turn, hesitated and glanced at me. "I feel danger for you, sir," he suddenly whispered. "Great danger."

Then he was gone, leaving behind the guests chuckling in amusement at the party piece and congratulating the host and myself on the fine piece of theatre.

Beth came to my side with a frown and handed me a slip of paper.

"I think I managed to get down the phonetics of what he said," she sighed. "I've no idea what language it's in. It might be gibberish, for all I know."

I drew her aside, away from the curious revelers.

"I've an idea that it is Irish," I said, a strange, cold fear lurking in my mind – a fear I could not articulate.

"What makes you say that?" She was curious.

I told her about the single word *púca*, which I recognised.

She smiled and shook her head. Beth had a BA in English.

"The word occurs in Anglo-Saxon and means goblin there as well. It is where we get the modern English 'puck' or 'pouke'. You must have read Kipling's *Puck of Pook's Hill* when you were a kid?"

"I thought it was Irish." I frowned.

"So it is. But it also occurs in Welsh as *pwca* and Cornish as *bucca*. You see, all those languages borrowed it from the Old Norse *púki*."

I stared at her in astonishment.

She chuckled. "I'm not really that academic. My thesis was on early Norse loan words in English. I know nothing else, but give me a Norse loan word and I'll bore the pants off you."

"All the same," I grinned back, "I believe it's Irish. I've a friend who has a contact at the Irish Embassy. He might be able to translate."

The next morning, at my office, I telephoned my friend and he told me that he would see what he could do. Then all thought of the incident was chased from my mind. Old man Greyson rang on my internal telephone and asked to see me. His voice was off, strangely subdued. Frowning, I hurried to his office.

"I'll get right down to it," he said as I entered and shut the door. "The company is about to go bust."

My jaw dropped. "Is this a joke?"

He shook his head sadly. "Not a bit of it. You'll recall that we've been pursuing the policy of the one big client?"

Indeed. In fact, it was my idea. Our advertising agency was a small one, with only a limited number of resources. It had been my plan to instigate a policy of consolidation by closing down our smaller accounts and relying on our big account which we could back with the entire staff at our disposal.

Greyson now thrust a copy of the *Financial Times* at me.

The company in which we had placed all our faith, a large frozen-food manufacturer, had announced that it was going into liquidation. An official receiver had been appointed.

I frowned. "But we must have assets to tide us over until we obtain new clients?"

Greyson shrugged. "We put all the financial assets we had into the last campaign for the company. They owe us a hundred thousand pounds. We've barely enough in the bank to pay everyone a week's wages in lieu of notice."

"We must be able to raise a loan?" I countered desperately.

"I've been trying. Advertising agencies are two-a-penny. We have no collateral."

"I'll think of something," I replied grimly, trotting back to my office. Of all the bad luck! How could something like this happen? The agency had been doing so well.

At lunchtime I was due to meet Beth at the reception of the

office block. She was late; in fact, she didn't show at all. I telephoned her office on her direct number but there was no reply.

It was late in the afternoon when my telephone rang.

An impersonal voice asked: "Do you know a Miss Elizabeth Atkins, sir?"

That cold, uneasy feeling started to creep over my limbs.

"I know Beth. Is anything the matter?"

The voice sounded suddenly troubled. "Did you know her well, sir?"

"Who the hell is this?" I demanded suddenly, fear making me angry.

"This is Rochester Row police station, sir. I'm afraid that there has been a traffic accident."

The coldness was unbearable.

"Beth … ?"

"Miss Atkins was involved in an incident with a motorcycle at —"

"For God's sake!" I nearly screamed. "How is Beth?"

"I'm afraid Miss Atkins died shortly after her admittance to Charing Cross Hospital. We found your name and telephone number in her address book and are trying to trace her next of kin. Were you a close friend, sir?"

"I was her bloody lover!" I snarled as I slammed down the receiver.

God knows how I fought my way out of the office back to the apartment, where a policeman confronted me. I was aware of sad, sympathetic utterances, mumbled words of condolence, of commiseration, of consolation. I was aware of people drifting to and fro like shadows and then … suddenly I was alone in the bedroom of Beth's apartment with the telephone jangling persistently beside me.

I reached out automatically.

It was a strange, lilting Irish voice. The man introduced himself as the acquaintance of my friend.

"This lot of nonsense you transcribed into phonetics," chuckled the voice, "now where would you have picked up such stuff?"

I tried hard to concentrate. "What do you mean?"

"Jesus!" exclaimed the man. "*Chughat an púca!* Beware of the Pooka, indeed! A pooka is –"

"I know what a pooka is!" I exclaimed. "What else does it mean?"

"'Tis only an old proverb: what a pooka writes, he deciphers himself."

The fear, the awesome dread, turned into mindless panic, causing me to slam down the receiver. My eyes turned unwillingly to the little green marble figure on the mantelshelf. There it was, grinning down at me, its grin wider, more malevolent than ever.

With a cry of rage I made a grab at it, thinking to throw it into the fireplace, to smash it into a thousand fragments. As I swept my hand upward I felt a terrible electric shock which threw me back against the wall.

I lay staring at the figurine in wide-eyed perturbation. My heart was palpitating with apprehension.

Beware of the Pooka!

This was no symbol of good luck! No charm for fortuity and prosperity. It was a symbol of my damnation!

Thoughts tumbled in my mind.

Jane! I had to see Jane! She would know what it meant, what to do. She would be able to help me out of this terrifying nightmare into which I had drifted. I crawled unsteadily to my feet and stumbled from the apartment.

It was twilight and raining by the time I arrived at our house – Jane's house – in the suburbs. I turned up the drive and pressed the bell savagely. There was no answer, but a light was burning in the hall. I pressed the bell again, letting it peal long and loudly. Then I heard a noise. Jane's figure appeared behind the frosted-glass panel of the door, fumbling with the locks.

She swung the door open and stood there, gazing in surprise. Her hair was tousled and she wore only a scanty dressing-gown.

"What do you want?" She frowned belligerently, having recovered from her astonishment.

"The Pooka!" I gasped. I could feel my face working in my anxiety. "Jane, the Pooka! It has a curse on it."

She stared at me for a moment before her faced creased into a smile. "You don't believe in curses, surely?" she chuckled cynically.

"For God's sake, Jane! I'm serious! So many terrible things have been happening to me – Beth's dead! My company's gone bust and there are countless other things which have happened. It's a curse! I swear it, Jane! I swear it! You must know … you must take it back. " I stood sobbing like a child.

"Take it back?" came Jane's sneer. "Why should I do that?"

I stared at her wild-eyed. "There was never bad luck with you. You can negate whatever curse it holds. You must take it back."

"Must I?"

It was then I caught a movement on the stair and glanced behind her.

John Graham stood hesitantly there, a trifle self-conscious. He was naked except for a bath towel folded around his middle. "Are you all right, darling?" he asked.

Jane gazed at me with a triumphant smile before turning. "Yes, John. He's just leaving." She turned back to me, her eyes suddenly filled with hate.

"Jane!" I cried in desperation. "For pity's sake!"

"Ah, pity and charity is something you know much about," she whispered softly.

"I don't understand. For God's sake, Jane, tell me what is happening to me. Why is it happening?"

"Every why has a wherefore."

She made to shut the door and then hesitated and stared coldly at me. "Take away the cause and the effect ceases. I trusted you and you took my trust and trampled it. I gave you my heart and you took it in your hands and crushed it. My love for you was not the love of a dog for the sheep, it was the love of a salmon for the river. You have hurt me beyond measure. Now you must pay.

144

Should I care now if you are pricked by the thorns which you planted?"

The door slammed in my face.

I heard her merry laugh mingling with the deep tones of John Graham's chuckle.

Shocked and numbed, I staggered away from the house, my mind in a turmoil. As I came out of the gate into the night-black street, head involuntarily down against the sheeting rain, a dark figure stirred by the bushes. It was the figure of a bent old woman.

"Bless you, sir. Can you spare a coin for an old woman, a coin for the sake of luck?"

The accent was familiar.

Habits of a lifetime take a long while to die. I turned away with a curse. My own state of mind made the violence of my reactions stronger. "Go and pollute your own country! How dare you bother people in a public street!"

The old woman chuckled. "No, you have not changed much, my fine *duine uasal* – my fine gentleman."

There was something in the voice, something about her which conjured up a vague memory.

I turned and frowned toward the black-shawled creature. "Do I know you?"

"Right enough, sir."

She moved forward slightly and her wizened features were briefly illuminated by the streetlamp.

"You!" I cried. "You were the one who gave us the Pooka! You caused the curse!"

"Not I," chuckled the old woman. "You caused your own bad luck, your own cursing. The Pooka was given to your wife. When you hurt her, that hurt rebounded on you. There is always a cause and effect."

I stared at her aghast, not wanting to believe what I was hearing and yet believing.

"I saw your character on your face ten years ago, when you treated me discourteously at Adrigole. I knew that someday you would hurt your wife. It was the same with her first husband."

"Her first husband?" I was totally bemused now. What did this crone know of Jane's first husband?

"She brought him to see me," she went on as if reading my thoughts. "He was the perfect gentleman. The suave English *duine uasal*. He treated me well, and she" – the old woman jerked her head toward my house – Jane's house – "she thought that me being a tinker would not matter to him. So she told him. I knew he wouldn't want her when he realised the truth. I gave her a pooka for protection."

There was a clawing in my stomach as I tried to fathom the meaning of what she was saying. "Are you talking about Garry Pennington?"

"That was his name," she assented.

"Pennington was killed in a car crash – " I began but was interrupted by her chuckle.

"So he was! So he was!"

"What are you telling me? The Pooka was responsible?"

"Oh no, no. *He* was responsible. Man is responsible for all his actions. He rejected her and hurt her."

"Rejected Jane? Hurt Jane?"

"Jane ... Sinéad ... whatever you call her in this country."

I tried to gather my thoughts and make a final attempt to understand. "Sinéad? How do you know Jane's real name? Why should Pennington have rejected Jane because she introduced him to you? How do you know Jane?"

The old woman's laughing was uncontrollable. "A fine mother I'd be if I didn't know my own daughter."

I staggered back a pace, fear clawing with icy hands at my heart.

Jane's mother! Now it made sense. And at that moment I knew that there would be no appeal. I read the cold glaze of hatred in the old woman's eyes just as surely as I had read the hatred in Jane's face. The sentence for my misdeeds had been passed. My fate was inevitable.

I tried to bring my gaze back to the old woman, but she had

gone into the blackness and driving rain of the evening.

There was nothing for it, nothing left but to return to Beth's apartment, back to the grinning imp-like figurine, back to the Pooka. Was it an instrument of retribution or justice?

VII

Tavesher

CNOC NA BHRÓN is one of those comfortless, unfrequented and isolated places that still exist in the wild landscape of the bare Kerry mountains on the border of Cork and Kerry. It is a gloomy solitude, high among the barren peaks that are among the tallest in the country. In English Cnoc na Bhrón means "The Hill of Sorrow," but this is an area where English is seldom heard, where the people cling to the ancient language of the country and traditions that were millennia old before the coming of Christianity. Cnoc na Bhrón is a desolate spot, wreathed in brooding melancholia and grieving friendlessness.

Perhaps I am getting ahead of my narrative. I ought to tell you what brought me, Kurt Wolfe of Houston, Texas, to that wild spot thousands of miles from my home. It is a simple story. I work as a surveyor for a mining corporation that decided it was worth the risk of undertaking a prospecting survey of some of the old, deserted copper mines of south-west Ireland. A century ago there were many such mines operating quite profitably. In those days Ireland had been ruled from England, so when England found it cheaper to extract its copper from Australia, the Irish mines found it impossible to compete and gradually, one by one, they were forced to close. My company was concerned with the viability of opening some of those mines once more.

I had made preliminary surveys of several mines in the region and was heading for the village of Ballyvourney. Here, according to my map, I would find a road that would lead me into the

Derrynasaggart Mountains to one particular peak, Cnoc na Bhrón. On the slopes of Cnoc na Bhrón stood an old mine called Pollroo, which I learned was a corruption of the Irish *An Pholl Rua*, which meant "The Red Hole" and doubtless had something to do with the fact that red copper was mined there. My notes showed that Pollroo was one of the last mines to be worked in the country and had not been entirely deserted until the turn of the century.

I found the village of Ballyvourney easily enough, but although I had a large-scale map of the district, I had difficulty finding the road to Cnoc na Bhrón. I was lucky enough to spot a police car parked in the village and drew up behind it. Two members of the *Garda Síochána* sat inside, and I approached them to enquire the way.

"You'd be an American, I'm thinking." said the moon-faced driver morosely, in response to my question.

I nodded.

"There's nothing up at Cnoc na Bhrón," the second man said.

I explained the purpose of my visit. The men exchanged glances with raised eyebrows.

"'Tis dangerous up at Pollroo; the mine has been deserted since the turn of the century. No one goes there these days."

I suppressed my impatience and said, "If you could point out the way to Cnoc na Bhrón ... ?"

After a further exchange of inconsequential conversation, they finally pointed me through a maze of farm lanes on to a small dirt track that I would have had no hope of finding if I had been left to my own devices. It was a small, narrow track that had once been paved with stones but was now overgrown. It twisted and climbed high into the mountains, passing many deserted stone crofts; ancient, roofless cottages.

In spite of the bleak aspect of the higher reaches of the mountains the weather was surprisingly mild, and the fact that this was usual was reflected in the wide variety of subtropical plants that occurred in the area. Predominant across the broad lower slopes was the purple mist of heather; fuchsias were also common and so, too, was the arbutus or strawberry tree, which grew in amazing profusion. It is an evergreen, flowering in the autumn and winter, and it has an edible fruit that, at first, reminds one of wild strawberries although the flavor is a trifle bitter.

I was lulled into a pleasant, warm feeling as I drove through this gentle, sunlit vista.

It came as something of a surprise, therefore, to turn my car across the shoulder of the mountain and come abruptly on a flat of land that constituted a plateau and a valley at one and the same time. It was as if a hand had suddenly been stretched across the face of the sun; I went from lightness into darkness. The area appeared as if some giant had scooped a large hole in the side of the mountain. The plateau was surrounded on three sides by a protective semicircle of black granite cliffs. The actual width of the plateau was probably a mile across and the same distance in depth. I could see a tarn, a small mountain lake, and the ruins of an old house. Beyond the house were ruined outhouses and buildings that I easily recognised as the deserted mine-workings. The sun did not seem to penetrate on to the plateau, and there was a peculiar stillness and rawness; a penetrating chill permeated the area.

I drove my car along the uneven track that skirted the tarn and halted it before the ancient, decaying house. According to the map I had, it was called Rath Rua and it appeared like so many of the stately houses of a bygone age that you find littered through the countryside of Ireland. It had once been the prosperous habitat of the mine owner and his family. A century of decay and neglect and the incursions of nature, insidious creeping weeds and hungry, devouring ivy, now disguised the once-grand aspect of the place. I climbed out of my car and stood staring up at its eyeless windows, its dark frowning exterior. Its great stones had obviously been quarried from the black granite of the surrounding circle of cliffs.

The atmosphere seemed damp here and I caught the whiff of bittersweet decomposition as a cold breeze blew its chill breath against me. I turned toward the tarn. It was quiet and still and very black. The water was obviously stagnant and on its surface were strange green stains. It took me a moment to realise that this was caused by copper ore permeating the lake, presumably from the disused mine. The realisation lightened my heart. If the ore was still staining the tarn, then there must surely be copper deposits left in the workings.

I glanced at my watch. It was midday and there was plenty of time to take some initial samples. Obviously, I did not mean to make a thorough survey there and then. In fact, I knew that I would have to get plans of the old mine-workings and perhaps a local guide in order to get to the copper veins in order to see if they could be reworked.

Behind the house were the remains of an overgrown path that led directly to the base of the black granite cliffs and the entrance to the mine. Its black, gaping mouth was nearly obscured by undergrowth. I returned to my car and pulled out a small haversack in which I carried the tools of my profession. I took out a flashlight, slung the haversack on my back and made my way carefully over the path.

If it was cold at the house, it was even colder here. Brooding blackness stretched out to envelop me. I switched on my flashlight and turned the beam along the walls, which had been hewn by the hand of man into that thick granite. The walls were damp and oozed with water. It was obviously seepage from the mountain draining through the innumerable cracks and crevices. From farther along the tunnel came the sound of gushing water making a noisy, echoing music.

I moved forward cautiously, swinging the beam to right and left. It was not long before I noticed that the tunnel was growing narrow; the roof began lowering over my head. The walls glittered with green-stained water and the floor was slippery with the slime of disuse. In fact, I had barely started along the tunnel when I slipped, struck out wildly for support, and fetched my head a crack against an overhanging thrust of granite. It stunned me for a moment but I retained my footing, rubbed my forehead ruefully and moved on – this time a little more carefully.

However, the conditions began to worsen. My mind was just forming the notion that the place was too treacherous to proceed further on my own when my feet slipped from under me again. This time my feet seemed to slide away from me. The torch fell from my hand and I cried aloud. I tried to catch hold of some object to save myself, but my forward momentum was unimpeded. Then I was falling; falling into utter blackness. I felt sharp rocks jabbing at me, scraping my flesh, tearing my clothes. Something cracked against my head but this time it was no mere stunning impact. For one terrible moment I felt fear; complete, heart-stopping fear stabbing like a knife in my chest as I realised that I was falling down a vertical shaft. I hit the bottom with a vague feeling of impact and then ... nothing. A deep, silent, black void enveloped me.

When I opened my eyes, the first thing that I became aware of was the cheerful, crackling fire roaring away in a rather ornate hearth. I blinked and frowned, trying to bring my surroundings into focus. I was apparently lying on a couch; the couch was in front of a large arabesque marble fireplace in which the vigorous fire played with logs of sweet-smelling pine. My gaze expanded to take in a large room, decorated in somber burgundy and gold, a touch too old-fashioned for my taste. Numerous prints and drawings covered the walls, and there were some exquisite pieces of period furniture about.

"Relax," said a voice close to me. "You're all right."

I turned my head slightly to see a tall man with pleasant features standing at the head of the couch. I made to sit up but groaned at the dull ache in my head.

"Steady," admonished the man in a gentle tone.

"What happened?" I mumbled, raising a hand to massage my temple.

"You've had a fall, old fellow," replied the man, moving around to stand in front of me. He reached forward and took my wrist between his finger and thumb in a most professional manner. His gray, deep-set eyes peered into mine and then turned

153

to examine my forehead.

"A slight contusion, but you'll be fine enough."

"What happened?" I demanded again.

"You fell down a shaft in the old mine," he replied.

The memory came flooding back.

"That was a damned stupid thing to do," I said ruefully.

"Very stupid. My name is O'Brien. Dr Phelim O'Brien."

I told him my name and asked, "Where am I?"

"Mothair Pholl Rua; it's a house close to the mine."

"I thought this spot was more or less deserted," I replied, lying back. "Have I been out a long while?" I asked, realising that the curtains were pulled and night had apparently fallen.

The doctor nodded.

"Is this your house?"

"More or less," O'Brien replied in a tone that roused my curiosity.

"How did I get here?"

"I brought you here."

"From the mine-shaft?" I raised my eyebrows in astonishment.

"I happened to be near by when you fell," he replied shortly, turning to the mantelpiece and picking up a pipe. He slipped into an armchair at the side of the fire and proceeded to light the pipe, all the while regarding me thoughtfully.

"You are an American."

"Guilty." I smiled. "And are you the local doctor?"

"No, no." He shook his head. "My practice was in Cork city. But that was years ago now."

"What brought you to these wilds then?" I asked. I suppose I was simply making conversation, because I was actually wondering whether I was well enough to drive back down to Ballyvourney to look for a hotel for the night.

"Oh, I came here a long time ago ..."

As he was not much more than forty years old, I remarked that it could not have been so long. He replied with a wry smile.

"When you live here, here in the midst of these mountains, so close to nature, time ceases to have any practical meaning."

"What made you give up a city practice for the remoteness of these mountains?" I asked, my curiosity now overcoming my initial diffidence.

"In the first place – a woman."

He stared disgustedly at his pipe, poked at it, relit it and tried a few experimental puffs.

"I was engaged to a girl at that time. It was she who wanted a taste of the country life. In those days there were quite a few great country estates on the market; places that had fallen into a state of dereliction and that one could purchase for a song."

"So you decided to buy one?" I nodded.

"That was the idea," he agreed. "I learned from an estate agent that this house, Mothair Pholl Rua, was for sale. I didn't tell my fiancée because I wanted to inspect the place first. One Sunday I climbed into my car – I had one of those new Fords – and drove out to Ballyvourney."

"And so you decided to settle here?"

"No."

I stared at him in surprise. "But here you are," I said.

"I did not want to stay." He frowned at me abruptly. "To be honest, Mr Wolfe, it is a tale that takes some believing."

It was plain that O'Brien wanted to tell the story, and I gave him full credit for the way he was catching my interest.

"Have you ever heard country people hereabouts speak of the *taibhse*?"

"Tavesher?" I echoed, trying to pronounce the Irish word with English phonetics. "What is that?"

"A *taibhse* is a phantom," he said solemnly. "Do you believe in such things?"

"Good Lord, no!" I smiled broadly.

"Neither did I ... until the day I came to Cnoc na Bhrón."

I glanced at him to see whether he was joking, but his face seemed solemn enough.

I sighed. "Tell me your story," I invited.

He stoked up his pipe and sat back. "Well, as I said, I drove to

Ballyvourney and then found the road for Cnoc na Bhrón. It was a pleasant enough day and I was driving along without a care in the world. The road was deserted and so I was driving at a cracking pace without a thought of meeting anything on the road. It happened very suddenly. I swung around a bend of the mountain road and, out of nowhere, an ass stood in my path. I didn't have a chance to halt in time and so I swung the wheel to avoid the creature. Now if I had swung to the right I would have gone straight off the side of the mountain and careened down into the valley below. So left I swung and went into a ditch that bordered the road. Down went the hood of the car and, as it ceased its forward motion, I was propelled into the windscreen and fetched my head a crack.

"I must have lost consciousness for a moment, for when I came to the damnable beast had ambled off. The car was so positioned in the ditch that I knew it would be futile to attempt to move it. So I decided to walk up to the house – Mothair Pholl Rua – which I could see in the distance. I half-hoped that there might be a telephone still working in the house from which I could ring down to the village and save myself a long walk. Well, there was no telephone ... but I am getting in advance of my tale.

"I walked up the mountain track toward the imposing edifice of the house. I knew enough, even from a distance, to say that it was not my sort of place. It was a solitary, isolated spot. You may think it ridiculous, perhaps, but I felt that there was something strange about the house. After all, what is a house but a lump of stones, wood and glass, thrown together by the ingenuity of man? A house is only an inanimate object, a lifeless, inorganic, abeyant structure. In spite of that knowledge I felt that there was something about it that threatened me.

"As I came to the stone wall that marked the borders of what had presumably been its gardens, I suddenly noticed a small boy sitting on the top of it. He was staring into space and whittling at a piece of wood.

"'Hello!' I called. To my astonishment the boy ignored me. I wondered if he was deaf. I walked toward him and called again.

I swear that he raised his head and stared at me ... no, stared through me as if I had no existence. Then, calmly as you please, he threw away the stick, put his clasp knife into his pocket, jumped down from the wall, cast a glance around him, and was bounding down the mountainside. He neither uttered a word nor looked back in my direction."

"Children can be strange at times," I volunteered, interrupting O'Brien's narrative.

The doctor looked thoughtfully at me and inclined his head in agreement. "So I thought at the time. Well, I continued on to the house and peered through the darkened windows. The estate agent had given me the key, and feeling rather ridiculous at my initial reaction to the house, I let myself in. The feeling returned even as I was dismissing my former reaction. The house was somehow unfriendly and forbidding. I felt cold and nervous. If that house had ever been filled with love, love had long since fled. I soon realised that my faint hope of finding a telephone still connected was to be dashed. I made up my mind to start walking down to the village. It would be a long walk, but I set off with a confident stride. I felt quite relaxed and well."

He paused and stared at me. "I emphasise the point because of what happened next. I had walked back as far as my car and proceeded not more than fifty yards further on when I was overtaken by the weirdest sensation."

"What sort of sensation?" I intervened.

"I felt sick; so sick and dizzy that I thought I was going to pass out. The attack, or whatever it was, was so acute that I was forced to sit down by the side of the road. My body seemed to grow ice cold, and an odd blackness hung before my eyes as if it were evening twilight ... yet I knew the time to be little after midday. I realised that in such a condition I could not continue down the mountain. Somehow, I thought, I would have to try to crawl back to the house and rest there.

"I did so, straining every limb. Imagine my astonishment, Mr Wolfe, when, as soon as I was but a few yards away from my car, I began to feel better. I paused; if I felt well enough perhaps I had recovered from whatever the attack was. I turned over the symptoms in my mind. The only thing I could think of was that it was a case of delayed shock arising from my accident. But I felt well enough now. I shrugged, turned, and started to walk down the mountain again.

"No sooner was I but fifty yards down the track when the same thing happened. In all my years as a doctor I had never experienced or heard the like of the sickness that I suffered. Eventually I made my way back to the house, let myself in and crawled to the very couch you now lie upon. This time it took me a little longer to recover, but recover I did."

He paused for a moment and stared into the fire. The dancing flames were reflected in his somber gray eyes.

I shivered. It occurred to me that in spite of the brightness and zestful play of the fire, I felt oddly cold.

Dr O'Brien saw me shiver. His lip drooped, and he made no comment.

"I lay on that couch for quite a while. It was dusk when I finally gathered myself together and decided to make a third attempt to walk down the mountain. It was then that I noticed a small fire burning outside the house.

"I peered through the window and saw that it was a campfire blazing away before a tent. From the light this campfire sent flickering into the darkness of the night, I saw a young man and a girl seated before it and cooking something over it. Now we get a lot of hikers and campers in these mountains and it was obvious that while I had been lying down, these two had chosen to make a camp for the night within the garden of the old house. Well, I was delighted. Here was company and I could get something to eat and drink from them. I went out of the house and across the wild tangle that had once been the lawn.

"'Hello!' I cried, well before I reached their friendly campfire. I took pains not to frighten them by a sudden appearance.

"They made no move to look up, though they surely heard my call. Instead, they bent to their food, chuckling and whispering to each other.

"I reached their campfire and stood before them.

"'Hello,' said I. 'Sorry to disturb you but I've had an accident down the road.'

"They ignored me.

"Then it was that I was swept by a sudden coldness. I noticed that while the fire leapt and crackled, it cast no warmth. The figures of the boy and girl seemed to have an odd ethereal quality about them, a silver flickering sheen. Their features, when I looked closely, were pale, so near transparent it seemed as if I could stare right through them.

"'What's the matter?' I cried, trying to keep the fear from my throat. 'Don't you hear me?'

"They continued talking – talking about the tramp across the mountains to Kenmare that they were planning for the next day.

"A sudden anger seized me. I reached forward to shake the boy by the shoulder.

"*A Dhia na bheart!* My hand – my hand went right through the shoulder. The boy had no corporal existence. His only reaction was to shiver slightly and turn to his companion and say, 'There's a chill wind up here.'

"I stepped back in horror.

"Was I having a nightmare vision? Of course, the old people often talked of seeing the *taibhse* – phantoms – shadows without any tangibility. I backed cautiously away from these ghostly campers, expecting that at any minute they would simply vanish from my gaze. They did not. I was sweating … yet at the same time I was cold with fear. I did not know whether to start immediately down the mountain path into the darkness or go back to the house and wait until dawn brought a friendly light to the scene.

"A hollow cough behind me made me spin around, wondering what new danger could threaten me.

"A man sat on the low stone wall of the garden border. He was old; his face was deeply etched. I could see his graven lines clearly, for he held a storm lantern in one hand. His dark eyes stared solemnly at me.

"'God between me and all evil!' I cried in Irish, for a terrible fear was upon me.

"'Amen to that,' replied the man.

"The relief flooded my body. 'You can hear me?'

"'I can.'

"'You can see me?'

"'I can again.'

"'*Buíochas le Dia!* Thanks be to God,' I said with a sigh. Then I turned my head. The wraiths were still seated at their ghostly campfire. "'Yet can you see those?'

"Again the man nodded.

"'But they can neither see nor hear me,' I cried in exasperation.

"The old man raised a shoulder in a shrug.

"'But that is the way of it.'

"'How do you mean?'

"'*Mo bhuachaill*,' he said, adopting a kindly attitude. 'My young man, you must know that they be phantoms. Up here in the mountains we dwell close to nature, seeing many things that those who dwell in the cities think are strange. But we do be all part of one universe, one world, where nature and supernature are two sides of one coin. There is no "natural" and no "unnatural," only what is and what is, do be."'

"If I had been told that I would be talking about higher philosophy with an old peasant high in the Derrynassaggart Mountains in the middle of the night while staring at a phenomenon I believed impossible, I would have thought the person who dared propose the idea to be insane.

"'Truly,' I asked the old man, 'you say that they are phantoms?'

"'*Sin é*. Right enough,' he replied. 'They be *taibhse*.'

"I stared at him, seeing the truth of the matter reflected in his solemn gaze. I reached up a hand and wiped the sweat from my brow. Then I brought my mind to more pressing matters.

"'Can you direct me to where I might rent a bed for the night?'

"'I would willing give you a bed but my cottage do be five miles walk from here and I must be at work. Try at the house.

Miss Áine will be there right enough.'

"He turned and walked rapidly away. I called after him, protesting that the house was deserted, but he vanished into the night. I cast a shuddering glance at the ghostly campers and decided that the only thing to do was take shelter in the house for the night.

"I went in through the door and halted. Whereas before the house had seemed cold, unfriendly, and forbidding, I was aware that it had grown warm, a soft friendly warmth. Whereas before the dust and cobwebs predominated, everything now seemed clean, as if someone had suddenly brushed, polished and tidied the place. Even the cold furniture, which I had thought rough, damp and near decay, was almost new and had a comfortable, lived-in feeling.

"I felt that I had had enough shocks for the day and was turning away when I heard the faint rustle of silk skirts. The door to the living-room opened abruptly and there stood a girl. *Dia linn!* She was beautiful. A slim slip of a girl with red-gold hair and grave green eyes. She looked like some goddess standing in the half-light of the lamp that she held in one hand. She did not seem in the least perturbed by my presence.

"I stumbled for the right words: 'I'm terribly sorry,' I said, 'I had no idea that the house was still occupied. The estate agent said that it had been deserted before the Great War.'

"The girl frowned, drawing her brows together gently as if perplexed. 'I'm sorry, sir,' she replied. 'I do not know what you mean.'

"I plunged on desperately: 'The estate agent told me that this house, Mothair Pholl Rua, was for sale and I –'

"She interrupted me with a smile. 'But this house is Rath Rua, sir.'

"'Then I am in the wrong house and have made a terrible mistake.'

"The girl smiled, but the frown did not leave her pretty face.

"'The house you are looking for is called Mothair Pholl Rua?' she asked, with a shake of her red-gold hair. 'But I have never heard of such a house and I have lived here all my life. My name is Áine FitzGerald. The estate and the mine belong to my father, Lord Cauley FitzGerald.'

"I introduced myself and told her that I regretted not having heard of her father. In turn, she invited me into the living-room and we sat before the fire and spent some time in idle chatter. I did not mention my experience with the ghostly campers, for fear of frightening my lovely companion. I did wonder why she appeared alone in the house.

"It was about then that I noticed the gray cold light of dawn creeping in at the window and I realised that I had not been to sleep. Strangely, I felt alert and refreshed. I began to apologise for my thoughtlessness in keeping the girl talking all through the night.

"She smiled softly at me and chuckled. 'Do not trouble yourself, Doctor,' she said sweetly. 'No one bothers to sleep here.'

"I frowned, thinking that I had misheard her. 'I should be on my way back to the village,' I said.

"A sad expression came on her pretty features. 'Alas, it is futile for you to try to walk back to the village.'

"'How so?' I demanded, suddenly feeling uneasy.

"'Ah, my poor doctor. Don't you know? I would have thought that a man of your intelligence would have been able to work it out.'

"I tell you, Mr Wolfe, a terrible cold fear began to creep upon me.

"Work what out?" I demanded.

"Why you will not be able to get beyond the point where your car crashed. You see ... you were killed there."

O'Brien paused, sighed, and kicked at the fire with the toe of his boot.

I gazed at him for a long time, wondering whether to laugh.

"The girl continued. 'The ghosts you thought you saw last night? They were living people. It is you who is dead.'

"Well, Mr Wolfe, I was shocked, I can tell you. In fact, it took me a long while to realise that the girl was right. And here I have been in this house ever since that day … I remember it well. May twelfth, 1929."

He sat back indifferently and began to rekindle his pipe.

I stared at the man for a moment and then snorted in disgust. "I do not find this a very amusing story, Doctor," I said, tight-lipped.

His gray eyes twinkled at mine. "It was not meant to be merely amusing, Mr Wolfe."

He turned and glanced at the curtains.

"But here is the first glimpse of dawn," he said, rising and going across to pull aside the heavy velvet curtains with a swish.

It was true; the cold gray light of dawn was filling the tall glass windows. I stood and shook my head. Dr O'Brien either had a bizarre sense of humor or else he was a little touched in the head.

From a distance came the purr of a motor-car engine.

"If I am not mistaken, Mr Wolfe" – O'Brien's voice was genial – "that sounds like a search party coming to look for you."

I joined him at the window. Across the mountain there was a good view of the old roadway, and in spite of the neutral effect of the gray early morning light, I could pick out the bright flash of the headlights of a car sweeping this way and that as it twisted and turned its way up toward us.

"Well, at least they can give me a lift to where I parked my car," I said. "Is the old ruined house near the copper mine far from here?"

O'Brien smiled broadly. "Your car is outside this house where you parked it."

My jaw gaped. "But I parked it outside the ruin, the old house called Rath Rua. What game are you playing, Doctor? Besides, you said that this place was called Mothair Pholl Rua."

"Rath Rua was the name of the house when it was young and alive. You should have learned that in Irish *mothair* means a ruin, Mr Wolfe. That is what people call Rath Rua now."

I snorted with indignation. I had seen the ruins of Rath Rua last night and this place was well kept. It was certainly no ruin.

The car halted outside. I looked through the window and saw

that it had a blue flashing light on its roof and the sign *Garda* on it. The Irish police. Here was some sanity at last.

"I'd better go out and tell them that I am all right," I said distantly.

O'Brien smiled softly but did not say anything.

I turned from the living-room and walked through the hallway and opened the massive doors. They led on to a large sweep of half a dozen steps to the driveway outside.

Directly below, at the foot of the steps, stood my car illuminated clearly by the lights of the police car and the pale gray of early morning. My mouth opened in astonishment. A number of thoughts raced through my mind, concluding with the thought that O'Brien himself must have driven the car here from the ruins where I had left it.

A car door banged and a moon-faced policeman strode up to my car and peered inside. His companion was leaning against the side of the police car with the door open and a microphone in his hand.

"'Tis the American's car right enough," called the moon-faced officer.

He had evidently not seen me and so I started down the steps with a grin on my face. "It's all right, officer," I called.

To my astonishment, they both ignored me.

"We'd best look through the old ruin first, but if he isn't there then I'm thinking we'll have to look in the mine next. Didn't I warn him it was dangerous up here?"

"You did, John-Joe," replied his partner.

"Now wait a moment," I demanded, growing slightly angry.

I stood in front of the moon-faced policeman as he turned from my car. Staring me straight in the eyes, the man took a step forward and walked right through me!

O'Brien's peal of near-maniacal laughter slowly roused me from the shock of it.

I turned to stare up at him as he stood on the steps of the house. "What – what's happened?" My voice was a shocked whisper.

"Don't you see?" O'Brien paused to wipe the tears of laughter from his eyes. "Don't you understand yet, you poor fool? You are just as much a *taibhse* as I am. You broke your neck when you fell down that shaft in the old copper mine. You are dead!"

I uttered a cry of disbelief, of terror. Never had I felt such a surge of blind panic. I turned down the steps of the house into the welcome light of that early morning; I turned to flee from this dark brooding place. As I did so, I lost my balance on the step, tumbled and fell heavily. The jarring shock knocked the senses from my head.

I regained them but a moment later; I had merely been stunned.

Yet it was cold and dark. Brooding blackness enveloped me. I found I held a flashlight in my hand and switched it on. Its beam reflected along the wall that had been hewn by the hand of man out of the thick granite. The walls were deep and oozed with water. It was obviously seepage from the mountain draining through the innumerable cracks and crevices. From farther along the tunnel came the sound of gushing water making a noisy, echoing music.

I stood bewildered for a moment, raising my hand to massage my aching head, feeling the smarting abrasion on my temple.

Then I felt a sudden desire to shout with laughter. I was in the old copper mine. As I entered, I had slipped and fetched my head a crack on the overhanging granite, which must have stunned me momentarily – *momentarily* – but in that moment what a strange fantasy had sped through my mind. I shuddered and then smiled ruefully to myself. The countryside with its countless legends and ghosts must be having more of an effect on me than I would have admitted. Well, I was recovered now. I hesitated a moment about pushing on into the mine; it was rather dangerous. Still, I ought to see all I could before starting back.

I moved forward cautiously, swinging the beam of my torch to right and left. It was not long before I realised that the tunnel was narrowing, the roof lowering over my head. The walls glittered with green streaks of water and the floor increased its slipperiness with the slime of disuse.

My mind was just forming the notion that the place was too

treacherous to proceed further on my own when my feet slipped from under me again. This time my feet seemed to slide away from me. The torch fell from my hand and I cried aloud. I tried to catch hold of some object to save myself, but my forward momentum was unimpeded. I was falling; falling into utter blackness. I felt sharp rocks jabbing at me, scraping my flesh, tearing my clothes. Something cracked against my head but this time it was no mere stunning impact. For one terrible moment I felt fear; complete, heart-stopping fear stabbing like a knife into my chest as I realised that I was falling down a vertical shaft. I hit the bottom with a vague feeling of impact and then ...

   Nothing.

VIII

Fear a' Ghorta

"**B**LESS ME, FATHER, for I have sinned."

Fr Ignatius had heard the words a million times or more. He could not begin to recall the times he had sat in the dark oak womb of the confessional box, oppressed by the odour of polished wood, the musty smell of the velvet curtains and the camphor-scented candles, while he sat on the hassock which served as a cushion but which did not ease the hardness of the wooden bench on which the priest was supposed to sit. He could not begin to recall the times he had heard the opening line of the confessional formula echoing from successive shadowy forms beyond the small fretwork grille. Fr Ignatius had served both as curate and priest in the Church of the Most Holy Redeemer, on New York's Third Street, for twenty years. Twenty years of confessions. He reckoned that he was now as broad-minded as anyone could be; nothing could shock him after listening to twenty years of sins from countless individuals. He had heard the opening line of the confessional ritual spoken in many tones – truculent, fearful, bored ...

"Bless me, Father, for I have sinned."

Yet the hoarse whisper of the voice which came through the lattice held a timbre which made Fr Ignatius stir uneasily. The emphasis on the words gave them an immediacy and a terrible urgency that the priest had never heard before. Fr Ignatius frowned into the gloom at the shadow beyond the grille.

"How long has it been since your last confession, my son?" he asked.

There was a pause and then the hoarse whisper came: "Twenty-five years, Father."

"Twenty-five years?" A priest was not supposed to sound so condemnatory but the words were wrenched from Fr Ignatius in an accusing tone.

"I last made a confession on the first day of August, 1848."

The priest made a rapid calculation.

"Indeed," he confirmed. "Twenty-five years lacking four weeks. Why do you come to make confession now? Why, after all this time?"

"It is a long story, Father."

Fr Ignatius turned, drew aside the velvet curtain and peered into the church. It was deserted. The man had obviously waited until last before coming to the box, waited until the last of the evening confessionals had departed.

"We have plenty of time, my son," he said, bringing his attention back to the shadow beyond the grille.

"Then perhaps, Father, I could tell my story without interruption? In that way I will confess all and you will be able to understand why it is that I have been so long in coming back to the sanctuary of Holy Mother Church."

Fr Ignatius listened to the cadences of the voice and then observed: "You are Irish, aren't you? I can tell by your accent."

The shadow gave a rueful laugh.

"Strange, after twenty-five years in New York I fondly thought that I had lost my accent. Is it so obvious that I am not a native of this city?"

"What is native, my son?" smiled Fr Ignatius. "We are all immigrants here."

"But you are not Irish, Father," observed the voice.

"I was born in Austria. My parents brought me here when I was small." The priest hesitated. He had heard of the clannishness of the Irish. "Would you prefer an Irish priest to hear your confession? Fr Flannery is in the presbytery and I am sure…"

The voice was firm. "No. It does not matter who hears my confession. A priest is a priest, isn't this so, Father?"

"We are merely the link to God, my son. Very well. Perhaps you had best begin."

* * *

"My name ... ah, perhaps that does not matter. When I had friends they call me Pilib Rua, Foxy Pilib on account of my red hair. Among the Irish here I am called *Fear a' Ghorta* which, in the Irish language, means the Man of Hunger. Why I have been given this name will become obvious as I proceed.

"My home was in the province of Connacht, in the west of Ireland, where I was weaned and educated for life. I was sixteen summers in my youth when I ran away from the drudgery of life on my father's croft. It was a terrible existence. We worked on the estate of Colonel Chetwynd, the English landlord who owned our part of the country. And a poor land it was. It was a place filled with poverty and where cold clung to your marrow and the rain was a constant and relentless downpour. There was no hope of improvement in our life for the poor sod which we worked was not ours to enjoy. We could work it but had to pay tithes and tribute to Colonel Chetwynd and if our poor land did not give us sufficient to pay the rent then the Colonel's bailiffs would evict us, throwing us off the land in which our fathers and our forefathers had dwelt for centuries. To prevent those evicted crawling back to their homes for shelter the Colonel's men would burn the thatch from the roofs. Our small corner of Ireland was no different from any other corner of our poor conquered land. That was why I could not bear to face a future there. So I ran away to sea. I joined the Royal Navy as a means of escaping from the drudgery of my life and voyaged abroad for five years until, falling from a rigging, I suffered an injury which drew me back to my native land.

"I landed in the city of Galway in August of 1848 when the famine was in its fourth year and the dead lay unburied on the roads and lanes of Connacht. Homeless beggars roamed the streets of the city, while others gathered on the quays trying to find a place in the emigrant ships. The worst sight of all was the children ... mere animated skeletons, some screaming for food, while many were past crying. They sat or lay, emaciated bundles of bone with scarcely any flesh, with only their eyes ... large, round eyes, staring beseechingly in muted suffering.

"I had heard of the extent of the famine in my voyaging. Indeed, I had heard it said that nearly a third of the population of the province of Connacht had already perished from the land by the time I set foot at Galway. Yet it had been impossible to visualise such suffering. As well as the suffering children there were those who had the famine dropsy, with bodies swollen to twice their natural size, the gums spongey so that the teeth fell out, the joints enlarged, the skin red where the blood-vessels had burst and the legs turned black. They peopled Galway city like wraiths.

"Among this swarm of figures from hell rode the well-fed English cavalry troopers and the administrators. Truly, after the centuries of struggle, could it be said that in those years of famine the English had finally conquered – conquered our spirit and our will.

"I walked from Galway north along the shores of Loch Corrib until I turned west and came by easy stages to my village. It nestled at the foot of some gaunt hills facing the brooding Atlantic sea. The people scarcely recognised me in their plight. Many had died. Indeed, 'twas to a cold and empty croft that I returned. My father, mother, and two young brothers had been dead a year since.

"'Why did you come back, Pilib Rua?' demanded Dangan Cutteen, who always acted as spokesman for the villagers. 'Weren't you better off sailing the seas than returning to this bleak place?'

"I told him my story and how the Royal Navy had put me ashore because I had fallen from a rigging and was no longer any use to them.

"Dangan Cutteen had scowled. 'And what are you here but another mouth to go hungry?'

"I was surprised at the bitterness in his voice. He was a man of fierce primeval passions but of equally fierce attachments. He was as hard and gaunt as the granite rocks and withal as protective to those he cared for as the bleak surrounding hills. From Dangan Cutteen I had learnt seacraft by going out with him since I was a sprogeen, scarcely walking from my cradle. Many is the hour we spent in his curragh while he would teach me not only the way the fish ran but also the old ranns and proverbs of our native tongue. In his rich baritone, which droned like the wind, he would sing the wild traditional songs of our forefathers as we fought the currents and the tides of that restless coast.

"Seeing the hurt in my eyes, Dangan Cutteen gripped me by the shoulders.

"'Yerrah, boy, let there be forgiveness at me. I am half insane with fear for our people. Nearly half the village has perished and I am helpless to aid them. The men grow desperate as they watch the old, the sick and the young grow wizened and frail before their eyes. God! God! What a fearsome sight it is to see the old and the young neither crying nor complaining but crawling over the potato ridges, turning sods of earth in the hope that a good potato might remain in the ground.'

"'But why are the people starving?' I demanded. 'It is only the potato crops that have failed, and the oats, grain and barley yield in abundance. Why, coming into Galway, for every famine relief ship I saw entering port, I saw six ships loaded with grain and livestock and wool and flax sailing for England.'

"Dangan Cutteen gave out a bitter laugh.

"'The people starve because the grain and livestock belong to the English landlords who own the land in Ireland. And we ... we Irish are but a poor, crushed and conquered people. We do not have the backbone to rise up and take what is ours that we might live. The English landlords threaten us with eviction if we do not pay our rents, and whole families die of starvation so that the lords of the land have their due.'

"'Surely the politicians ...?'

"Dangan Cutteen spat.

"'A curse on their dead ones!' he pronounced. 'There is devastation in the land and what do the lickspittle representatives say? John O'Connell, the son of Daniel O'Connell whom the people hailed as "The Liberator", rose in the English Parliament and said: "I thank God I live among a people who would rather die than defraud the landlord of rent." Aye, they die, they die, the Irish, in their tens of thousands to feed the English landlords.'

"I heard hatred in Dangen Cutteen's voice. It was a hatred I came to share. Yes, I'll admit that. *An Gorta Mór* left hatred behind it. Between Ireland and England the memory of what was done has and will endure like a sword probing a wound. There have been other famines in Ireland and doubtless there will be other famines to come but the days of the Great Hunger will never be forgotten nor forgiven.

"During the first few days I stayed in my village, I joined with Dangan Cutteen and the others in putting out to sea in the curraghs in search of fish. Yet even the fish had apparently deserted their normal feeding grounds along the coast, perhaps sensing the presence of the terrible spectre of hunger which stalked the land. Several of the women of the village protested at their menfolk putting to sea for in their weak, starving condition; they felt that they would not have the strength to fight its contrary moods. But Dangan told them that there was only death before them anyway so was it not better to look for death on the water rather than passively wait for it on the bleak land?

"Came the day when Dangan Cutteen ordered the people of the village to gather together. He had decided to make a final appeal to the lord of the land, Colonel Chetwynd, to release some of the produce and livestock he was keeping in his barns. The people walked slowly in a body up the steep road to the great white-walled mansion which was the seat of Colonel Chetwynd's estate. It lay about a mile east of the village. With the afternoon sun slanting its golden rays across it, it looked a beautiful and peaceful place. It seemed a place at odds with the terror that was oppressing the land.

"Colonel Chetwynd was obviously warned of our coming

and, as we approached the big house, we saw him standing at the top of the great stairs that led to the main doors. At his side was the weasel-faced overseer of the estate, a man named Brashford. I recall him well. He had been brought over from England to manage the estate for the Colonel twenty years before. Brashford made no pretence at hiding the fact that he carried a revolver in his pocket. I was sure that a corresponding bulge in the Colonel's pocket concealed a similar weapon. Also, posted about the estate, there were half a dozen English soldiers sent up from the Galway garrison in case of trouble.

"The soldiers were there not specifically for us but because there were rumours of a rising against the English throughout the country. I have never known a time when there were not such rumours, although I was too young to remember the uprising of 1798 and 1803. It seemed that the Young Irelanders were determined to make another attempt to establish a republic in Ireland before the year was out and English troops were flooding into the country in preparation.

"As we approached Colonel Chetwynd I saw there was a disdainful look on his fat, bloated features. It was at least six years since I had previously seen the man who was the sole arbiter of our lives and fortunes. He had not changed except that he appeared to me more dissolute, more debauched than before. There was no hunger nor want about his replete figure.

"'What do you want here?' His voice was nasal and he called in English.

"We halted, unsure of ourselves. Then Dangan Cutteen moved forward. He was unused to speaking English and his voice was slow, soft and considered.

"'Why, your honour, we want food.'

"'Food?' Colonel Chetwynd gave a sharp bark of laughter, like the bark of a fox at night.

"'Your honour, we work on your estate. We know you have enough livestock, hogs and cattle, and sheep, and enough grain to keep us from harm. Yet we starve and sicken and die. We are in desperate need, your honour.'

"Colonel Chetwynd grimaced, his mouth ugly.

"'Am I to be a philanthropist, issuing alms out of altruism?'

"'I have no understanding of those words, your honour,' replied Dangan. 'Is there not an abundance of food on your estate?'

"'No business of yours,' snapped the Colonel. 'It is my property and on it depends my income. Do I have to explain the principles of business to the likes of you?'

"'You do not, your honour, for we are not discussing the principles of business but the principles of humanity. Our people are dying almost daily from *An Gorta Mór*. Our potatoes, on which we rely, are blighted, our own pigs and fowls are long since dead, and now our old folk, the wee ones and the frail and sick are dying. Yet in your barns is food a-plenty.'

"It was then that the overseer, Brashford, whose face was almost apopletic with rage, interrupted.

"'I know this man, Colonel. Dangan Cutteen by name. A troublemaker if ever there was one. Let me drive these swine from the estate.'

"Colonel Chetwynd smiled thinly.

"'No, Brashford. No. Mr Cutteen has a good argument here. He seems to be stating the law of supply and demand. He and his people want food. We have food.'

"For a moment we stood silently, not one of us sure that we had heard the Colonel aright. Few of us had subtle English and we thought that our interpretation might be at fault. Dangan took a pace, frowning.

"'Are you willing to give us the food, your honour?' he asked hesitantly.

"Colonel Chetwynd threw back his head and guffawed loudly.

"'By the pox, no! I am willing to sell you the food. You must pay the price that I would get were I to ship it to England.'

"It was then that we realised the bitter humour of the man and a murmur of suppressed rage ran through us.

"Dangan Cutteen did not lose his temper.

"'Your honour, you know that we have no money. We work

on your estate to earn for the rents and tithes you claim for our poor hovels. We have to provide our labour to you in order to remain on the land which was our forefathers' land long before you and yours came to it. For this we must be grateful, but the only extra money we have, in a good year, is when we can sell any abundance and surplus of our own produce at the market. There has been no surplus from our small potato plots since the start of the famine. We have no money.'

"Colonel Chetwynd was smiling evilly now and nodding his head.

"'Then we have no business to discuss, Mr Cutteen.'

"He made to turn away and Dangan Cutteen spoke sharply at last:

"'God forgive you, your honour!'

"Colonel Chetwynd glanced back. 'The question is settled, Cutteen. Business is business. You have no money. I am not a charity. My produce goes to England.'

"'And we are simply to starve to death?'

"'Are there no fish left in the sea?' Brashford interrupted again.

"'None that we can take,' replied Dangan.

"'Then eat grass,' replied the overseer. 'Didn't His Highness, the son of our Gracious Sovereign, Queen Victoria, suggest that the Irish nation could save itself by eating grass, for aren't the Irish capable of eating anything?'

"The weasel-faced overseer laughed uproariously at his sally and the red-coated soldiers joined in his mirth.

"Dangan Cutteen stood there a moment more, his face twisted in a scarce-controlled rage. 'But Colonel ...' he began slowly.

"'Have I not made myself plain, Cutteen? There is no more to talk about. I don't care a damn about your people. Eat the bodies of your dead for all I care!'

"He turned and stormed into his great, rich house leaving us standing there. Had Dangan told us to charge it and set it afire, I don't doubt that we would have met our end there and then. Brashford and the soldiers seemed to sense what was running through our minds for they lined up their revolvers and rifles and stood waiting. But Dangan Cutteen turned away and we followed him back to the village.

"That afternoon lots were drawn as to who should crew a three-man curragh and go to sea in search of fish. Dangan wanted to go and I, likewise, for we were still fairly healthy. But the lot fell to others and these were proud men, these men of the West, and none would change their seats in the boat. No sooner had the black dart of the curragh vanished beyond the headland than a wind came up, whistling and crying like the banshees of hell. The curragh did not return home. By dusk we gathered on the foreshore, silent and ghastly, and we waited; waited until dusk gave way to night. The grey murderous sea was empty of any craft.

"It was in the grey light of the morning that a man from the neighbouring village of Raheenduff came to us to tell us that a curragh had been washed ashore there upside down.

"'They are all away,' the man said of the crew, which is a way of saying in the West that all had perished.

"A strange look come upon the features of Dangan Cutteen then.

"He gave a long sigh. '*Ní chuimhníonn cú gortach ar a coileán*,' he said softly.

"I thought it a strange time to utter the old saying which means 'a hungry hound does not remember its whelps', which is to say that necessity knows no law.

"Dangan beckoned to Seán and Iolar, who were his brothers and closer to him than anyone. 'We have work to do,' he told them and he left without a backward glance to any of us.

"That night I sat in my cabin trying to keep the spectre of hunger away by boiling the edible carrigeen seaweed, which grows along the shoreline, into a soup. I had decided that I must leave the village while I was still healthy and perhaps find a berth on a merchantman bound for the New World. It was true that I felt more remorse this time than when I had first run away to sea years before, for was I not leaving my fellow villagers and comrades to their deaths?

"It was then that there came a sharp rap on the door and opening it I beheld Iolar in the gloom.

"'Dangan has sent me,' he said. 'If you want to eat, there is food to be had.'

"'What?' I cried, 'From where is the food come?'

"Iolar raised a finger to his lips and shrugged.

"'Follow me, Pilib Rua, and you shall see.'

"I was surprised when he led me through the darkened village and up the steep path to the old caves in the hills above the village. Few knew of the existence of these caves for this was where the villagers had sheltered during the devastations of Cromwell, when the English could take the head off any Irish man, woman or child and receive a £5 reward for doing so; a time when the English soldiers could ride down on villages and take off the young men and girls to ship them as slaves to the Barbados. The caves had been our secret shelter in those days.

"I was startled to see the entire remnants of the village gathered in the caves when Iolar led me in. Everyone stood in silent wonder around a great roaring fire. I, too, stared in bewilderment at the great roasting spits that were turning over the flames while on them were cuts of meat which cracked and sizzled as their natural greases dripped on to the fires which cooked them. And the smell … ah, the sweet smell of roasting pork!

"And Dangan Cutteen was there, grim-faced and silent as he supervised the roasting.

"What miracle had he wrought to bring us such a plentiful supply of meat?

"Each person was given meat and each person ate their fill without stinting. Not a word was spoken while we sat and made ourselves replete with the feast.

"Only when the people began to move drowsily back towards the village did I seek out Dangan and asked: 'Where did the food come from? Did you steal it from the estate of Colonel Chetwynd? If so, we will be in trouble from the English soldiers on the morrow.'

Dangan Cutteen glanced at me without a change of expression

on his grim features.

"'The meat came with the courtesy of Colonel Chetwynd,' he said softly. Then he turned away after the villagers, leaving me alone in the cave staring at the dying embers of the fire, staring at the smouldering bones which lay behind.

"It was the bones that first raised some tiny pricking in my mind ... bones which belonged to no pig that I knew of. A chill began to run down my spine and sent my stomach heaving.

"Some instinct made me turn towards the back of the cave, seizing a piece of wood from the fire to act as a torch. I held it aloft and moved forward.

"I did not have to look far.

"There, in a heap at the back of the cave, were the blood-stained but easily recognisable clothes that I had last seen worn by Colonel Chetwynd. And by them lay a torn and stained coat that Brashford had been wearing. I stood like a statue, not wishing to believe what I now knew to be true. When Colonel Chetwynd had said to Dangan Cutteen: 'I don't give a damn about your people. Eat the bodies of your dead for all I care!' he had sealed his own fate. He had pronounced his own sentence for his crimes against us.

"Such was the horror that overcame me that I fled crying with terror from the cave and did not stop at the village but went on to Galway. At Galway I persuaded the captain of a merchantman to give me a berth, working my passage here to New York."

* * *

The hoarse whisper from the shadow beyond the grille halted a moment and Fr Ignatius heard the sound of an emotional swallow.

"I have not been able to tell this story for twenty-five years, Father. Please ... please ... I must have absolution."

Fr Ignatius hesitated. It was a grim story, a horrendous story. But God must be the judge. He was merely the instrument and he was moved to pity for the owner of the hoarse voice; pity, in spite of the terrible tale, for the fault lay clearly not with the man but those conditions which had forced the man into his grotesque sin.

"Please, Father!"

The pleading tone of the man's voice tugged at his soul. Fr Ignatius stirred himself.

"I will absolve you, my son," he said slowly, "even though the sin you have committed is beyond anything that I have ever heard in my years as a priest. I will absolve you because your story has moved deep compassion in my soul. Before you leave this church you must recite five decades of the rosary and make an offering ... that I shall leave to your conscience and God."

The figure behind the screen let forth a deep shuddering sigh. "God bless you, Father, for you have charity of mind and spirit."

"It is God's will to move me to compassion, my son," replied Fr Ignatius, "and I am but an instrument of His infinite goodness and His compassion. Make a good Act of Contrition, my son."

The figure beyond the lattice bent its head.

"Oh my God, I am heartily sorry for having offended Thee. I beg pardon for all my sins. I detest them above all things because they offend Thy infinite goodness who are so deserving of all my love and I am firmly resolved by the help of Thy grace never to offend Thee again and carefully to avoid the occasion of my sin."

The ritual Act of Contrition was recited mechanically as Fr Ignatius had often heard it recited. Yet it fell strangely on his ears for what had gone before had prepared him to hear some more emotional declaration of intent. But he shrugged. The Act of Contrition was said and was meant.

"*Absolvo te ab omnibus peccatis tuis in nomine Patris et Filii et Spiritus Sancti ... Amen!*"

He made the sign of the cross.

The figure behind the grille sat with its head bowed for a moment and then came the long, drawn out sigh again.

"Am I truly absolved in the eyes of God and the Church for what I have done, Father?"

Fr Ignatius frowned. "Do you doubt the rituals of the Church, my son?" His voice rose sharply.

"No, Father. Yet it seems that I have shouldered the burden of this guilt for so long that it is strange that it should be cast from me in a single moment."

"God, in His infinite wisdom, so ordained His priesthood to forgive sins however great," responded Fr Ignatius with pursed lips. "From this moment on your sins no longer exist. You are reborn into the world in the eyes of God as innocent as if you were a newly born child."

There was a silence behind the grille. Then the voice came, sounding almost triumphant. "Then I am reborn as pure as if the last twenty-five years had never existed?"

"Of course, my son."

"It is a wonderful feeling, Father."

Fr Ignatius smiled and was about to gently dismiss the strange confessionalist when the fretwork grille that divided the confessional box splintered into fragments. A thick, hairy arm thrust through towards the priest, the squat, dirty fingers grasping the started man's throat and choking off his cry of alarm.

Fr Ignatius was aware of the grotesque face in the shadows, the wild staring eyes, blood-veined and burning like the coals of hell. He was aware, too, of the large twisted mouth, the blood-red lips drawn back to show pink gums from which sharp white teeth ground against each other.

The voice was clearly triumphant now. "I am innocent again. But your confessional has not dismissed the craving, the terrible longing ... you see, Father, the terror and horror I felt when I ran wildly from that cave, twenty-five years ago, was not at the fact that I had eaten human flesh. It was at the realisation that I had enjoyed it. Enjoyed it in spite of the knowledge of what it was. I am innocent again. Therefore I must sin again. There will be others to hear my future confession but now ... now I must have meat again ... succulent human meat ... I cannot live without it!"

IX

The Dreeador

THE LARGE, RED-FACED man in the ludicrously loud check shooting jacket and Inverness cape had been annoying him ever since he boarded the train at Dublin. He had fondly thought that he was going to have the first-class compartment to himself when, without warning, the man had squeezed himself through the door, followed by a languid young man and an equally pale and apathetic-looking young woman. They had spread themselves in the far corner of the compartment and, after casting an inquisitive glance in his direction, proceeded to ignore him.

Well, that was fine by him, for he was in no mood for trivial conversation with strangers, simply to pass the time. He sat back, a newspaper spread before him as if he were reading it. Yet he was not reading it. He was too exhausted, too weary. So much had happened during the last six months. His doctor had said that he needed rest. Peace and relaxation had been emphasised. But soon the rolling monologue of the red-faced man banished all thoughts of quiet concentration. He had a loud bark of a voice. His moustache quivered as he spoke. He phrased his sentences as if they were terse, sharp commands like an army officer on parade. The unwilling listener placed the red-faced man as an Indian Army officer, retired.

The pale young man and woman seemed to be related to him and, indeed, at one point confirmed this by calling him "uncle". As the train rattled through the countryside, westward from

Dublin, the listener came to learn that it was their first visit to Ireland and that they had come to spend a vacation with their uncle. He, on his part, proceeded in his nasal bark to show them the countryside as the train passed through it. And as the hours sped by, the listener's mind was battered almost into a comatose state by the perpetual monologue. He began to pray that the journey would soon end for he tried, unsuccessfully, to drown in his own thoughts but the man's voice had the ability to pierce them.

He was wondering whether he should attempt to get out of the compartment at the next station and seek a more congenial nook in which to travel when something the red-faced man said arrested his attention. He had taken out a silver Hunter watch and, glancing at it, said: "We'll be coming to Michelburnetown soon."

The name had no affect on the young man and woman.

"You'll see Coolarrigan Castle on the hill to your right overlooking the town. Nice place. But a rum do. Rum do."

"Coolarrigan Castle?" enquired the girl, smothering a yawn. "That sounds imposing."

The red-faced man shook his head.

"Nice house. Never was a castle. Georgian manor. Owned by the Michelburne family. Moderate fortune. Pleasant enough. Rum do, all the same."

"I've noticed most of the Irish gentry call their houses 'castles'," interposed the young man, airing some knowledge of the eccentric ways of the Anglo-Irish.

"Why do you say it was a 'rum do', uncle?" pressed the girl.

"Bit of a mystery. Sir Garth Michelburne was found dead six months ago. Heart attack apparently. Grandson inherits house and title. Baronet. But he's been in South Africa for ten years. Married out there, so they say. Now wife's dead. Rumour has it, he's coming back to take over Coolarrigan. Rum cove, they say. Fought against the Boers, though. Military Cross and all that."

"Why does the grandson inherit and not the son?" asked the young man in a voice which seemed to lack any interest in obtaining a reply to the question.

"Bad business. Father and mother had died a short time before Sir Garth. They say it was from some strange wasting illness. I heard they were both reduced almost to skeletons. Bad business."

The train suddenly slowed and came to a halt with a protesting squeal of brakes.

A raucous voice sang out: "Michelburnetown! Michelburne-town!"

The unwilling listener stood up in his corner of the carriage and opened the door, noticing with satisfaction the look of surprise on the face of the red-faced man as he observed him alighting.

Costello, the station-master, looked pretty much the same as the newly alighted passenger had last seen him ten years ago.

The uniformed functionary came across with a dazed expression on his broad face.

"Mister Giles, is it?" he asked uncertainly, and when the passenger smiled and nodded, Costello's expression broadened briefly into a smile of welcome. "Mr Giles ... *Sir* Giles. Welcome home, sir." And then, remembering what had brought him, he added uncomfortably: "We're sorry for your troubles, Sir Giles."

Sir Giles nodded and turned into the carriage to take out his bags, deriving some silly sense of enjoyment at the mortification on the face of the red-faced man. It was, he supposed, malicious pleasure at the man's embarrassment. A small compensation for having been bored by him all the way from Dublin. He heaved his bags out of the compartment and slammed the door.

"There's a carriage from Coolarrigan waiting in the station yard for you, Sir Giles," Costello said as he turned to dispatch the train on its journey.

Sir Giles waved acknowledgment and turned off the tiny platform, walked around the station house and into the yard beyond. Sure enough, waiting there was the ancient pony cart that he knew so well. An immaculately groomed black mare was harnessed to it. The driver of the carriage was standing by the horse's head, His back was towards Sir Giles and the white hair curled out from under his cap. Old Connery had been the driver for as long as he could remember and, presuming the man to be him, he cried out: "Connery! How is it with you?"

But the man who turned to face him was a stranger.

"Is it Sir Giles?" he asked, smiling quizzically at him.

"I am," Sir Giles replied, frowning a little. "I don't recognise you, though. I thought you were Connery, the stableman."

"I am Finnerty, sir," the man replied gravely, his expression seeming to mask some hidden humour but whether at the situation or something else, Sir Giles could not tell. "Your late grandfather, rest his soul, took me into his service eight years since."

He was a small, rotund man, with a fair skin and white hair, a snow-white colour with no trace of grey in it at all. The mop of untidy hair poked out from under the cap he was wearing. His eyes were light. Sir Giles swore that he could not tell whether they were grey or blue, or merely colourless, reflecting the changing skies. His cheeks were red and his face wore a perpetual grin, like the proverbial grin of the Cheshire Cat from *Alice in Wonderland*. It was hard to estimate his age. He could have been anything from mid-fifties to mid-sixties. He carried himself with the manner of a young, active man.

"If you'll be giving me your bags, sir, we can be off to Coolarrigan."

Sir Giles handed him the bags and he threw them into the trap with such a casual nonchalance that Sir Giles winced, hoping nothing would break in the process. He stepped into the vehicle and a moment later, Finnerty had cracked his whip and the horse was prancing out of the yard and away up the long road which led to Coolarrigan. It was ten years since Sir Giles had seen the old house in which he had spent most of his childhood, that part, of course, which was not spent at the gloomy public school to which his parents had sent him in the English Home Counties. It would be hard to visualise the old place without his bluff, hard-drinking, hard-riding grandfather. Sir Garth had been known far and wide. He boasted he could drink any man under the table and set out to prove it on numerous occasions. Sir Giles supposed his grandfather had led a full life. After all, he had been in his late eighties when he had died and death has to come to us all sooner or later. But he had been a tough man and all the family firmly expected him to make it to his one-hundredth birthday.

Sir Giles's father had been the opposite of that. A painstaking, studious man, interested in finances, bookkeeping and ensuring that the Coolarrigan estate was well run, while his mother was always sewing or engaging in some charitable work. They were both gone now. It was sad. He had never envisioned being Sir Giles, squire of Coolarrigan.

He bit his lip, to hide the tension within him. He doubted if he would have even returned to this place had it not been for Ethel. Ten years ago Giles had left Coolarrigan to join his regiment in South Africa. Mafeking, Talana Hill, Stormberg, Magersfontein, Colenso, Spion Kop, Paardeberg and Bloemfontein. Tombstones on the road to his manhood. After the treaty of 1902 he left the army and settled in Durban and there he had married Ethel. Life was good. They had an ostrich farm in southern Natal and did very well.

Then six months ago it seemed the entire Michelburne family were cursed. The news of the death of his mother and father, and then his grandfather, exactly in the manner recounted by the red-faced man, had reached him just as poor Ethel had been stricken with a fever. She did not recover. For some months he wandered lost and lonely around his farm. Eventually, his doctor suggested he needed peace and quiet. A holiday away from the farm to recuperate. That was why he decided to return to Coolarrigan; perhaps to exorcise the ghosts there.

And here he was gazing up at the grey Georgian walls of the three-storyed house. It seemed cheerless in the early evening. Deserted. No lights shone in welcome from its windows. It was as grey and bleak as the surrounding countryside.

"Where is everyone, Finnerty?" he demanded, as the man drew the trap to a halt before the front door, a front door which remained closed, no one opening it in greeting and admittance to the warm, friendly interior.

"*Everyone*, Sir Giles?" Finnerty demanded in an irritatingly amused tone.

"You know what I mean," Sir Giles replied, scarcely concealing his exasperation. "Where are the servants?"

Finnerty had jumped down from the driving box and opened the door of the trap for Sir Giles. His head was held to one side.

"Well now, I'm afraid you'll find that all the domestic staff" (was there an ironic tone in his emphasis?) "left the house after the funerals. At the time there was no word that you would come home and it was thought that the old house might be shut up and sold. Most of them went off to Dublin to find other positions."

Sir Giles bit his lip in annoyance.

"Well, who is here then? There must be a cook or a house-keeper?"

"Oh, I'm afraid that you will find that I'll have to do for you," Finnerty said with a sigh, reaching forward and taking the bags from the carriage. "I've been running the place since the funerals."

Sir Giles stared at him in astonishment.

"You mean there are no other serv ... domestic staff in the house apart from yourself?"

Coolarrigan in the old days had employed no less than fifteen servants.

Finnerty smiled sadly. "There is only myself to do everything, Sir Giles."

Sir Giles sniffed in annoyance at this unwanted problem. "Well, we will have to see about hiring new staff as soon as possible."

"Staff is hard to come by, Sir Giles, especially in these parts and in these times," replied the man.

"But what about the estate, the estate workers and management?"

Finnerty's smile broadened even more.

"Now don't go worrying about that, Sir Giles. You've only just arrived and there will be plenty of time, I'm thinking, to turn your head to those matters."

Sir Giles's voice rose sharply. "Are you saying that the estate has been left idle?"

"Bless you, no. It's being run as best as it can. I've been checking on affairs from time to time."

Finnerty was beginning to irritate Sir Giles with his bland, patronising tone. He spoke to him as if he were a child who had to be mollified from time to time.

Sir Giles was about to reply when he checked himself and turned for the door of the house.

"Well," he snapped, "it's been a long journey and I am tired and hungry. Will it be too much to expect some supper?"

"Surely not, Sir Giles. You'll find supper already laid in the dining-room," Finnerty responded without changing his expression or his tone.

Sir Giles ate the cold meats and salad dishes without enthusiasm. There was a chilled wine ready and a fine quality brandy to savour afterwards as he sprawled in front of the fire which blazed merrily in the hearth of the dining-room. He was left to his own devices. Only once did Finnerty put his head round the door, grinning away: "Is everything to your satisfaction, Sir Giles?"

He grunted more to disguise his irritation with the man than to make any answer. Finnerty withdrew.

Afterwards he began to wonder whether his irritation was simply a question of tiredness. After all, Finnerty seemed to have done pretty well with the supper and the house seemed to be spotless and in no way gave the impression of being neglected. Well, perhaps things would not look so bleak to him in the morning.

Although he went to bed exhausted from his journey, he did not rest easy during the night. Once he came awake and found himself listening to the high wind buffeting the ancient stones of the house; listened to its irritating chattering in the chimney of the room. And then, above its irksome noise he heard the cry of some animal. It was a lonely, heart-wrenching cry such as he had often heard wild dogs give out on the lonely Natal veldt. The cry seemed to come, oddly enough, from the very depths of the house itself. It was a long-drawn-out cry, as if of lonely despair.

In spite of his troubled sleep Sir Giles rose early to the pleasant smell of eggs and bacon issuing from below and washed, shaved and dressed with alacrity. There was no one in the dining-room but there was a grand breakfast laid out for him with a pot of steaming coffee.

"Good morning, Sir Giles," smiled Finnerty, entering the room. "Is everything to your satisfaction?"

"It is, Finnerty," he replied, perhaps a little too sharply. "It is my intention to ride the estate and see for myself how it is being run. Will you have the manager meet me outside in fifteen minutes?"

Finnerty shuffled his feet awkwardly, though still smiling. "I was thinking that I had made it clear last night, Sir Giles: there is no estate manager."

Sir Giles raised an eyebrow in surprise and Finnerty went on. "You see, Sir Giles, the estate manager also left soon after the funeral and we have not been able to replace him."

Sir Giles checked himself in an exclamation of annoyance. "And I suppose all our workers have gone as well?" he sneered.

Finnerty shook his head, the smile broadening again. "Oh no, Sir Giles. We have a full workforce. But it is myself who is giving the orders to them."

Sir Giles stared at Finnerty for a moment and then said, "I think I will ride across the estate and see what is going on for myself."

"Perhaps you would like me to ride with you across the estate?" Finnerty suggested ingenuously.

Sir Giles stood up. "Fifteen minutes, outside. I suppose we still have horses left and a means to saddle them?" he added waspishly.

Finnerty's smile grew broader. "That we have, sir. Don't worry your head. I'll see to the saddling myself."

Sure enough, fifteen minutes later he was waiting with two saddled mares outside the house. Sir Giles began to feel a little churlish at his manner with Finnerty for he could not fault the way the estate was kept. A group of men in the fields greeted Sir Giles with familiarity, some remembering him from when he was a small child on the estate. They seemed happy enough and no one had any grumbles or complaints. And all the while Finnerty rode beside with his easygoing manner and broad smile.

At the end of the inspection of the estate Sir Giles found the need to apologise as best he could to the good-natured Finnerty. It seemed he had done the man a disservice for the estate was being well handled.

"You seem to be running Coolarrigan very well, Finnerty," Sir Giles said tritely.

"Thank you, Sir Giles."

"You will excuse any bad temper that I may exhibit," he added lamely. "I have been told to rest. I need peace and quiet. So I will need to leave matters in your capable hands."

"That you may do, and safely, Sir Giles," Finnerty replied readily. "You must rest until your heart's content and have not a worry in the world."

That night Sir Giles was awakened by a muffled sound from beyond his bedroom door. He lay in the darkness trying to identify it. It sounded like a sobbing and as he strained to listen he realised that it *was* sobbing, the sound of a woman's suppressed anguish.

He rose from his bed and crossed to the door, flinging it open with a quick twist of the handle. The corridor was empty. Frowning, he ventured out, casting a look in each direction. Nothing stirred in the gloom. He was about to turn back when he heard the sound again, this time from the end of the corridor.

Hesitating for only a moment, he strode along it. According to Finnerty he and Sir Giles were alone in the house. By the Lord Harry! Was Finnerty entertaining a woman from the village and not telling him? Sir Giles could scarcely believe that the man would take such liberties.

The corridor gave on to a longer passageway which stretched the length of the house. He came into this passage and peered along it. The sound seemed to be coming from the far end. Slowly he walked along and the noise of the grieving cry did not diminish. He stood hesitantly before the door of what had been his parents' bedroom. Indeed, the sobbing sound was coming from behind it. A rage shook him. If Finnerty were "entertaining" some woman from the village, how dare he do it in this room of all rooms? With fury, he threw open the door and entered.

The chamber was thick with dust and there was no light there. It smelt musty and had clearly not been used for a long time. There was no sign that anyone had entered. He felt bewildered and suddenly very cold. Ice cold.

The next morning he awoke feeling surprisingly weak and his head ached abominably. Curiously enough he seemed to retain quite an appetite.

He decided to approach Finnerty indirectly and asked him whether there was anyone else staying in the house. As he suspected, Finnerty denied knowledge of such a thing. Sir Giles decided to press the point and Finnerty's eyes grew round and wondering, staring at him curiously. Eventually Sir Giles gave up; the way he was feeling, he wondered whether he might be sickening for something.

He asked Finnerty to drive him in the pony-trap down to the village in order to look in on Mr Keogh, the lawyer, as there were some papers regarding the estate in Natal which he hoped had been sent through for the lawyer to sort out.

Finnerty was driving at a rapid pace along the road into Michelburnetown. Too rapid, Sir Giles thought, for he had cause to cry out to Finnerty to ease off when the carriage hit a stone and he was pitched head first against the side of the vehicle. Finnerty merely grinned and drove on.

At the crossroads he did ease off, for otherwise he would never have been able to negotiate the turn.

There at the crossroads, astride an ancient tricycle, sat a curious apparition, an elderly man clad in black, with black gaiters, a black hat under which a shock of greying hair tumbled. He had a hawk face, pale and cadaver-like, and bright, shining eyes. His shirt and collar proclaimed him to be of a priestly calling.

Finnerty was about to pass by when the man held up his hand in an effort to stay him.

"Sir Giles, is it not?"

He spoke in a high-pitched, precise voice.

"Wait!" Sir Giles instructed, as Finnerty made to drive by, ignoring the man.

"'Tis only the Protestant minister," grumbled Finnerty but, nevertheless, stayed the horses.

"I am Sir Giles," Giles said, leaning from the pony cart.

The man edged nearer on his creaking means of transport, his pale face staring intently up to Sir Giles.

"My name is Forrestal, sir. Reverend Forrestal."

"Good day, sir," replied Sir Giles politely.

"Is it, sir? Is it?"

Sir Giles started at the intense tone in the minister's voice.

"I have stopped to warn you, sir. Yes, warn you," he went on with an impatient wave of his hand, as if Sir Giles were about to interrupt him. However, Sir Giles was too surprised at the man's attitude to make any comment. "There is evil at Coolarrigan Castle. I buried your father and mother and your grandfather. Pray God I don't have to bury you. Beware the evil at Coolarrigan!"

His voice rose in a tone akin to hysteria, one hand raised, palm outward, as if invoking a blessing.

Finnerty suddenly whipped the horses and the carriage sped on, leaving the old minister in the roadway, astride the tricycle, shouting something after them and shaking his hand.

"Who the devil is that?" Sir Giles demanded of Finnerty, astonished by the encounter.

The man chuckled dryly and shrugged. "Devil is in him, sure enough," he replied shortly. Sir Giles was perturbed for he was not used to treating ministers of the church in such a manner, especially as he confirmed from Finnerty that the Rev. Forrestal was the local Anglican minister. All the Michelburne family had followed the Anglican faith right back to the day when their ancestor had landed in Ulster and become Governor of Derry, when it was under siege from the risen Irish. It was rude to have left him in the roadway and Sir Giles told Finnerty so but he simply shrugged.

"How can you reason with a man who is insane?" he demanded truculently.

Well, truly, Mr Forrestal's behaviour was decidedly bizarre but that did not mean he was insane. After all, he was the local vicar and that made Sir Giles one of his flock. If memory served him right, there were very few Anglicans in Michelburnetown for all the Irish were Catholics in those parts and only the gentry would worship at the local Anglican church. Even then the congregation wasn't large for the Michelburnes had built their own private chapel at Coolarrigan where, in the old days, the family worshipped rather than go down to the village church.

Sir Giles felt that he owed a duty to visit the minister and apologise for his coachman's exceedingly bad manners. Was it eccentricity which caused the old man to behave in such a way? What did he mean by saying that there was evil at Coolarrigan?

He made up his mind to ride into Michelburnetown the next day and see him.

Sir Giles's business with the lawyer, Keogh, concluded satisfactorily, and he spent the rest of the day at Coolarrigan. The encounter with Rev. Forrestal had reminded him of a sad duty. At the back of the house stood the old Gothic-style chapel which Sir Godwin Michelburne had erected at the start of the nineteenth century. He had built the chapel on an earlier construction for in the chapel and in a vault beneath were the tombs of several generations of Michelburnes. Sir Giles's grandfather and his parents had been interred there and he took some white lilacs from the kitchen garden late that afternoon and wandered across to the building in order to pay his respects.

The chapel was full of the pretensions of the Anglo-Irish landed gentry, with stone statues in armour, coats-of-arms emblazoned and plaques to numerous ancestors; memorials to the men who had come to Ireland to conquer and to settle.

Finnerty said that Sir Garth Michelburne and Sir Giles's parents had been interred in the vault below the chapel and he made his way to the wrought-iron gates which separated the main chapel from the flight of stone steps circling downwards. Finnerty had thought to provide him with a lamp and he paused to light it before he ventured down into the musty crypt.

There were the coffins, resting on trestles, only brass plates announcing the names of their occupants. He laid his gifts of flowers on each coffin lid and stood, head bowed, in remembrance of his family.

The wick of his lamp suddenly spluttered and gave out. Frowning, he shook the lamp and heard no swish of paraffin in the bowl. How stupid! The oil had run out and neither he nor Finnerty had thought to check it beforehand. He judged where the stairs would be in his mind's eye and turned.

God help him! A cold hand brushed his own and a voice whispered close to his ear:

"Poor Giles! You must beware!"

He dropped the lamp in his consternation.

There came a long sighing sob.

"Mother?" he cried uncertainly, for his immediate reaction was to recognise the voice as that of his dead parent. It sounded so like her soft, cajoling tones.

"Beware, Giles," came the reply.

"Of what? Who are you?"

Something cold brushed him again and this time a harsh male voice said: "Your soul is damned, boy. Beware!"

He shivered and swore the voice was that of Sir Garth, his grandfather. He fought against the terrible feeling of being turned to stone and started to run blindly towards the stairs. The next thing was that he had smashed into something hard and measured his full length on the foul-smelling stone slabs of the crypt.

Then Finnerty was bending over him, concern in his pale eyes.

"You seem to have had a tumble, Sir Giles," he observed with a wry smile as he helped him to his feet.

What explanation could he give without appearing insane?

Finnerty helped him back to the house where he rested for the remainder of that afternoon.

Later he felt annoyed with himself for Sir Giles was not an imaginative man nor given to believing in ghosts, goblins or any form of supernatural manifestations. He knew there must be an explanation for what he had seen and felt. But for the moment he could not work it out. He was too tired.

Indeed, he was exhausted but that did not stop him from awakening in his restlessness during the night.

Again he heard the long-drawn-out sobbing from beyond his door. Yet he was too weary. He turned and buried his head into the pillows and tried to drown out the sound. It was a long time before it died away.

The morning was bright, the sky was without a hint of clouds and the sun already, cast its warmth from behind the tree-line of the eastern hills. It was a pleasant ride down into Michelburnetown. There were only a few people astir, some of whom greeted him civilly enough. He rode through the town, if town it should be called, for in truth it consisted of one main street with a collection of houses gathered along either side, crushed and ill-spaced. Behind the collection of houses stood the railway station and beyond that stood the Anglican church with the vicarage next door.

He dismounted at the gate and hitched the reins of his horse to the post.

The place looked deserted, as if both house and church were derelict, unused for many years. Frowning, he went up the weed-strewn path and knocked on the door. For a long time there was no answer; so long that he thought that no one was at home. Then there came a rattle of a chain, the creak of a bolt and the door swung open.

An elderly woman stood looking suspiciously at him.

"I am looking for Mr Forrestal," Sir Giles said with a smile.

"Then you best look in the church," she snapped, swinging the door shut.

Frowning at this unfriendly reception, he walked across the

overgrown lawn, through a paint-peeling wooden gate and over the jungle-like growth of the churchyard. The great doors of the flint-faced, ugly building were not locked but it took a good push to creak them open. He entered the semi-gloom of the interior.

"Mr Forrestal?" he called softly.

His voice echoed back mockingly from the vaulted interior.

He shuffled forward, screwing up his eyes in the dim light of the building.

There seemed to be no one about, though in the middle of the main aisle of the church, just before the altar, a coffin stood on two trestles. It was open, the lid resting on the floor beside the trestles. There was an overpowering smell of camphor. Curiosity made him walk forward to peer into the coffin in the semi-gloom.

There was no mistaking the hawk-like features of the Rev. Forrestal as he lay just as pale as he had been in life, stretched solemnly in the coffin.

Sir Giles's jaw dropped and he turned swiftly.

At the door of the church stood a fair-haired young man with a solemn face.

"Who are you?" Sir Giles demanded in his agitation.

"Blake, Sir Giles. My name is Blake. I am the curate here." His voice was mild and so soft that Sir Giles had to listen hard to hear it.

"How do you know who I am?" was Sir Giles's next question, born from the logic of his answer.

The young man shrugged. "Who else would you be in this place?"

There was no faulting his judgment. Sir Giles realised that what he had, at first, thought to be a soft Irish brogue was, in fact, an American accent.

"What happened to Mr Forrestal?" he then demanded.

"He is dead."

"I know that," he replied irritably. "How? I saw him on the road only yesterday."

"He was found dead in the Awbawn this morning. He drowned."

The Awbawn was the large river which meandered through Michelburnetown.

Sir Giles began to gather his composure, softly cursing himself for his moment of panic.

"I'm sorry to hear that," he replied. "When will the service be held? I would like to attend although I only met the man once."

"Ah," the young curate shook his head, "the body will be entrained for Dublin for burial there. Mr Forrestal was a Dublin man."

"If there is anything I can do ... ?"

"I'll let you know," replied the curate.

Sir Giles hesitated.

"You are an American, Mr Blake," he observed.

"I was born in Boston and grew up there," the curate confirmed, his tone seeming to indicate that he did not wish the conversation to proceed.

There was little else to be said. Sir Giles went to his horse and mounted. As he did so, he saw the old woman who had answered the door of the vicarage frowning at him from a crack in the curtain. He turned, observing the young curate closely watching his departure.

Sir Giles found on the journey back to Coolarrigan that his horse had suddenly become a little skittish and nervous. Several times he had to pause to calm her. It was only at the third or fourth time that he saw that something had been poked under the saddle and it was clear that this was irritating the horse. He halted and extracted it and found that it was a wedge of paper; good quality paper, almost of parchment quality. To his astonishment he saw that it was addressed to himself and signed by Mr Forrestal. It was a letter written on the preceding day.

He dismounted by the roadside and found a convenient stile to sit upon in order to read the letter properly.

"Sir Giles," Mr Forrestal had written. "I am putting pen to paper merely in case I am unable to see you this evening. It is my intention to attempt to see you after dinner in order to try, once again, to warn you of the danger which threatens you. However,

I am well aware of *his* power and *he* may stop me. So this is merely a safeguard. If I don't succeed in seeing you, I will try to get this note to you.

"Sir Giles, if you value your life, indeed, if you value your immortal soul, I pray you leave Coolarrigan. It has become soulless and evil stalks the happy rooms in which you once played as a child. Vengeance is mine, saith the Lord. But a terrible vengeful creature is loose in the shadows of the great house. Go! Go, if you value all that is good and sweet in this life and the next."

Sir Giles paused and frowned, shaking his head. In truth, the poor man was demented. Something, however, made him read on.

"There is a curse on the family of Michelburne. It started when your grandfather, Sir Garth, was a young man at the time of the Great Hunger.

"Your grandfather, Sir Garth, demanded the fruits of Coolarrigan while the poor people starved. Perhaps he did not do it with evil intent, perhaps he did not know precisely what was happening. There was a man called Tórna who lived on the estate. Indeed, it was said that his ancestors had lived on the land there long, long before the coming of the family of Michelburne, that they went back into the mists of time. Tórna, so it was told locally, boasted that he was descended from the ancient druids of Ireland, knew their secrets and their power. Well, one by one, the family of Tórna grew sick. Hunger struck their cabins, starvation and disease visited their hovels. And all the time Sir Garth, safe in London, demanded his rents and the produce of the estate. Tórna's sons died, then all his daughters and also his wife. Then Tórna himself fell ill. That was when he pronounced a fearsome curse. He said that one day, when the years shall number two companies of warriors, Sir Garth would have to answer to the Tórna; that Sir Garth and his seed would vanish from Coolarrigan and the seed of Tórna would triumph and be the lords of the land. Tórna vanished soon after. It was thought that he had died and his body vanished among the tens of thousands of other famine victims. However, over the years it was claimed that Tórna had been seen about the estate of Coolarrigan, never aging, never growing older.

"The curse has always puzzled people in its interpretation. What did it mean, when the years shall number two companies of warriors? Like other ancient Indo-European peoples, the Irish language and culture is filled with numerological symbolism. Five months ago, soon after the death of Sir Garth, I happened to mention the matter to an antiquarian acquaintance and he pointed out that in Irish mythology, a company was thirty-three men. That there were thirty-three gods of the Tuatha Dé Dannan at the First Battle of Mag Tuired when the Tuatha claimed Ireland from the Fomorii, the gods of evil and darkness. The number thirty-three had a time-honoured place in the tradition of the Indo-European people. The answer lay, therefore, in the traditional multiplication by an even number, in this case two, of the thirty-three. It was exactly sixty-six years ago when Tórna pronounced his curse.

"It is my belief, Sir Giles, that Tórna has returned and is seeking revenge. Do not ask me how such a thing is possible. I am a minister and therefore I do not lightly say this. I do not presume to know the mysteries which are beyond our understanding but neither can I scoff and dismiss the power of evil and darkness. If God exists, then so does the Devil. I do not believe that the death of Sir Garth, nor that of your mother and father, were God's will. When I learned of the death of your wife and your return here I knew the terrible vengeance of Tórna, the self-professed wizard, was working. Oh, Sir Giles! You are the last of the Michelburne family. There is great danger here. Leave this place and go. I am sure Tórna has returned."

Sir Giles stared at the letter not knowing what to make of it. The rambles of a crazed mind? Most assuredly. Yet just how did Mr Forrestal come to be drowned in the Awbawn? It was not called "white river" (such being the import of its Irish name) for nothing, for it was a fearsome torrent above Michelburnetown where the leaping salmon displayed themselves in spectacular aerobatics to reach their spawning grounds. Why had the old woman pressed the letter under his saddle, for it could surely be none other than her hand that had done so? And why had she not wished Blake, the young curate, to see it?

Sir Giles was a pragmatic and phlegmatic man who did not believe in the supernatural any more than he believed in ancient curses. Yet someone was trying to make him think that there was some supernatural force at work at Coolarrigan. Could some descendant of Tórna, or even one of the locals who knew about the curse, be trying to use it to scare him, or, indeed, exact some vengeance of past wrongs, real or imagined?

Suddenly his blood tingled. What if Tórna had a son or some other relative who had been sent to America at that time perhaps …? Forrestal thought Tórna had returned to wreak vengeance on his family. What of Blake, for he was an American! Oh, come now! He laughed nervously at his sudden flight of imagination. He was as bad as Forrestal with his supernatural ravings. Did he really think that Blake was going round committing murder? Still, he rubbed the side of his nose thoughtfully, there was something strange going on at Coolarrigan and perhaps he should go into Templemore, the nearest large town, and see the local inspector of the Royal Irish Constabulary. If there were any doubts about the deaths of his parents and grandfather then the inspector would know or be able to advise him.

When he returned to Coolarrigan he realised that he must be sickening for a cold. He had broken out into a sweat, and shivers caused uncontrollable spasms in his body. The old adage about "feeding a cold, starving a fever" seemed true for he had also developed quite an appetite. As usual, Finnerty had laid out the luncheon in the dining-room and Sir Giles did not eat sparingly. When Finnerty came in to clear away the plates Sir Giles sat back, deciding to chance the smoking of a cheroot as an aid to the digestion, and feeling a little better.

"Tell me, Finnerty. Have you heard of a man called Tórna?" The question was asked abruptly.

Finnerty's smile broadened as it invariably did when he was

asked a question.

"Now would that be Tórna," he corrected Sir Giles's pronunciation gently, "who is editor of the *Gaelic Journal,* a very learned gentleman from Cork who writes poetry and the like in the ancient language of Ireland under that name?"

"No," Sir Giles shook his head.

"Ah well, would you be meaning the famous Tórna Eigeas or the Learned, as you would say it in English? He was a great druid and poet who was fosterer of Niall of the Nine Hostages. He died in the fifth century. 'Twas said that his feats of magic caused thousands to travel to Tara, the seat of the High King, from every corner of Ireland."

Sir Giles gave an exasperated sigh.

"No, I do not mean that Tórna either."

"Well," Finnerty left carrying the plates, his voice drifting back over his shoulder, "those are the only men of that name who are, as yet, famous in Ireland."

That night Sir Giles came awake once more, listening to the wind moaning about the house. As it rose and fell he imagined that he heard words framed in its cadences. He sat up and grew chill for he was hearing words. Whispered words close to his head.

"Poor Giles. The curse is on the Michelburnes. We are all doomed, Giles. There is no escape."

He started up and lit a spluttering candle with nervous fingers and peered about.

There was no one in the room.

"Damn it!" he swore softly. "I know this is a hoax and I'll get to the bottom of it yet."

The voice gave a sad, soft moan. It sounded as if it had came from the back of the wooden four-poster. He peered under the bed and behind it, knowing full well there was no recess into which a person could crawl. But he had to make sure. As he was standing in indecision the whispering became suddenly clear.

"Go to the window, Giles. Go to the window if you seek proof of my warning."

The view from his bedroom window gave on to the chapel at the back of the house. The moon was up in a cloudless sky and its pale white light lit the front of the chapel and the small stone courtyard before it with an ethereal brightness.

He caught his breath.

A man was kneeling on the steps of the chapel, shoulders bent forward so that Sir Giles could not see his face. He could see his hands tied behind him and a rope was around his neck, one end of which was in the hand of a tall shadow that stood to one side. The shadow was draped in black and in its other hand Sir Giles saw it held a great scythe. It was hooded and, in his horror, Sir Giles realised it was how he had come to visualise the Angel of Death, the Grim Reaper.

Then the kneeling figure raised his head and the wide, pleading eyes stared straight into the face of Sir Giles.

"Grandfather!" he cried in recognition.

There was a shrill peel of demoniacal laughter throughout the room and the black figure with the scythe suddenly raised a white skeletal hand; raised it and beckoned, beckoned towards Sir Giles!

There was a terrible sensation rising in the back of his head and Sir Giles seemed to plunge forward into a bottomless pit.

When he awoke he found himself burning with a fever. His body felt cold yet his head was on fire, with sweat pouring from his aching temples. His extremeties, however, were icy. He could see the bright sunlight filtering through the curtains. He tried to stir but felt so exhausted that he fell back on the pillow. He had difficulty in reaching to the old bell-rope and tugging it.

It seemed an interminable time before the broad, smiling face of Finnerty poked around the bedroom door.

"I need a doctor, Finnerty," croaked Sir Giles. "I'm feeling terrible."

Finnerty came forward and reached out a hand to touch his perspiring forehead.

"Begging your pardon, Sir Giles, but a good stiff tot, perhaps mixed with lemon and honey, and you will be as right as ninepence. 'Tis a rare country cure, so it is."

Sir Giles shook his head. Whatever it was it had been seizing hold of him for the last couple of days. He needed a doctor, an outsider, to tell about the terrible visions he had been having.

"I need the doctor," he repeated.

Finnerty shrugged. "Very well. The local doctor is Gaffney. I'll have to go into Michelburnetown."

Sir Giles begged him to be as quick as possible.

It was not until well after midday that he heard the sound of Finnerty's horse coming back and with it the rattle of a carriage. A round, ruddy man in a long grey overcoat and rimless spectacles came into the room carrying a small black Gladstone bag.

"Sir Giles? I'm Dr Gaffney."

He bent over the bed, felt Sir Giles's forehead, and thrust a thermometer into his mouth, chattering away all the time.

"The town has heard of your arrival. We would have called to make your acquaintance except we thought we'd give you a day or two to settle in first. I'm distressed that your first days here are marred by illness but ... " he took the thermometer out of his mouth, glanced at it, and shook it, "I'm delighted to say that it is only a chill. A day or so and you'll be up and fine."

Sir Giles frowned.

"Are you sure, Dr Gaffney? Are you certain that all I have is a simple chill?"

"I'm willing to stake my professional reputation on my diagnosis, Sir Giles. Of course, if you want a second opinion you are entitled to one. You would have to send to Templemore or Thurles, for there is no doctor nearer."

He had straightened up, sniffing a little, as if offended, so Sir Giles reached out a hand to stay him. "I did not mean to question your diagnosis, Doctor. I just wanted to reassure myself that it is merely a chill."

Dr Gaffney nodded, still a little stiffly. Sir Giles gestured to a chair by the bed and he hesitated and then seated himself.

"Truly, Doctor, I am a little worried."

He raised an eyebrow as he examined Sir Giles's face.

"Worried?"

"I have had what I believe are called hallucinations."

He leaned forward, frowning slightly. "In what manner do you mean this?"

"I believe that I have heard my mother and father, walking the corridors of Coolarrigan. And last night I saw my grandfather."

Gaffney peered forward with a frown. "*Saw* him?"

"Last night," repeated Sir Giles. "In the grounds outside that window, by the old chapel."

Gaffney reached forward and placed his pudgy hand against Sir Giles's brow, pursing his lips thoughtfully. "Well now, it's not unusual to hallucinate when one is in a fever."

"Yet it was before I was in the fever," Sir Giles insisted. "And I have heard whisperings. I have heard my mother's voice calling me by name."

"I see." He looked disconcerted. "When and where did these … er, whisperings … occur?"

"At night. Here in my bedroom, in the corridor outside my parent's old bedroom and in the vault beneath the chapel."

The doctor compressed his lips and was silent.

"No, Doctor, I am not mad," Sir Giles assured him. "I have seen these things but I do not ascribe them to the supernatural." He lowered his voice. "I think someone is trying to frighten me away from Coolarrigan for some reason. Even trying to persuade me that I am going crazy."

Gaffney's eyebrows shot up but Sir Giles went on: "Tell me, Doctor," he raised himself on an elbow and gazed intently at the round-faced man. "Have you heard of a local man called Tórna who died about sixty years ago?"

Gaffney blinked, staring at Sir Giles thoughtfully for a moment before nodding slowly.

"Who has not heard the name in these parts?" he replied.

"Tell me what you know about him."

"He was a very wise man," the doctor admitted. "Oh, this was before my time. I merely repeat what the locals say. He is quite a legend in these parts for they regarded him as the local healer, a wizard, if you like. He was called the 'Dreeador', which is the native word for a magician. They used to say that if any man or beast fell ill in the district, then Tórna would be sent for and the affliction would be made well." Gaffney sniffed and added sourly, "That would have made my job superfluous."

"Did he die in the famine?" pressed Sir Giles.

"He did, indeed. He and all his family. So much for his vaunted power if he could not heal his own."

"But local people claim they have seen him since?" Sir Giles's voice was sharp and probing.

Gaffney looked surprised. "Who told you that?"

"And this Tórna, the Dreeador, as you call him," Sir Giles went on remorselessly, "didn't he curse my family, blaming the famine deaths on us?"

Gaffney stirred uncomfortably, as if he knew the truth of the matter and was not prepared to admit it.

"I am not fully acquainted with the local folktales, Sir Giles," he replied distantly. "The Irish peasant is much given to such prattlings. Tales of curses, of the supernatural, come pouring out of every quarter compounded, I believe, by the illicit distilling of poteen. I treat more people from the affects of bad illegal spirits than I do for common colds."

"Doctor," Sir Giles lay back on his pillows, his eyes fixed on Gaffney, "I suspect Blake, the curate, of being the son of the Dreeador, the son of this Tórna. I think he is trying to frighten me away from Coolarrigan for some purpose I cannot fathom. Perhaps he had a hand in my grandfather's death or in that of my parents and does not want me to find out."

Gaffney smiled. It was a patronising smile, the face of a man trying to humour someone not quite sane.

"I hardly think Mister Blake is in his late sixties, for the son of the Dreeador, if still alive, would be at least that age. Wasn't the curse pronounced sixty-six years ago?"

Sir Giles stared at Gaffney for a moment, suddenly realising the man's logic. He bit his lip, frustrated. It had not occurred to him about the passage of time since the 'Great Hunger'. Of course anyone who had been even a babe in arms during 1844-48 would be in his sixties now! How stupid he felt. Then he relaxed. He was about to suggest that Blake could be a grandson or some other relative who knew of the curse but Gaffney was standing up, trying to disguise his impatience.

"Besides, Sir Giles," Dr Gaffney's voice was heavy with irony, "I attended both your parents in their illness and also examined your grandfather after his heart attack. I signed their death certificates. There was nothing strange about their deaths."

Sir Giles stared at him, his mind in a turmoil. All his suspicions and conclusions suddenly seemed ridiculous. Had he let himself be misled by Forrestal's ravings? But what of the voices, the things he had seen? He bit his lip. Was he really going mad?

Gaffney reached forward and patted his hand. "I think you are suffering from your chill, strain and an active imagination, Sir Giles. I'll give you a sedative and come back to see you soon. The chill will go soon and with it the fever and then the hallucinations will be gone."

He took a bottle from his bag, poured some of it into a water glass, told Sir Giles to drink it and left with a cheery wave of his hand. Sir Giles watched him go, making no effort to drink the potion. Hearing him stop outside the bedroom door and begin to speak in a low voice, presumably to Finnerty, something stirred Sir Giles's curiosity as if he were reluctant to let go of his theory. Someone *was* trying to frighten him away from Coolarrigan. He was certain! He slipped from the bed and went softly to the door.

"I'm worried, Finnerty," came Gaffney's soft accent. "He has some morbid curiosity about the past. Says he sees visions of his dead relatives. Macabre sensitivity. Know if there is a history of insanity in the family?"

Finnerty's voice was not clear but Sir Giles had heard enough. Even his doctor believed that he was going insane. Perhaps he was. He could just hear the gossip in the village. It would all fit in, wouldn't it? The deaths of his grandfather and his parents, the death of his wife, the return to Coolarrigan to brood in isolation; and then they would say he had a morbid obsession about the time of the Great Hunger. Was it all some terrible plot arranged by the Dreeador?

He returned to bed just as Finnerty came in, smiling as ever.

"Can I get you anything now, Sir Giles?"

He shook his head and retreated further into the terrible sense of isolation which had spread over him. In desperation he reached for the concoction left by Dr Gaffney and swallowed it. He eventually fell into a deep sleep.

It was dark when he awoke. There was the sound of sobbing again. In spite of his reeling head and the feeling of weakness, he determined to come to grips with his tormentors. He would not let these phantoms slip through his fingers again.

He slipped out of bed and flung wide his door. As he expected, the corridor was deserted and he hastened along to the end of the corridor. He paused and peered towards his parents' bedroom door from beyond which he believed the sobbing was coming. To his horror a figure stood outside the door. The pale figure of a woman. He froze for a moment. A terrible coldness seized him. It was his mother. The pale face was turned towards him.

Then the illogicality of the vision struck him.

"Beware, Giles ... " it started to say but before the words were out of its mouth he had launched himself down the corridor towards it as if he were hurling himself down a rugger pitch. Outrageous anger overcame any momentary fear he had for he was sure it was some trick. He was sure that the "hallucinations" were manufactured for his benefit by the Dreeador, or whatever Blake called himself.

The apparition gave a scream and tried to turn the handle of the door but he had reached it, flung himself upon its warm, corporeal frame which was as alive as he was.

He swung the woman round. Her face was caked with make-up to elongate the features and make them pale and wan. Her eyes stared at him, pale and frightened.

"So you are real?" he snarled angrily.

Then it seemed her eyes focused beyond his shoulder, her lips curled back in a malevolent grin and she gave a deep throaty chuckle.

Sir Giles had a split-second warning of someone behind him but it was too late. A moment later his world exploded into blackness.

When he recovered his senses he found himself stretched on his back in a cold, musty chamber which was so dark that he could hardly see a yard or two in front of him. It took him a while before he could gather strength to move. His temples throbbed in agony and violent pains caused his stomach to spasm. Groaning in the effort, he sat up. He appeared to be lying on a long stone bench. He blinked in the semi-gloom and peered about.

The only soft grey light came from a tiny grill set high in the chamber. The odours of the place now assailed his nostrils – a bitter-sweet stench of decay and of things rotting.

It was then that he knew where he was!

He sprang to his feet with a cry of terror.

He was in the Michelburne family vault underneath the chapel at the back of Coolarrigan.

He stumbled forward, smashing into something which barred his path. Then he lost his balance and fell, knocking it over. It was a long box of wood, rotten wood. It crashed to the ground with him on top of it, disintegrating. His hand, held forward to cushion the impact of his fall, broke through the decayed wood and touched something beneath, a pulpy mass and brittle bone.

He sprang back with another cry.

A grille grated at the far end of the terrible chamber and flickering lamplight illuminated the place. He found himself staring down at a shattered coffin and the putrid remains of a decomposing body.

"So you're awake, Sir Giles?" came Finnerty's taunting voice.

He scrambled to his feet and turned to stare at the shadow behind the lamplight.

"Finnerty! What does this mean?"

His question, he silently admitted even as he spoke it, sounded feeble in the circumstances.

There came a hollow chuckle.

"Surely you can work it out, Sir Giles? I am Tórna."

Sir Giles stared at the man, incomprehension setting his features.

"You are the last of the Michelburnes, Sir Giles. And with your passing, my revenge will be fulfilled."

"*Your* revenge?"

"I am Tórna," repeated Finnerty.

"But..." a thousand thoughts cascaded in rapid succession through his mind as he tried to cling to some reality, "but what good will your killing me do you?"

"It will cause the souls of my people to rest in peace, the people who slaved on the estate of the Michelburnes during the Great Hunger and who were left to starve to death by the roadside while the Michelburnes profited and grew fat. Now it is your turn, Sir Giles. You will remain a prisoner here in the vault. You will starve to death here as my family starved to death amidst the prosperity of your estate. You will feel the embrace of the Great Hunger as your grandfather and your parents did before you."

He tried to understand Finnerty but somehow he could not take his words in. Then his eyes widened as he realised the man's implication.

"Yes, Sir Giles," confirmed Finnerty in answer to the horrified question that was framed in his eyes. "They, too, were brought to this chamber and ended their days here. Your grandfather was so stubborn he lasted sixty days before he succumbed to the peace of death."

"Please ..." Sir Giles found himself crying. "Please! What do you want? I am a rich man, there is the Coolarrigan estate. Take what you want but do not do this terrible thing."

"Oh, I shall take the Coolarrigan estate anyway," chuckled Finnerty. "Your will leaves everything to your wife."

"Bu ... but Ethel is dead," Sir Giles cried in frustration, trying to understand the man.

"I am not talking about your first wife, Sir Giles. I am talking about Lady Aileen Michelburne." Finnerty's voice was mocking.

Sir Giles stared blankly. Then he caught sight of another figure behind Finnerty's shoulder, the figure of a woman. She came forward into the light. He could only recognise her by those pale, malevolent eyes, the same eyes as Finnerty. Gone was the caked make-up and the wig which had made her appear like his mother. Aileen Finnerty was an attractive woman. But she was staring at him with a malicious and hostile sneer which distorted her beauty.

"You don't remember?" she asked, jeeringly. "Yesterday, in a private service, you married me, Giles. You needed companionship and love after the misery and loneliness of the last six months. Why, surely you remember? Didn't Mr Blake, the curate, perform the ceremony? I have the certificate duly signed and witnessed."

Finnerty was chuckling in self-satisfaction.

"Yes, Sir Giles, Coolarrigan will be the property of the Tórna Finnerty and his family just as I foretold it would." His voice was savouring the sweetness of his revenge.

Sir Giles held his hands to his head and groaned aloud in anguish as he realised the fiendish plot which had been laid.

"How can Blake, a man of the cloth, a churchman, subscribe to this … this atrocity?" he demanded, trying to hold on to some hope.

Finnerty chuckled more loudly.

"Because his name is Blake Finnerty. He is my son."

Behind Finnerty and the girl Sir Giles saw the jeering face of the young curate. He stepped back with a groan.

So Finnerty's web was complete and he was trapped.

Yet he tried to hang on to one more slender thread of hope in this hour of desperation.

"How can you prove that you did not murder me? If you starve me to death, as you threaten, then who will sign a death certificate? Dr Gaffney will not grant it."

"Why then did he grant the death certificates for your grandfather and for your father and mother?" came the smug reply.

The thought had already struck Sir Giles even when he had been speaking. A coldness welled in the pit of his stomach. "Is he also in this monstrous plot?"

"Indeed. But purely for money. He is a greedy man and greedy men are not altogether trustworthy. So when he has served his purpose ... " Finnerty shrugged. "And now, Sir Giles, you know everything you need to know. You know why you and your family are doomed to extinction. Soon, very soon now, my curse will be fulfilled. Twice thirty-three years have passed and the power is mine!"

Sir Giles stared at the man in utter bewilderment. "Tell me, Finnerty, since you mean to kill me, tell me one more thing. What relationship are you to this man Tórna, whom you call the Dreeador; the wizard who died in the famine? Are you his son? Do you do this out of mere vengeance or are you just a common murderer and thief?"

Finnerty's face contorted in a scowl which caused shivers down Sir Giles's back.

"You still do not understand? I *am* Tórna! I am the Dreeador! I could not die without fulfilling my purpose."

It seemed suddenly as if his whole demeanour changed. His voice rose abruptly in harsh, grating accents.

"You puny fool! You have no conception of the power of hate, how it can animate man over the years. Once you, the last of the Michelburnes, are dead then so shall I sleep – but with the curse fulfilled. Hate and the ancient knowledge has animated my frail body over the years. Now it is done. You and your kind have come to this land and sought to destroy or enslave us. We, who have lived here from the early mists of time's beginning, we are of the Dé Dannan, sprung from the loins of the ancient gods of Éireann. We are possessed of the ancient knowledge and we will remain when you and your kind have descended back into the mud pit from which you have crawled. Sleep well, Sir Giles – last of the Michelburnes."

The door grated shut with a hollow clash, shutting him in total darkness.

For a moment he stood staring into the blackness as his mind tried to digest the completeness of the terrible vengeful plot that had been revealed. Yet his reaction was not one of terror or fear.

It was a surge of fury; fury at the urbane Finnerty, Tórna Finnerty, and his loathsome children. There was no doubt that Finnerty was truly mad, imagining himself to be some ancient witch-doctor who had died over sixty years ago. He and his brood thought that they had devised the perfect murder; tried to drive him insane with their pseudo-apparitions and sepulchral voices. Anger rather than fear filled him now.

He felt his way towards the door and tested its strength. He would find a way out of this vault and teach these damned upstarts a lesson. No peasant's spawn would get the better of him – wizard or no wizard. Madman or not.

Something moved in the darkness behind him.

There came a low moaning sound. The sound of a woman sobbing in anguished despair.

He found the hairs on the nape of his neck standing out.

Then a voice, he *knew* it was his mother's voice, said sadly at his ear: "Poor Giles! We tried to warn you. We tried our best."

For a moment he stood rooted to the spot. The blood in his veins turned to ice. Then, spurred on by the terror and suffocating darkness, he let forth a great scream of horror and flung himself against the rusting iron, pounding futilely on the ancient metal with bare hands, shrieking for mercy.

X

Daoine Domhain

OW SHOULD I start? Do I have time to finish? Questions pour into my mind and remain unanswered, for they are unanswerable. But I must get something down on paper; at least make some attempt to warn people of the terrible dangers for mankind that lurk in the depths. How foolish and pitifully stupid a species we are, thinking that we are more intelligent than any other species, thinking that we are the "chosen" race. What arrogance – what ignorance! What infantile minds we have compared to ... But I must begin as it began for me.

My name is Tom Hacket. My home is Rockport, Cape Ann, Massachusetts. My family history is fairly typical of this area of America. My great-grandparents arrived from County Cork, Ireland, to settle in Boston. My grandfather, Daniel, was born in Ireland but had come to America with his parents when only a few years old. Neither my father nor I ever had the desire to visit Ireland. We had no nostalgic yearnings, like some Irish-Americans, to visit the "old country". We felt ourselves to be purely American. But grandfather Daniel ... well, he is the mystery in our family. And if I were to ascribe a start to these curious events then I would say that the beginning was my grandfather.

Daniel Hacket had joined the United States Navy and served as a lieutenant on a destroyer. Sometime in the early spring of 1928 he went on leave to Ireland, leaving his wife and baby (my father) behind in Rockport. He never came back; nor did anyone in the family ever hear from him again. My grandmother, according to my father, always believed that he had been forcibly prevented from returning.

The US Navy took a more uncharitable line and posted him as a deserter. After grandmother died, my father expressed the opinion, contrary to his mother's faith in Daniel Hacket's fidelity, that his father had probably settled down with some colleen in Ireland under an assumed name. If the truth were known, he always felt bitter about the mysterious desertion of his father. However, my father never sold our house in Rockport; we never moved. And it was only towards the end of my father's life that he revealed the promise he had made to grandmother. She had refused to move away or sell up in the belief that one day Daniel Hacket would attempt to get in touch if he were able. She had made my father promise to keep the old house in the family for as long as he could.

No one asked that promise of me. I inherited the old wooden colonial-style house, which stood on the headland near Cape Ann, when my father died of cancer. My mother had been dead for some years and, as I had no brothers or sisters, the lonely old house was all mine. I was working as a reporter for the *Boston Herald* and the house was no longer of interest to me. So I turned it over to a real estate agent thinking to use the money to get a better apartment in Boston itself.

I can't recall now why I should have driven up to the house this particular week. Of course, I made several journeys to sort through three generations of family bric-à-brac which had to be cleared before any new owner set foot in the place. Maybe that was the reason. I know it was a Tuesday afternoon and I was sifting through a cardboard box of photographs when the doorbell buzzed as someone pressed firmly against it.

The man who stood there was tall, lean with a crop of red-gold hair and a broad smile. I had the impression of handsomeness in spite of the fact that I noticed he wore an eye-patch over his right eye and, on closer inspection, his right shoulder seemed somewhat misshaped by a hump. When he spoke, it was obvious he was Irish. That did not make him stand out in itself for Boston is an Irish city. But he possessed a quaint old-world charm and courtesy which was unusual. And his one good eye was a sharp, bright orb of green.

"Is this the Hacket house?" he asked.

I affirmed it was.

"My name is Cichol O'Driscoll. I'm from Baltimore."

"That's a long journey, Mr O'Driscoll," I said politely, wondering what the man wanted. At the same time I was thinking that his first name, he pronounced it "Kik-ol", was an odd one for an Irishman. "Did you fly up this morning?"

He gave a wry chuckle.

"Ah, no. Not Baltimore, Maryland, sir. But the place which gave it its name – Baltimore in County Cork, Ireland."

It would have been churlish of me not to invite him in and offer him coffee, which he accepted.

"You are a Hacket, I presume?" he asked.

I introduced myself.

"Then I'm thinking that Mrs Sheila Hacket no longer lives?"

"She was my grandmother. No. She has been dead these fifteen years past."

"And what of her son, Johnny?"

I shrugged. "My father. He died three weeks ago."

"Ah, then I am sorry for your troubles."

"But what is this about?" I frowned.

"Little to tell," he said in that curious Irish way of speaking English. "As I said, I am from Baltimore which is a small fishing port in the south-west of Ireland. A year ago I purchased an old croft on Inishdriscol, one of the islands that lie just off the coast, to the west from Baltimore. I am refurbishing it to make it into a holiday cottage. Well, one of my builders was pulling down a wall when he found some sort of secret cavity and in this cavity he came across an old oilskin pouch. Inside was a letter addressed to Mrs Sheila Hacket at Rockport, Massachusetts, with a note that if she no longer lived then it should be handed to her son, Johnny. The letter was dated 1 May 1928.

I stared at the man in fascination.

"And you have come all this way to deliver a letter written sixty-three years ago?"

He chuckled, shaking his head.

"Not exactly. I have business in Boston. I own a small export business in Ireland. And so I thought I would kill two birds with one stone, as they say. It is not a long run up here from Boston. In fact, I had to pass by to get to Newburyport where I also have business. I thought it would be fascinating to deliver the letter if Sheila or Johnny Hacket survived after all these years. But I didn't really expect to find them. When the people in the local store told me the Hacket house still stood here, I was fairly surprised."

He hesitated and then drew out the package and deposited it on the table. It was as he said, an old oilskin pouch, not very bulky.

"Well, I guess you have a right to this."

He stood up abruptly, with a glance at his wristwatch.

"I must be off."

I was staring at the package.

"What's in it?" I asked.

"Just a letter," he replied.

"I mean, what's in the letter?"

His face momentarily contorted in anger.

"I haven't opened it. It's not addressed to me," he said in annoyance.

"I didn't mean it like that," I protested. "I didn't mean to sound insulting. It's just ... well, don't you want to know what it is you have brought?"

He shook his head.

"The letter is clearly addressed. It is not for me to examine the contents."

"Then stay while I examine it," I invited, feeling it was the least I could do to repay the man for bringing it such a distance.

He shook his head.

"I'm on my way to Newburyport. I've a cousin there." He

grinned again recovering his good humour. "It's a small world." He paused, then said: "I'll be passing this way next week on my way back to Boston. Purely out of curiosity, I would like to know whether the letter contained something of interest. Maybe it's part of some local history of our island Inishdriscol."

"What does that mean?"

"Driscoll's Island. The O'Driscolls were a powerful ruling clan in the area," he responded proudly.

In fact, I arranged to meet Cichol O'Driscoll the next week in Boston because I had to return there to work on the following Monday morning. I watched him walk off down the drive, for presumably he had left his car in the roadway. I remember thinking that it was odd to come across such old-world charm and courtesy. The man must have flown a couple of thousand miles and never once attempted to open the letter he had brought with him. I turned to where it lay on the kitchen table, picked it up and turned it over and over in my hands. It was only then that I suddenly realised the identity of the hand which had penned the address.

How stupid of me not to have realised before but it is curious how slow the mind can work at times. The date, the handwriting – which I had recently been looking at in the papers I had been sorting out – all pointed to the fact that here was a letter from my grandfather, Daniel Hacket.

My hands suddenly shaky with excitement, I opened the oilskin and took out the yellowing envelope. Using a kitchen knife, I slit it open. I extracted several sheets of handwriting and laid them carefully on the flat surface of the table.

> Inishdriscol,
> near Baltimore,
> County Cork,
> Ireland.
> 30 April 1928

Dearest Sheila,

If you read these words you may conclude that I am no longer part of this world. Courage, my Sheila, for you will need it if these words reach you for I will require you to make them known so that the world may be warned. You must tell the Navy Department that they were not destroyed, that they still exist, watching, waiting, ready to take over ... they have been waiting for countless millennia and soon, soon their time will come.

Today is the feast of Bealtaine here. Yes, ancient customs still survive in this corner of the world. This is the feast-day sacred to Bíle, the old god of death, and I must go down into the abyss to face him. I do not think that I shall survive. That is why I am writing to you in the hope that, one day, this will find its way into your hands so that you may know and warn the world ...

But first things first. Why did I come here? As you know, it was purely by chance. You will recall the extraordinary events at Innsmouth a few months ago? How agents of the federal government, working with the Navy Department, dynamited part of the old harbour? It was supposed to be a secret, but the fact of the destruction of the old seaport could not be kept from those who lived along the Massachusetts coast. In addition to that operation, I can tell you that my ship was one of several which were sent to depth-charge and torpedo the marine abyss just beyond Devil Reef. We were told it was merely some exercise, a war-game, but there was considerable scuttle-butt as to why the old harbour should be destroyed at the same time that the deeps were depth-charged. Some sailors conjured up visions of terrifying monsters which we were supposed to be destroying. There was talk of creatures – or beings who dwelt in the great depths – which had to be annihilated before they wiped out mankind. At the time we officers treated these rumours and tales with humorous gusto.

When the operation was finished and we returned to port the officers and men who had taken part in the exercise were given an extraordinary four weeks' leave; extraordinary for it was unprecedented to my knowledge of the service. I now realise that it was done for a purpose: to stop the men from talking about that strange exercise. The idea being, I suppose, that when they returned they would have forgotten the event and there would be no further speculation about it.

Well, four weeks' leave was facing me. I had always wanted to see the place where I was born. Do you remember how you insisted that I go alone when it was discovered little Johnny had scarlet fever and, though out of danger, would not be able to make the trip to Ireland and you would not leave him? I was reluctant to go. Ah, would to God I had not done so. Would to God I had never set eyes on the coast of Ireland.

I took passage to Cork, landing at the attractive harbour of Cobh, and set out to Baltimore, where I had been born. The place is a small fishing port set in a wild and desolate country on the edge of the sea. It stands at the end of a remote road and attracts few visitors unless they have specific business there. The village clusters around an excellent harbour and on a rocky eminence above it is the O'Driscoll castle which, I was later told, has been in ruins since 1537. The only way to approach it is by a broad rock-cut stair. Incidentally, practically everyone in the town is called O'Driscoll for this was the heart of their clan lands. When the sun shines, the place has an extraordinary beauty. The harbour is frequently filled with fishing-boats and small sailing ships and there are many islands offshore.

On local advice I went up to the headland which they call the Beacon hereabouts. The road was narrow and passed between grey stone walls through open, stony country. From this headland there is a spectacular view of the islands. The locals call them "Carbery's Hundred Isles". Opposite is the biggest, Sherkin Island, on which stands the ruins of another O'Driscoll castle and those of a Franciscan friary, also destroyed in 1537. Beyond is Inis Cléire or Clear Island with its rising headland, Cape Clear, with yet another O'Driscoll castle called Dunanore, and four miles from the farthest tip of Cape Clear is the Fastnet Rock.

Everyone in the area speaks the Irish language, which has put me at a disadvantage and I now wish my parents had passed on their knowledge to me. All I have learnt is that Baltimore is merely an Anglicisation of *Baile an Tigh Móir* – the town of the big house – and that some local people also call it *Dún na Séad* – the fort of jewels.

There was a certain hostility in the place, for it must be remembered that the War of Independence against England is not long past and that was followed by a bitter civil war which ended in 1923, only five years ago. Memories of that terrible time are still fresh in people's minds and colour their attitude to strangers until they are able to judge whether the stranger means them harm or no.

Within a few days of arriving in Baltimore I found that I had not been born actually in the village but on one of the nearby islands called Inishdriscol, or Driscoll's Island. I soon persuaded a fisherman to take me there, it being three miles from Baltimore harbour. It is a large enough island with a small village at one end and a schoolhouse at the other with its overall shape resembling the letter "T".

I was able to hire a cottage close by the very one in which I had been born. The owners, Brennan told me, were away to America to seek their fortune. Brennan is the only one who speaks English on the island. He is a curious fellow combining the functions of mayor, entrepreneur, head fisherman, counsellor ... you name it and Brennan fits the role. Brennan is his first name, at least that is how I pronounce it, for he showed me the proper spelling of it which was written *Bráonáin* and the English of it is "sorrow". Naturally, he is also an O'Driscoll and, for the first time, I learnt the meaning of the name which is correctly spelt *Ó hEidersceoil* and means "intermediary". Names mean a great deal in this country. Our own name, Hacket is, unfortunately, not well respected here for in 1631 two corsair galleys from Algiers sacked Baltimore, killed many of the inhabitants and carried off two hundred to be sold as slaves in Africa. They were guided through the channels to the town by a man called Hacket, who was eventually caught and hung in the city of Cork. Ah, if only I had knowledge of this language, how interesting these arbitrary signs we use would become.

In lieu of any other companion to converse with I have been

much thrown together with Brennan and he has been my guide and escort on the island. Indeed I found no close relatives although most people knew of my family and several claimed distant kinship. After a while I settled down to a life of lazy fishing and walking.

It was after I had been on the island a few days that two more visitors arrived, but only for a few hours' stay on the island. Brennan told me that one was some representative of the English government and the other was an official of the Irish government. Apparently, during the War of Independence, a number of English soldiers and officials had disappeared, unknown casualties of the conflict. It seems that there had been a small military post on the island: a captain, a sergeant and four men. One night, the captain disappeared. It was assumed that he had been caught by the local guerrillas, taken away and shot. All investigations had proved fruitless in discovering exactly how he had met his end. No one on the island had talked. Nor had the guerrillas, many of whom were now members of the Irish government, issued any information on the subject. Now, nine years after the disappearance, the English government, in cooperation with the Irish Free State government, were attempting to close the case.

I met the English official while out walking one morning and we fell into conversation about the problem.

"Trouble is," he said, "these damned natives are pretty close."

He blandly ignored the fact that I had been born on the island and could, therefore, be classed as one of the "damned natives".

"Nary a word can you get out of them. Damned code of silence, as bad as Sicilians."

"You think the local people killed this Captain...?"

"Pfeiffer," he supplied. "If they didn't, I'm sure they know who did. Maybe it was a guerrilla unit from the mainland. There wasn't much activity on the islands during the war although there was a lot of fighting in West Cork. A lot of bad blood, too. Political differences run deep. Take these people now ... they don't like the Irish government official that I'm with."

"Why not?"

"He represents the Free State. This area was solidly Republican during the Civil War. They lost, and they hate the Free State government. I suppose they won't tell us anything. Damned waste of time coming here." I nodded in sympathy with his task.

"Well, if you give me your card, perhaps if I hear anything ... any drop of gossip which might help ... I could drop you a line. You never know. They might talk to me whereas they would not talk to you."

He smiled enthusiastically.

"That would be pretty sporting of you, Lieutenant." He pronounced it in the curious way that the English do as "left-tenant".

"When did your man disappear?"

"Nine years ago. Actually, exactly nine years ago on April 30." He paused. "You are staying at the pink-wash cottage near the point, aren't you?"

I confirmed I was.

"Curiously, that's where Captain Pfeiffer was billeted when he disappeared."

The officials left the island later that day and I raised the subject with Brennan. I had been a little arrogant in assuming that because I had been born on the island, and was of an old island family, that I would be trusted any more than the officials from Dublin and London. I was an American, a stranger, and they certainly would not divulge the hidden secrets of the island to me. Brennan was diplomatic in answering my questions but the result was the same. No one was going to talk about the fate of the captain.

A few days later, I had almost forgotten Pfeiffer. Brennan and I went out fishing. We were after sea trout: *breac* as he called it. Brennan took me out in his skiff, at least I describe it as a skiff. He called it a *naomhóg*, a strange very light boat which was made of canvas, spread over a wooden frame and hardened by coatings of pitch and tar. Although frail, the craft was very manoeuvrable in the water and rode heavy seas with amazing dexterity. A mile or two from the island was a weird crooked rock which rose thirty or forty feet out of the sea. Brennan called it *camcarraig* and when I asked the meaning of the name he said it was simply "crooked rock". Brennan reckoned the sea trout ran by here and into Roaring Water Bay, close by. So we rowed to within a few yards of the pounding surf, which crashed like slow thunder against the weed-veined rock, and cast our lines.

The fishing went well for some time and we hauled a catch that we could not be ashamed of.

Suddenly, I cannot remember exactly how it happened, a dark shadow seemed to pass over us. I looked up immediately expecting a cloud to have covered the sun. Yet it was still high and shining down, though it was as if there was no light coming from it. Nor were there any clouds in the sky to account for the phenomenon. I turned to Brennan and found him on his knees in the bow of the boat, crouching forward, his eyes staring at the sea. It was then that I observed that the water around us had turned black, the sort of angry green blackness of a brooding sea just before the outbreak of a storm, discoloured by angry scudding clouds. Yet the sky was clear.

I felt the air, dank and chill, oppressive and damp against my body. "What is it?" I demanded, my eyes searching for some explanation of the curious sensation.

Brennan had now grabbed at the oars and started to pull away from the crooked rock, back towards the distant island shore. His English had deserted him and he was rambling away in eloquent Irish and, despite his rowing, would now and then lift his hand to cross himself.

"Brennan," I cried, "calm down. What are you saying?"

After some while, when we were well away from the crooked rock, and the sun was warm again on our bodies and the sea was once more the reflected blue of the sky, Brennan apologised.

"We were too near the rock," he said. "There is an undercurrent there which is too strong for us."

I frowned. That was not how it had seemed to me at all. I told him so but he dismissed me.

"I was only fearful that we would be swept into the current,"

223

he said. "I merely offered up a little prayer."

I raised an eyebrow. "It seemed a powerful long prayer," I observed.

He grinned. "Long prayers are better heard than short ones."

I chuckled. "And what was the prayer you said? In case I have need of it."

"I merely said, God between me and the Devil, nine times and nine times nine."

I was puzzled. "Why nine? Wouldn't seven be a luckier number?"

He looked amazed at what he obviously thought was my appalling ignorance.

"Seven? Seven is an unlucky number in these parts. It is the number nine which is sacred. In ancient times the week consisted of nine nights and nine days. Didn't Cúchulainn have nine weapons, didn't King Loegaire, when setting out to arrest St Patrick, order nine chariots to be joined together according to the tradition of the gods? Wasn't Queen Medb accompanied by nine chariots and ..."

I held up my hand in pacification at his excited outburst.

"All right. I believe you," I smiled. "So the number nine is significant."

He paused and his sea-green eyes rested on mine for several seconds and then he shrugged.

That evening I went to Tomás O'Driscoll's croft which served as an inn, or rather a place where you could buy a drink and groceries from the mainland when they came in by the boat. The place is called a *síbín*, or shebeen, as it is pronounced in English, which signifies an unlicensed drinking house. Several of the old men of the island were gathered there and Brennan sat on a three-legged stool by the chimney-corner, smoking his pipe. As I have said, everyone looked up to Brennan as the spokesman for the island and the old men were seated around him talking volubly in Irish. I wished I could understand what they were saying.

Two words kept being repeated in this conversation, however. *Daoine Domhain.* To my ears it sounded like "dayn'ya dow'an".

Only when they noticed me did a silence fall on the company. I felt a strange uneasiness among them. Brennan was regarding me with a peculiar expression on his face which held a note of … well, it took me some time before I reasoned it … of sadness in it.

I offered to buy drinks for the company but Brennan shook his head.

"Have a drink on me and welcome," he said. "It is not for the likes of you to buy drinks for the likes of us."

They seemed to behave strangely to me. I could not put my finger on it for they were not unfriendly, nor did they stint in hospitality, yet there was something odd – as if they were regarding me as a curiosity, watching and waiting … yet for what?

I returned to the croft early that evening and noted that the wind was blowing up from the south, across *camcarraig* and towards the headland on which the handful of cottages on the island clung precariously. Oddly, above the noise of the blustering wind, stirring the black, angry swells which boomed into Roaring Water Bay and smacked against the granite fortresses of the islands, I heard a whistling sound which seemed less like the noise of the wind and more like the lonely cry of some outcast animal, wailing in its isolation. So strong did the noise seem that I went to the door and stood listening to it just in case it was some animal's distress cry. But eventually the noise was lost in the howl of the wind from the sea.

"Out of the mouths of babes and sucklings …" the Bible has it, and I was reminded of the saying two days later when I happened to be fishing from the high point beyond my cottage, where the seas move restlessly towards the land from the *camcarraig*. It was a lazy day and the fish were not in a mood for taking the bait. Nonetheless I was content, relaxing, almost half asleep.

I was not aware of any presence until I heard a voice close to my ear say something in Irish. I blinked my eyes and turned to see a young girl of about nine years old, with amazing red-gold hair which tumbled around her shoulders. She was an extraordinarily attractive child, with eyes of such a bright green colour they seemed unreal. She was staring at me solemnly. Her feet were bare and her dress was stained and torn but she had a quiet dignity which sat oddly on the appearance of terrible poverty. Again she repeated her question.

I shook my head and replied in English, feeling stupid.

"Ah, it is a stranger you are."

"Do you speak English?" I asked in amazement, having accepted Brennan as the only English-speaker on the island. She did not answer my superfluous question for it was obvious she understood the language.

"The sea is brooding today," she said, nodding at the dark seas around *camcarraig*. "Surely the *Daoine Domhain* are angry. Their song was to be heard last night."

"Dayn'ya dow'an?" I asked, trying to approximate the sounds of the words. It was the same expression which had been used in the shebeen a few nights ago. "What is that?"

"Musha, but they are the Fomorii, the dwellers beneath the sea. They were the evil ones who dwelt in Ireland long before the coming of the Gael. Always they have battled for our souls, sometimes succeeding, sometimes failing. They are the terrible people: they have but a single eye and a single hand and a single foot. They are the terrible ones, the Deep Ones: the *Daoine Domhain*."

I smiled broadly at this folklore so solemnly proclaimed by this young girl.

She caught my smile and frowned. Her face was suddenly serious. "God between us and all evil, stranger, but it is not good to smile at the name of the Deep Ones."

I assured her that I was not smiling at them. I asked her what her name was but she would not tell me. She turned to me and I saw an abrupt change in her expression. Abruptly a sadness grew in her eyes and she turned and ran away. That left me disturbed. I wondered who her mother was because I felt I ought to go to the child's parents in case they thought I had deliberately scared her. I should explain that I meant the child no harm in case it was afraid of something I had said or of some expression on my face.

I was packing my rods when Brennan came by. I greeted him

and my first question was about the child. He looked mighty puzzled and said that there was no child on the island who could speak English. When he perceived that I was annoyed because he doubted my word, he tried to placate me by saying that if I had seen such a child, then it would have come from another island or the mainland and was visiting.

He offered to walk back with me to my cottage and on the way I asked him: "Who exactly were the Fomorii?"

For a moment he looked disconcerted.

"My, but you are the one for picking up the ancient tales," was his comment.

"Well?" I prompted, as it seemed he was going to say nothing further on the subject.

He shrugged. "They are just an ancient legend, that's all."

I was a little exasperated and he saw it for he then continued: "The name means the dwellers under the sea. They were a violent and misshapen people who represented the evil gods in ancient times. They were lead by Balor of the Evil Eye and others of their race such as Morc and Cichol, but their power on land was broken at the great battle at Magh Tuireadh when they suffered defeat by the Tuatha Dé Dannan, the gods of goodness."

"Is that all?" I asked, disappointed at the tale.

Brennan raised a shoulder in an eloquent gesture. "Is it not enough?" he asked good-humouredly.

"Why are they called the Deep Ones?" I pressed.

A frown passed across his brow.

"Who told you that?" his voice was waspish.

"Were you not talking about the Deep Ones in the shebeen the other night? Dayn'ya Do'wan. Isn't that the Irish for Deep Ones? And why should you be talking of ancient legends?"

He seemed to force a smile.

"You have the right of it," he conceded. "We talk of ancient legends because they are part of us, of our heritage and our culture. And we call the Fomorii by this name because they dwell in the great deeps of the sea. No mystery in that."

I nodded towards *camcarraig*. "And they are supposed to

dwell near that rock?"

He hesitated, then said indifferently, "So legend goes. But a man like yourself does not want to dwell on our ancient tales and legends."

It was as if he had excluded me from my ancestry, ignored the fact that I had been born on the island.

Then he would talk no more either about the girl or the Deep Ones, the Fomorii, or the *Daoine Domhain*.

Two nights later as I was eating my supper in the main room of the tiny two-roomed cottage, I felt a draught upon my face and glanced up. I was astonished, for there standing with her back to the door was the little girl. The first thought that filled my mind was how quietly she must have entered not to disturb me. Only the soft draught from the door, supposedly opening and shutting, had alerted me. Then I realised that it was curious for a young child to be out so late and visiting the cottage of a stranger. I knew the islanders were trusting people but this trust bordered on irresponsibility.

She was staring at me with the same sadness that I had seen in her eyes when she had left me on the cliff top.

"What is it?" I demanded. "Why are you here and who are you?"

I recalled Brennan had claimed there was no such girl on the island. But this was no apparition.

"You have been chosen," she whispered softly. "Beware the feast of the Fires of Bíle, god of death. The intermediary will come for you then and take you to them. They are awaiting; nine years will have passed at the next feast. They wait every nine years for reparation. So be warned. You are the next chosen one."

My mouth opened in astonishment, not so much at what the girl was saying but at the words and phraseology which she used, for it was surely well beyond the ability of a nine-year-old to speak thus.

Abruptly as she came she went, turning, opening the door and running out into the dusk of the evening. I hastened to the door and peered into the gloom. There was no one within sight.

I have strong nerves, as well you know, but I felt a curious feeling of apprehension welling in me.

That night I was awakened by an odd wailing sound. At first I thought it was the noise of the wind across the mountain, whistling and calling, rising and falling. But then I realised it was not. It was surely some animal, lonely and outcast. The cry of a wolf, perhaps? But this was a bare rock of an island and surely no wolves could survive here? It went on for some time before it died away and I finally settled back to sleep.

The next morning I called by Tomás O'Driscoll's place and found Brennan, as usual, seated in the little bar-room. Once again he refused to accept a drink from me and instead offered me a glass of whiskey.

"Brennan," I said, my mind filled with the visit of the young child, "you are frugal with the truth because there is a little, red-haired girl living on this island. She can speak English."

His face whitened a little and he shook his head violently even before I had finished. "There is no one here like that," he said firmly and demanded to know why I asked.

I told him and his face was ghastly. He crossed himself and muttered something in Irish, whereupon Tomás behind the bar replied sharply to him. Brennan seemed to relax and nodded, obviously in agreement at what Tomás had said.

"What's going on here?" I asked harshly. "I insist that you tell me."

Brennan glanced about as if seeking some avenue of escape.

I reached forward and grabbed him angrily by the shoulder.

"No need for hurt," he whinged.

"Then tell me," I insisted firmly.

"She's just a tinker girl. She and her family often come to the island to lift the salmon from the rock pool at the north end of the island. They must be there now. I swear I didn't know the truth of it. But that's who she is. Tinkers are not good people to be knowing. They say all manner of strange things and claim they have the second sight. I wouldn't be trusting them."

He looked down at his glass and would say no more.

All at once I had a firm desire to quit this island and these strange people with their weird superstitions and folk ways. I might have been born on the island but they were no longer my people, no longer part of me. I was an American and in America lay reality.

"Can I get a boat to the mainland, to Baltimore, today, Brennan?" I asked.

He raised his eyes to mine and smiled sadly.

"Not today nor tomorrow, Mr Hacket," he replied softly.

"Why so?"

"Because this evening is May Day Eve. It's one of our four main holidays."

I was a little surprised.

"Do you celebrate Labour Day?"

Brennan shook his head.

"Oh, no. May Day and the evening before it is an ancient feast-day in the old Celtic calendar stretching back before the coming of Christianity. We call it Bealtaine, the time of the Fires of Bíle, one of the ancient gods."

I felt suddenly very cold, recalling the words of the tinker child.

"Are you saying that tonight is the feast of the god of death?"

Brennan made an affirmative gesture.

The girl had warned me of the feast of the Fires of Bíle when some intermediary would come for me and take me to ... to them? Who were "they"? The Deep Ones, of course. The terrible Fomorii who dwelt beneath the seas.

I frowned at my thoughts. What was I doing? Was I accepting their legends and folklore? But I had been born on the island. It was my reality also, my legends and my folklore as much as it was their own. And was I suddenly accepting the girl's second sight without question? Was I believing that she had come to warn me ... about what? I must be going mad.

I stood there shaking my head in bewilderment.

I *was* going mad, even to credit anything so ridiculous.

"Have a drink, Mr Hacket," Brennan was saying. "Then you will be as right as ninepence."

I stared at him for a moment. His words, an expression I had frequently heard in the area, triggered off a memory.

"Nine," I said slowly. "Nine."

Brennan frowned at me.

But suddenly I had become like a man possessed. Nine years ago to this day had Captain Pfeiffer disappeared from the very same cottage in which I was staying. The girl had said something about them waiting every nine years for reparation. Nine was the mystical number of the ancient Celts. The week was counted by nine nights and nine days and three weeks, the root number of nine, gave twenty-seven nights which was the unit of the month, related to the twenty-seven constellations of the lunar zodiac. Nine, nine, nine …! The number hammered into my mind.

What was I saying? That every ninth year these people made some sacrifice to ancient pagan gods whom they believed dwelt in the depths of the sea – the *Daoine Domhain*, the Deep Ones? That the English army captain, Pfeiffer, had been so sacrificed nine years before, nine years ago on this very night?

I found Brennan looking at me sympathetically.

"Don't worry, Mr Hacket," he said softly. "There is no joy in that. It does no good to question what cannot be understood."

"When can I get a boat to the mainland?"

"After the feast is done." He was apologetic but firm.

I turned and left the shebeen and began to walk towards the point.

Brennan followed me to the door for he called after me.

"There's no fear of it. I'll come along for you tonight. Tonight."

I turned and strode through the village street and made my way to the north end of the island. I was determined to find the tinker child and demand some explanation. It was not a big place and eventually I came across a collection of dirty, rough-patched tents grouped in front of a smouldering turf fire at which a woman of indiscernible age was turning a large fish on a spit.

231

There seemed no one else about.

I climbed down the rocks to get to the encampment which was sited on the beach, a fairly large strip of sand. The woman, brown-faced and weatherbeaten, clearly someone used to the outdoor life, watched me coming with narrowed eyes. There was suspicion on her features. She greeted me at first in Irish but when I returned the reply in English she smiled, her shoulders relaxed and she returned the greeting in kind.

"A grand day, sir. Are you staying on the island for the fishing then?"

"I am," I replied.

"Ah. By your voice you would be American."

I confirmed that I was. I was looking about for some sign of the girl but there seemed no one but the woman, who, now I came to observe her more closely, resembled the child with her mass of red hair.

"My man is fishing," the woman said, catching my wandering gaze.

"Ah," I said in noncommittal tone. "And do you have a child?"

"My girl, Sheena, sir."

The suspicion was back in her eyes.

"I thought I saw her a while ago," I said.

The woman shrugged.

"That you may."

"Is it right that you have the gift of second sight?" I demanded abruptly.

The woman looked taken aback and studied me for several long seconds before replying.

"Some of us have. Is it a fortune that you are wanting?"

I nodded.

"I'll be charging a shilling."

I reached in my pocket and handed over the coin which the woman took with alacrity.

"Is it your palm you wish read or shall I see what the tea-leaves say?"

I was about to reply when the flap of the tent moved and there stood the child. She regarded me with her large solemn, sad eyes and seemed to let out a sigh.

"He is the chosen one, Mother. He has already been warned," she said softly.

The woman stared from me to the child and back again. Her face was suddenly white and she threw the coin back at me as if it had suddenly burnt her hands.

"Away from here, Mister." Her voice was sharp.

"But ..."

"Have you no ears to hear with? Did you not hear what Sheena said. She is gifted with the second sight. She can see beyond the unseeable. If you value your soul, man, heed her warning. Now be away." She glanced about her, her face showing that she was badly frightened. "Sheena, find your father ... we must leave this place *now*."

Slowly I retreated, shaking my head in wonder. At least I had proved to myself that I was not hallucinating. The girl, Sheena, existed. A tinker girl with, supposedly, the gift of second sight, who gave me a warning ...

I walked up to the point above my cottage and sat on a rock gazing out across the dark brooding sea towards *camcarraig*. What nightmare world had I landed in? Was I losing all sense of reason? Was I accepting shadows for reality? Did I really believe that the girl had some strange power to foresee evil and warn me about it? I was the chosen one. Chosen for what purpose? And what had really happened to Captain Pfeiffer nine years ago, nine years this very night?

I shivered slightly.

The sea was a mass of restless blackness and far away, as if from the direction of *camcarraig*, I heard the strange cry which had disturbed my slumber on the previous night; a soft, whistling wail of a soul in torment.

It was while I sat there listening that I recalled the words of the child.

"You have been chosen. Beware the feast of the Fires of Bíle,

233

god of death. The intermediary will come for you then and take you to them. They are waiting. Nine years will have passed at the next feast. They wait every nine years for reparation. So be warned. You are the next chosen."

Abruptly I heard Brennan calling to me from the doorway of the shebeen.

"There's no fear in it. I'll come along for you tonight."

Brennan O'Driscoll. O'Driscoll who had explained the meaning of the name Ó hEidersceoil – *intermediary!*

Brennan was the one who would take me to the Deep Ones!

I rose then and began to scour the island in search of a boat, any boat, any form of floating transportation to get me away from this crazy nightmare. But there was none. I was alone, isolated and imprisoned. Even the tinkers had apparently departed. I was left alone with the islanders. Left alone to my fate.

That was this afternoon, my darling Sheila. Now it is dusk and I am writing this by the light of the storm lantern on the table in the tiny cottage. Soon Brennan O'Driscoll will come for me. Soon I shall know if I am truly crazy or whether there is some reality in this nightmare. It is my intention to take these pages and wrap them in my old oilskin pouch and hide them behind a loose brick in the chimney-breast of this cottage. In the hope that, should anything happen to me this evening, then, God willing, this letter will eventually reach your beloved hands or those of young Johnny, who may one day grow to manhood and come seeking word of his unfortunate father. Soon it will be dark and soon Brennan will come ... The intermediary; intermediary between me and what? What is it waiting out there in the deep? Why do they demand reparation every nine years and reparation for what? God help me in my futility.

Daniel Hacket.

Thus was the writing on the browning pages ended as if hurriedly. I sat for a while staring at those strange words and shaking my head in disbelief. What madness had seized my grandfather to write such a curious fantasy?

The wind was getting up and I could hear the seas roaring and crashing at the foot of the point where our house stood, gazing eastward towards the brooding Atlantic. The weather was dark and bleak for a late April day and I turned to switch on the light.

That something had deranged my grandfather's mind was obvious. Had he remained living on the island? Surely not, for the US Navy's enquiries at the time would have discovered him. But if he had disappeared, why hadn't the natives of this island, Inishdriscol, reported he was missing? Had he thrown himself into the sea while his mind had been so unbalanced and drowned, or what had taken place ? The questions flooded my thoughts. I suddenly realised that he had written the curious document, which so clearly demonstrated his warped mental condition, exactly sixty-three years ago this very night. It was April 30. A childish voice echoed in my mind, reciting the nine times table -- seven nines are sixty-three!

I shivered slightly and went to the window to gaze out at the blackness of the Atlantic spread before me. I could see the winking light from the point further down the coast which marked the passage to Innsmouth, and far out to sea I could just make out the pulsating warning sweep of the lighthouse at Devil Reef beyond which was sited one of the great deeps of the Atlantic. Deeps. The Deep Ones. What nonsense was that?

As I stood there, my mind in a whirl, staring out in the darkness beyond the cliff edge, I heard soft whistling, like a curious wind. It rose and fell with regular resonance like the call of some lonely outcast animal. It whistled and echoed across the sea with an uncanniness which caused me to shiver.

I pulled the curtains to and turned back into the room.

Well, the old-world Irishman had surely brought me an intriguing story. No wonder my grandfather had never returned. For some weird reason he had gone insane on that far distant Irish island and perhaps no one now would know the reason why.

I would have much to ask Cichol O'Driscoll when I saw him. Perhaps he could set forth an investigation when he returned to

Baltimore in order to find out how my grandfather had died and why no one had notified my grandmother of either his death or disappearance.

I frowned at some hidden memory and turned back to my grandfather's manuscript.

"They were a violent misshapen people who represented the evil gods in ancient Ireland. They were lead by Balor of the Evil Eye and others of the race such as Morc and Cichol ..."

Cichol! With his one eye and hump-shaped back!

I could not suppress the shiver which tingled against my spine. I tried to force a smile of cynicism.

Cichol O'Driscoll. O'Driscoll, the intermediary. April 30, the eve of Bealtaine, the feast of the Fires of Bíle. Seven times nine is sixty-three ... *Daoine Domhain.* The Deep Ones. "They wait every nine years for reparation."

Then I knew that I would be seeing Cichol O'Driscoll again. Very soon.

Outside the wind was rising from the mysterious, restless Atlantic swell, keening like a soul in torment. And through the wind came the whistling call of some lonely outcast animal.

XI

Amhránaí

I HAVE PLAYED the tape a dozen times now; played it and am unable to believe; unable to understand what curious transformation has happened. The studio technicians have gone now, gone with derisive laughter and gibes, convinced that I am playing some trick on them. Yet if any trick has been played it is on myself.

And is it some trick, or ... ? Surely the alternative is too bizarre to accept.

I sit alone in the studio running the tape back and forth, staring through the glass of the control room into the gloom of the studio itself, with its deserted music-stands, abandoned chairs and discarded sheet music – deserted by the musicians at the end of the recording session. I sit alone listening to the tape and yet hardly hearing it now.

Instead I hear *her* voice: soft, slightly breathless, a restful, easy soprano. The melodic tone rises and falls like a summer breeze. The ancient Gaelic rhythms and words caress my ears.

Do not neglect me or reject me because I'm poor.
Take, oh take me, and ne'er forsake me for lack of store!
Would to heaven I were at even with him who broke
    my heart,
With him only, in a valley lonely, ne'er, ne'er to part!

I wipe the sweat from my brow as I sit listening yet find myself shivering at the same time. Shivering as if icy hands were clutching at my spine.

Can it have been only a few days ago since I sat in this same studio control room with Art Kirwan who runs the small record company for which I work as a producer? Oh, we aren't a large company not even as Irish companies go. Shannon Records of Dublin is no giant but we are what is known as a "growing company", growing both in size and reputation but we have a long way to go to really be able to compete with Gael-linn or Claddagh. Still, two of our singles have made it into the Irish "Top Ten" and one of them has even reached the "Top Twenty" in Britain. That is no bad thing for our reputation.

I was doing some mixing for our latest single offering when Art came into the control room.

"Is that the MacAuley single?" he asked and when I nodded, he sniffed. Art sniffed as others would grunt or say "oh".

"What's wrong?" I asked, easing the headphones from my ears and switching off the tape.

"Our distributors are telling me that they can't persuade the outlets to stock large quantities of singles any more. The public want LPs, cassettes, compact discs ... the age of the seven-inch vinyl single is over."

He paused and stroked the bridge of his nose as if contemplating a bleak future.

"Well, it was coming," I offered, unhelpfully. "The trade press have been on about it for some time now."

Art didn't appear to hear me. He went on:

"I've decided we'll have to ditch this single. No use producing a record which no one is going to stock. Can MacAuley record enough to turn this into an album?"

I shrugged. MacAuley was one of our more temperamental rock singers. A young man from the West Cork *Gaeltacht*, an Irish-speaking area, who had become what is described as a "teenage rebel", rebelling against his upbringing and social values. At least, that is what we said on the publicity blurb of the record sleeve. He had even Anglicised his name from Seán Mac Amhlaoibh to John MacAuley as a sign of his rejection of his parents' values. His rebellion was, in my opinion, outdated. Personally, I didn't like the young man and, I guess, he didn't like me.

"Maybe," I replied. "But he probably won't like it."

"Get hold of him and arrange some sessions. Tell him it's urgent. We've promised our distributors a new MacAuley release and I am going to keep to it ... with an album not a single."

When Art makes up his mind there is little to be done to shift him

Sighing I reached for the phone and rang MacAuley's house in Clontarf. The first thing the young man did when he started to make money was to buy a house in a wealthier suburb of Dublin. His girlfriend answered.

"John's down to West Cork to see his folks," she replied with a touch of annoyance in her voice, as if this were some personal insult to her.

I must admit to being surprised by the fact. As I said, MacAuley was supposed to have totally rejected his West-Cork *Gaeltacht* roots and that meant his folks as well.

"How long will he be down in Cork?" I asked, telling her who I was and that it was urgent I reach him as soon as possible.

"He didn't say," she replied, unbending her air of superiority for a moment. "I think there was some trouble at home and the local priest phoned him and asked him to go down. It might be a few days. It might be a few weeks. He didn't want to go but the priest was insistent."

I pursed my lips at the mouthpiece in a wry gesture. It would be a pretty powerful personality, priest or not, to make young MacAuley do anything he did not want to.

"Can you give me his phone number down there?"

The girlfriend laughed at the idea.

"His parents aren't on the telephone. Not in that godforsaken little backwater."

"But you do have the address?" I pressed in desperation.

She gave it and a fruitless five minutes with the operator confirmed that she had been right: MacAuley's family were not on the telephone. When I told Art, I knew what he would say.

"Then you'd best drive down there and find him. We don't have time to waste."

The city of Cork is just over 160 miles from Dublin but it was late afternoon by the time I reached it and found myself in a nice little traffic jam as I attempted to negotiate the city centre to take the road for Macroom and West Cork. It took me fully three-quarters of an hour to cross the city centre.

The delay was annoying for it was dusk when I reached the village of Ballyvourney, a further forty miles from the city, which is regarded as the centre of the West Cork Irish-speaking district. *Baile Bhúirne*, the rocky place, is its real name.

I halted the car at the crossroads and consulted the map.

MacAuley's village was not too far away now but it was several miles over a mountain road which rose to meander through the Derrynasaggart Mountains before me, a rough track-like ribbon of a road. Dusk was beginning to creep across the jagged granite thrust of the mountains, which seemed to rise like a wall of towering barren rocks, though heather-covered in places. It was hard to believe that some people still farmed here in these heights of over a thousand feet. There was scarce feeding for the small, sure-footed mountain sheep among the peat bogs which now gave cover for grouse where once the majestic eagle had its home. And among these boulder-strewn fields was Gortstrancally, the tiny hamlet where MacAuley came from. The map I had with me was bilingual so that I could see that the Anglicised distortion was actually *Gort Srón na Caillí* (field of the hag's nose).

I set the car into gear and began to ascend into the mountains, twisting along the narrow track where there was scarcly room for one car. But cars are very few in this part of the country and I encountered none coming in the opposite direction nor, in fact, any other vehicle or pedestrian. Dusk spread itself languorously over the mountains and before I knew it night had fallen over the treacherous landscape. I began to worry for, according to the map, I should have reached Gortstrancally by now. After all, I not only had to see MacAuley but also to find my way back to the main road and get some lodgings for the night. I glanced at the clock on the dashboard and could not believe the time it was taking to negotiate the few miles.

At a bend on the shoulder of the mountain a sign, half hidden in the stone hedgerow, caught my eye. It was wooden and leaned at a drunken angle. I halted to read it. The letters were incised in Gaelic form. *Baile an Ghort.* The village of hunger. I smiled thinly and wondered what they were hungry for.

Then a sound caught my ear and something made me switch off the car engine to hear it.

High above me on the mountainside a pipe was playing. It was piping a jig and I could make out faint laughter and the clapping of hands. I peered upwards and could see a faint, flickering light not far away. The headlights of my car showed that the wooden sign pointed to a small track, a path which seemed cut, step-like, into the mountainside.

I had come to the conclusion fifteen minutes before that I had lost my way and realised that here was an excellent opportunity to get directions. These mountains were not so densely populated that I would have other opportunities. And so, restarting my engine, I pulled the car over to the far side of the bend to allow any other traffic using the road to pass though, as I have said, there was probably little prospect of it on such a deserted mountain track.

I took my pocket torch and, after a moment's hesitation, reached for the small cassette player which, out of habit, I always kept in the car. Listening to the piper on the night air, I felt it might be worth recording a tune or two.

Then I set out, up the uneven and awkward path which led upwards between the two stone hedges. It was curious, for after a climb of some minutes I seemed to pass through a suffocating yellow mist bank into the clear night air of the upper mountain. Here it was chill and the air was crystal underneath a canopy of ultramarine in which bright white lights flickered as a million stars danced in the heavens.

I had not realised that I was so close to the buildings for before me, looming up in the semi-light, were clustered a half-dozen crofts, thatched and with whitewash discernible even in the half-light. They clustered round a moneen, a village green, or so I thought it to be. And here was a large fire around which people were gathered with musicians among them. The piper had just finished playing and a burst of hand-clapping showed the appreciation of the audience.

As I moved forward one of the party turned, saw me, and whispered to his neighbour. The people grew silent and turned to watch my approach to the fire. I could not see their expressions but I sensed the curiosity on their faces.

"Good evening," I called to them.

There was a whispering and then someone stepped forward.

It was a man, elderly by his stooped shoulders, country breeches tucked into his Wellington boots. He moved a step in my direction

"*Dia dhuit,*" he greeted in Irish.

"*Dia's Muire dhuit,*" I replied automatically.

The old man sighed as if in relief.

"Ah, you have the Gaelic? That is good for though I have some English it is poor."

The man was ancient but there was nothing frail about his sturdy, mountainy figure, in spite of his rounded shoulders. His toothless gums clenched on a foul-smelling briar which caused my nose to itch from a distance of several paces.

"You are a stranger," he went on in Irish.

"I am," I replied. "I am trying to find the road to Gortstrancally."

I was proud of my fluency in the language, having made a special point of my studies at school and having persuaded my parents to send me to Irish-speaking areas during the summer in order to improve my knowledge.

"Is it so?" he nodded. "Then you will find it a long and difficult road this night. It could take you many hours in the dark. Best to come near the fire and warm yourself. We'll find you a bed and you can continue your journey in the morning."

"But am I so far away from Gortstrancally?" I asked, surprised that I could have been so far off my route.

The old man nodded. "Too far to journey this night," he affirmed.

"But I cannot impose myself on your hospitality," I protested feebly.

"And would we not be providing a bed for a stranger?" he demanded as if affronted. "Whist, man, come and have a dram and warm yourself."

He led the way back to the fire where a fiddler, seated on a three-legged stool before the fire, was striking up a tune. It was a merry, infectious tune and it was joined by a piper seated near him playing the *uileann* pipes, his elbow working the wheezy bellows. And soon the people were clapping their hands and stamping their feet. A pottery mug was pressed into my hands by a grinning hag of a woman. The aroma of the whiskey with its peaty taste was delicious.

"Is it a *céilí* you're having?" I asked the old man, stating the obvious.

"Is it not Lughnasa?" he returned with an air of controlled patience. "Doesn't everyone celebrate?"

It had not registered that this was the last evening of July and, in recent years, there had been a fashion to resurrect some of the old pagan Irish celebrations such as the Feast of Lughnasa, one of the four great festivals of the Celtic year.

My attention was suddenly attracted by a young girl stepping into the circle of light by the fire. She had the high cheekbones so characteristic of the country folk, fair skin with a touch of rose red on her cheeks, light blue eyes and raven black hair. I've heard the French call such a colour combination *yeux de pervenche*. Her beauty owed nothing to fashion or artifice. It was a beauty that made my heart skip a beat. Her slim figure was clad in a crimson homespun skirt and she wore a white blouse over which a tight black bodice was laced.

She moved forward and stood expectantly. Hands straight to

her sides, a slight smile on her red lips. Waiting.

Then a young man came forward to face her. He was a typical country lad, sturdy and muscular. He seemed dressed in his best.

The fiddler had played sixteen bars of a double jig. Then the dancers began to move. How they complemented each other! I almost grew jealous of the young man as his masculine vigour offset her feminine grace. His hands hung loosely by his side as he expressed himself through the intricate, grinding steps – they seemed to describe the gaiety and joy of living. She stood in repose until it was her turn to move forward with a sedate beauty of movement, her lighter steps seemingly more graceful, more effortless, hands clasped before her. Her face was a sphinx-like mask, only a slight smile hovering on her lips now and then betrayed the pleasure of the dance.

I had scarcely seen traditional dancing better performed.

The dance ended and immediately the fiddler slid into a noisy eight-hand reel.

I turned back to the old man.

"You are fairly isolated in this place," I said, more to make conversation than anything else.

He made a gesture like spitting but confined himself to the mime rather than the action.

"Isolated? Were we not driven here long ago from the fertile inland by the planters?"

I smiled. "That was long ago."

"How long is memory? We were driven into the bleak mountains to suffer and die at the leisure of the planters. Many of us did die in the winters before we could make our first crops grow. Yet we did not all die. We reclaimed little fields from the stony hills, reclaimed the earth from the marsh, bog and rock at the cost of our blood and sweat. And life became a struggle against nature as we tried to shut out the encroaching dour wilderness and claim what little land we could."

"But it was so long ago," I repeated. To hear the old man tell it, it was as if he had lived the terrible days of the confiscations and plantations, when Cromwell ordered the Irish nation west of the Shannon on pain of death; when he had pronounced that the Irish could go "to Hell or Connacht!"

The old man gave a repetition of his spitting mime. "We are the children of that sorrow. The memory will always be with us. We must be constantly vigilant for the marsh and bog, the heather and bramble, the rock and stone from the eroded mountainside wait outside our boundary hedges, ever watchful and waiting to reclaim their own. Spend only a day or so away from the field and when you return you will find boulders pushing through the soil, the heather gnawing at the ground. It is waiting, ever waiting."

Strange, but I felt a shiver at the intensity of his words,

Then I was aware of a sadder note to the fiddler's tune. I looked up and there was the young girl who had danced so entrancingly. She stepped forward demurely, hands clasped softly together in front of her; eyes downcast.

The fiddler played a few bars and I recognised the tune of the old song *An Draighean Donn*, the Blackthorn Tree.

An instinct made me reach into my pocket for the little cassette recorder and set it on the wooden bench beside me with a click of the switch. I was an enthusiast for recording traditional songs and I was hoping to persuade Art to issue a new recording of songs sung by traditional singers rather than professionals. There was still a lot of good traditional talent in Ireland.

The girl's voice was a soft soprano, melodious and sighing like a gentle breeze. She had already sung the first verse, *Fuaireas féirín lá aonaigh ó bhuachaill dheas,* when I noticed that her eyes were raised and gazing with a smile into mine.

> There's many thinking, when they're drinking, that I'm surely theirs,
> But to their pleading I'm unheeding with his whisper in my ears.
> His dear face has all the grace of mountain and of lea,
> And his bosom is like the blossom of the blackthorn tree.

How sweet and enticing her features. I felt the blood in my cheeks and pulled nervously at a pottery mug of whiskey in my hands in an attempt to hide my gaucheness. A smile wreathed her lips at my awkwardness and still she sang, gazing directly at me.

> *'Tis but folly to scan holly or more lofty trees,*
> *When in the bushes where water rushes we find heart's*
>   *ease.*
> *Though the rowan so high is growing, its berry is tart,*
> *While near the ground fruit sweet and sound will charm the*
>   *heart.*

I looked nervously around but everyone sat with their eyes fixed intently on the *amhránaí*, the sweet singer; they had no eyes for me. They were oblivious also to the audacious message of the girl's gaze directed towards me.

> *I'm thine, love, be mine, love, and heed not gold,*
> *I'm thine, love, be mine, love, nor sheep in fold,*
> *Take me – I've no baby as yet unborn,*
> *Take me – should you forsake me, I'll die forlorn.*

The song came to an end in eerie silence. Then, with an abrupt change of mood, the fiddler slid into an eight-hand reel and the girl disappeared into a throng of dancers.

I found myself sweating a little as I switched off the cassette recorder and replaced it in my pocket.

I turned to the old man.

"Who is the young girl?"

"The *amhránaí*?" he smiled. "That is Emer Ní Muirgheasa. And sadly is she named."

I frowned.

"Sad? The name means something to do with the sea, doesn't it?"

He nodded slowly. "Choice of the sea, it is. And sad for she was wed for two weeks when her husband, Eoin, went off to Kenmare to seek work on the fishing boats and within a further week was drowned out by the treacherous Skelligs. It was the sea's choice, *mhuise!*"

He added the emphatic with a jerk of his head.

The reel came to a halt but almost before the dance had ended the fiddler was striking up another tune, a jig, and suddenly I found the girl standing before me, smiling down at me. Her hands were stretched out invitingly towards me.

I stumbled to my feet, blushing.

"I haven't danced a jig in years," I began but her cool hands had taken mine and led me into the line of happy dancers.

I do not know how I succeeded in remembering the steps of the dance. I had not danced since I was a boy at school. Somehow I survived, my eyes following the dexterity of my partner as she slipped and weaved through the complex figures of the dance with a gay smile on her lips.

Somewhat out of breath I stood smiling uncertainly at the girl as the dance ended. I did not know what to say.

Then I found the people apparently dispersing.

The dancing had ended. The *céilí* was over.

The old man was at my side.

"We will find you a bed this night so that you may continue your journey tomorrow," he said.

"There is a bed in my cabin," came the soft breathless soprano of the girl.

"Indeed there is," avowed the old man. "Then there is an answer to the matter. *Oíche mhaith, a mhic.*"

Before I had time to return his "good night", the old man was gone.

The girl and I were alone on the moneen by the dying fire. She smiled at me almost coquettishly before turning and walking towards the end of the village.

"I ... ah, I hope I am not putting you to any trouble," I said awkwardly as I made to keep up with her. "I was heading for Gortstrancally when I seemed to lose my way."

"No trouble in it," she called over her shoulder. `What is to be, must be."

We reached a grey old stone croft at the end of the village and she went inside. I followed to find myself in a large single room with a great fireplace at one end in which a turf fire smouldered.

I stared around in amazement.

It was as if I had walked into a folk museum, as if I had been transported back into the last century.

"Don't let the heat out," ordered the girl sharply for, I confess, I stood open-mouthed on the threshold. Sheepishly, I entered and closed the door behind me.

"You have made a marvellous," I frowned trying to think of the Irish word for a replica, "a wonderful copy of what a croft must have been like a hundred years ago."

The girl gazed at me a moment and shrugged.

"It's only a poor cabin," she said indifferently. Yet the furnishings were surely genuine antiques. I had never seen the like. A grandfather clock in the corner gave a musical hollow tick-tock. That was surely ancient.

"I'm sorry," I suddenly realised the lateness of the hour. "I am keeping you up. Where shall I sleep?"

The girl turned to me and again I saw the mocking, mischievous smile on her lips.

"You do not know?" she breathed softly.

I'm thine, love, be mine, love, and heed not gold,
I'm thine, love, be mine, love, nor sheep in fold.
Take me – I've no baby as yet unborn,
Take me – should you forsake me I'll die forlorn!

I could scarce believe it was happening to me as she took a pace towards me, bringing her soft warm body forward against me, her face upturned, her lips parted invitingly. I hesitated only for a moment before I decided to surrender to fate.

I had a strange sense of plunging into a deep mysterious pool as I lowered my lips to hers. Somewhere, perhaps it was only in my imagination, I heard the soft, plaintive wail of a distant piper.

I came awake with a sense of unease. Emer lay warmly beside me in the wooden cot. A blanket covered us. It was still dark but I glanced at my watch and saw, by the luminous dial, that it was not far off dawn. I could hear the hesitant beginnings of bird-song some way behind the croft. The girl was deep in sleep. The sound of her breath was gentle even in her slumber. The turf hissed on the fire and the only other sound was the all-pervasive ticking of the grandfather clock in the corner.

Gently I eased myself from the cot, trying not to disturb her. It was chilly in the early dawn and I threw my clothes on hurriedly. I do not know what made me leave the bed and dress so early. I suppose it may have been a combination of my desire to get away early to find Gortstrancally and the fact that I had my overnight bag in the car on the road below. I am a fastidious person and knowing I had my toilet things in my bag I thought I would seize the opportunity of my wakefulness to go down to the car and bring them back to the croft. It would be good to have a wash and shave before I went on my way.

I let myself out of the croft to see a dull grey light, which heralded dawn, low down behind the mountains across the valley.

The village was sleeping.

I made my way carefully down the path which led to the roadway. A little way down I suddenly found myself plunged into a freezing mist, a swirling greyness which caught at the breath with icy fingers and assailed the nostrils with a nauseous odour. I found myself stumbling along the path, scuffing my toes against the uneven stony surface. Then I tripped, and with a grunt as the wind went from my body, I found myself, with grazed shins, tripping over the low stone wall and falling on the other side of it.

I lay on the ground for a moment cursing silently and regretting that I had been so stupid as to attempt to make the journey down to the car simply because vanity dictated that I needed my toilet bag.

As I lay there I abruptly became aware of heavy steps ascending the pathway. It is hard to describe but the tread was a squelching sound, like the stamp of wet rubber boots. I turned on my side and was about to call out a rueful greeting but something stopped me. Even now I do not know what it was. Some awesome premonition, cold and heart-clutching.

Perhaps it was the smell. The odour of the sea coupled with the stench of rotting fish and seaweed; a reek of such putridness that I felt the bile rise in my throat.

The sound of the steps passed by on the other side of the low wall. I had the impression of a figure passing, thickset and heavy. The mist hid us both effectively. Then the odour was past too.

Frowning, I climbed to my feet and felt my limbs to ensure that I had suffered no more than a bruising and loss of dignity and then I climbed back over the wall and continued downwards.

Like passing through a door, suddenly I was through the mist and out into the grey dawn light. In fact, dawn had come up with a rather startling abruptness since I had left the village. There was my car parked on the bend of the road exactly as I had left it.

The air was now full of noisy, querulous bird-song. I took my canvas overnight bag from the car and started back up the mountain path with a light heart.

I did not know what good fortune had ordained my meeting with Emer but I knew that some chemistry had worked between us that night. Fate had ordained our meeting. Fate ... and a rock singer named John MacAuley. I grinned at the idea, as I swung up the path back towards the village and Emer's croft.

It is hard to describe the attraction we felt; an almost terrifying lustful fascination in which we had allowed all natural barriers to fall away in order to satiate our passions.

It was as if we had been doomed to meet.

I moved upwards smiling happily in my new-found infatuation. Strange, how things seen at night are so different by the light of the day. The path to the village looked so overgrown and disused now. I found the gate in the stone hedge and paused. My eyes focused on the village. The mist had cleared and the early daylight brightened the mountainside as the first rays of the sun peaked over the eastern mountain tops.

I stared in horror at the buildings, letting my bag drop to the ground from nerveless fingers.

The moneen, where the people had danced the night before, was a jungle of bramble and heather. The crofts, which had seemed so neat and whitewashed in the comfortable firelight, were crumbling, their roofs caved in, creepers covering some of the ruined walls and spilling in through the windows.

My heart began beating wildly.

I turned to the end croft, the cabin I had left just a few moments before.

It was old and gave the appearance of disuse and neglect like the others.

I ran to the door, rotten, its paint peeling, and pushed it open, knowing full well what I would find.

The roof was gone but I could recognise the configuration of the room. There was little doubt but that I recognised it. There was the same fireplace where a short time before a healthy turf fire had hissed. There was the corner where the grandfather clock had stood and there ... there was the rotting wooden frame of a cot where only a brief span of time had surely passed since Emer and I had made love on its eiderdown mattress.

My mind whirled in a dizzy sickness trying to find reason in this insanity.

Suddenly I heard a soft soprano voice whispering through the shell of the ruined croft.

I'm thine, love, be mine, love, and heed not gold,
I'm thine, love, be mine, love, nor sheep in fold.
Take me – I've no baby as yet unborn,
Take me – should you forsake me I'll die forlorn.

Then the voice was cut short by a terrible piercing shriek of terror.

Fear rooted me to the spot for a moment and then I turned and was running in blind panic as if my very life depended on it, hastily snatching up my bag as I sped through the gap in the stone hedge and stumbled my way down to the roadway below. As if in fear of the hounds of hell on my heels, I threw myself into the car, praying it would start in the chill morning air. It did so on a single turn of the key, and soon I was accelerating along the mountain road.

I did not stop until I reached the next village some miles away; Gortstrancally, as it turned out. I halted the car in the square by a small church and sat shivering, sweat pouring from me, trying to make sense of the experience and yet unable to believe what my own senses had told me.

A moment later I was conscious of a black-clad figure halting by the car.

"Good morning," came a cheery voice. "Are you in trouble?"

The rotund, red-faced features of a smiling priest peered down at me.

I forced an answering grimace. "I'm all right, Father," I replied. Then: "Is this Gortstrancally?"

"It is so."

"I'm looking for John MacAuley. I'm from Dublin."

The priest smiled indulgently. "Ah, that would be young Seán Mac Amhlaoibh. He'll be at Seán Mór's house across the square. That's his father's house. His mother has been ill, but, *buíochas le Dia*, she is recovering now."

"Thank you, Father."

He half turned and then hesitated. "Are you sure that you are not troubled?" he pressed. "You don't look well."

I shook my head

"It is just an early morning start, Father," I tried to sound jocular. Then I hesitated. "But perhaps you could tell me something. On the road here I passed a sign for a village called *Baile an Ghort*. Do you know anything about the place?"

The priest's eyes widened slightly.

"Ah, is it the name which interests you? The village of hunger?"

I nodded, not wishing to commit myself further.

The priest rubbed his chin.

"It was during the time of the Great Hunger. That little village was severely hit. Not one person survived. It's been a village of ghosts and memories since 1847. That's why it was renamed the village of hunger in later years. But no one has ever lived there since."

I stared at him for a long time. My face must have been a mask of horror. Yet he seemed oblivious of me.

"Twice in a year tragedy shook the village. Twice in a year. You'll find people who will tell you that the two tragedies are not unconnected."

"Two tragedies? How do you mean?"

"Well, when God, in His infinite wisdom, allowed the village to be destroyed in the time of the terrible hunger, it was said it was merely retribution for the first tragedy which had befallen the place."

"What tragedy was that?" I demanded, my voice rising a little in my agitation.

"Why, a girl was murdered there by her husband."

I felt the icy chill creeping over me again.

"Do you know the details?"

The priest guffawed wryly.

"Everyone knows the tale in these parts. However, my son, it is not really a pleasant story. The man had just married. His wife was said to be very comely. But there being no work in these parts during the early years of the Great Hunger, he went off to Kenmare to work on the fishing boats. Then came the report that he was drowned. But not long afterwards, he returned and, so 'tis said, found his wife sleeping with a stranger ... a traveller who had sought hospitality in the village. Half demented, in great fury, the husband killed his wife."

"Then what happened?" I pressed, almost hoarse in my fascination.

"Neither the husband nor the stranger were ever found. Of course, the police made enquiries and, curiously, the fisherfolk at Kenmare took oath that the husband had been drowned weeks before the murder, as they had previously reported. He had fallen overboard near the Skelligs and been washed away. The evidence conflicted, for one of the villagers swore that he had seen the husband enter the cabin where his wife was. This was about dawn on the day she was discovered dead. The police refused to believe him and the stranger was blamed for the murder."

"Did they find the stranger?"

"No," the priest shook his head. "As I said, neither the husband nor the stranger were ever found. There was an end of the tragedy. Except some people felt it was God's retribution when the entire population of the village were destroyed in the Great Hunger. Many hereabouts at the time accused the villagers of hiding the husband. What was his name?"

"Ó Muirgheasa," the name dropped unwillingly from my lips.

The priest frowned a moment.

"Yes. I think you are right. So you've heard the story before?"

I shook my head.

The priest shrugged. "Well, a strange tale and God's curse on the place ever since."

Then he pointed across the square. "You'll find young Seán at Seán Mór's house there. Good luck to you."

Two days later, back in the studio in Dublin, I at last found the courage to take out my cassette recorder and place it on the table before me. I sat looking at it for a long time, running my hands over it like some icon, fearful of what it would reveal to me.

I recalled her soft, breathless soprano voice as she sang ... and her song was meant for me, for me alone.

Perhaps it was fate; perhaps I had managed to record an enchanted piece of folk music which would be forever immortalised – an eternal love song.

Summoning my courage, I rewound the tape and pressed the "play" button.

My heart beating wildly, I waited as the tape began to come alive with background noise. The music *was* there.

Whoso resents me will not prevent me, my love is yours.
Whoso resents me will not prevent me, through all time's wars.
May who resents it be demented and nevermore thrive!
O my dearest, 'tis you who tearest my heart alive!

The words seem to take on a new meaning but it was not the

words which chilled my heart. It was the voice that sang them; an ancient, shrill voice, the cackling of old age beyond measure.

These stories have first appeared in a wide variety of magazines and book anthologies in several countries. Three of them were also published in Irish, one of them prior to the English version, in the magazine *Feasta*. These were "Aisling", *Feasta*, October and November 1985; "The Samhain Feis", which appeared as "*Feis na Samhain*" in November 1984; and "The Pooka" as "*An Púca*", *Feasta*, November 1986.

The first English language appearance of the stories were "Aisling", *Weirdbook* (USA), October 1985; "Deathstone", *Winter Chills* (UK), January 1987; "My Lady of Hy-Brasil", *Kadath* (Genova, Italy), autumn 1983; "The Samhain Feis", *Hallowe'en Horrors*, ed. Alan Ryan, Doubleday (USA), 1986; "The Mongfind", *Weirdbook*, October 1990; "The Pooka", *Shadows 8*, ed. Charles L. Grant, Doubleday, 1985; "The Tavesher", *Shadows 8*, 1986; "Fear a' Ghorta", *Final Shadows*, 1991; "Daoine Domhain", *Weirdbook*, summer 1992. "The Dreeador" and "Amhránaí" are published here for the first time.